I0550010

THE LUCIFER STRAIN

by
KEVIN PAUL TRACY

The Lucifer Strain

ISBN: 978-0-9972606-2-5

Cover Art by Donna Murillo.

For Jimma,
In Loving Memory

ACKNOWLEDGEMENTS

Thanks to Disney (no, not that one,) Tatsumoto,
and my big sis.

CHAPTER 1

"I'm here to see Dr. Reisen," Lainie Parker told the receptionist through the half-open sliding pane of glass. The window was set into one wall of the waiting room, festooned with signs such as "Please have Payment on Day of Treatment" and "Please do not leave children unattended."

"You mean Dr. 'Ray-zon?'" the receptionist said, a distracted young woman in flowered scrubs and drooping bun.

Lainie consulted the appointment entry on her cell phone. "I'm sorry, it's pronounced 'Raisin?'" She nearly dropped her tablet computer but trapped it between her elbow and her hip.

"It's spelled R-E-I-S-E-N," the receptionist droned. "It's pronounced 'Ray-zon.' Who may I say is asking."

"I'm Lainie Parker. I'm sorry, Dr. Lainie Parker. I have an interview with her this morning at ten."

Upon hearing the word 'doctor' prefixed to Lainie's name the receptionist straightened in her seat and met Lainie's gaze with more attentiveness. Upon hearing the word 'interview' her eyelids drooped again and she turned to her computer. "I'll let Dr. Reisen know you're here. She's running behind this morning. Have a seat and she'll be with you as soon as she can."

Recovering her tablet, Lainie stepped back from the receptionist window and scanned the waiting room. This was no ER, nor even a proper hospital, so the waiting room was richly appointed and appeared virtually unused. Even now, deserted. She took a seat.

Lainie's phone buzzed again. It never really stopped, which had ceased to surprise her – men requested companionship at all hours of the morning, noon, and night.

Very soon after she'd been cleared of all charges a year ago, Orin – sad, sweet, geeky Orin who lost his job because he'd inadvertently helped Lainie steal confidential company records – had called her with a business proposition. He'd created a very particular app for smartphones and tablets and wanted Lainie to work for him administering it.

She resisted him for many months, but after graduation and no jobs to be had anywhere, the money dried up and Lainie became desperate. She agreed to partner with him on a temporary basis only. That'd been eight months ago and she was making more money now than she'd ever made at Capris.

It was not a job of which she was particularly proud, she would certainly never be able to put it on her resume. But it paid the rent and put food on the table. More than that, she had been able to pay off a good portion of her student loans and was well on the way to being financially flush for the first time in her whole life.

She was restless and stood up. "Can I have a look around?" The receptionist eyed her for a moment, then shrugged.

The Reisin Clinic for Developmental Impediments was not the top clinic fo gpr children in the country. In point of fact it wasn't even one of t gphe top ten. Unlike the top ten, however, this one was hiring. Having finally graduated what Lainie Parker needed more than anything else was a job. A respectable one.

She strolled out into a hall from which the muted sounds of pounding could be heard above the even more distant sounds of children laughing and playing. She peered into the narrow, meshed windows of some of the rooms to see equipment such as phoropters and keratometers for eye exams; scales and calipers for weight and body mass; toys and puzzles to assess spatial and relational conceptuality; etc.

School districts around the country had waiting lists to choke a whale. And why not, with their three-month summer hiatuses and the diamond-encrusted solid-gold pension packages extorted for them by an iron-fisted union that put Hoffa's Teamsters to shame? Private schools were even more backed-up, with their higher salaries and academic puritanism. And besides, Lainie had always had a sense that she wanted to work more directly on developmental disorders than trying to mainstream children who really needed more personal attention.

The pounding got louder as Lainie approached a door that was ajar. She peered into a music room. A young, impeccably dressed couple stood in the center looking miserable. They were clearly distressed, but in a resigned way, as if they'd given up hope. The insistent banging made the woman winced repeatedly and jump under the man's arm.

"Jeremy, could you please do that a little quieter?" the man snapped.

The woman placed a hand on his chest to calm him, which appeared to work. "Please, Henry, he can't help it."

To one side sat a little boy of perhaps three years with sandy hair and wearing a 49ers jersey. He'd wedged a pair of bongos in the center of his crossed legs and was hitting them with a pair of maracas with much verve and concentration. He didn't smile, but he seemed entirely absorbed by what he was doing. Lainie focused on him, watching his expression intently as he banged and banged and banged.

He was listening to the sound, and seemed soothed by what he was hearing.

"Excuse me," the woman turned to Lainie. "Do you know how much longer Dr. Reisen will be?"

Lainie stepped into the room. "I'm sorry, I don't actually...can I ask..." She gestured to Jeremy.

"Diagnosed autistic," the man, Henry, said. He offered Lainie his hand. "I'm Henry Jacobson. This is my wife Mary. That's..."

"Jeremy," Lainie said, approaching the boy. "Hi, Jeremy, I'm Dr. Lainie Parker. How are you?"

Jeremy flinched away from her. He stopped pounding long enough to turn himself away from her, then resumed.

"He isn't responding to any of the standard treatments," Mary told Lainie. "Mirroring, puppeting, recitation, it all seems to bother him more than help."

"All he wants to do is make noise," Henry said, an edge to his voice. "He does it mostly to drown us out when we try to speak to him, or when the TV is on. They let us wait for the doctor in here, the music room, because music is about the only thing that seems to quiet him, and not always that."

Lainie set her tablet on a nearby table and sat cross-legged next to Jeremy. She nodded her head to the steady, unbreakable rhythm of the pounding, then lifted her hands and clapped to match it. Once she was in sync with the noise exactly Jeremy appeared to cock an ear toward her. The exuberance of his own pounding seemed to relent a little.

"That's amazing," Mary said., but as soon as she spoke Jeremy resumed pounding as hard and as loud as ever. Still, she shouted over him, "Mirroring has never worked with him before."

"I may not be mirroring," Lainie said. She cast about her and saw what she was looking for on a shelf propping up some song books. "Can you hand me that metronome?"

Henry looked. "The what?"

"The thing that looks like an upside-down pendulum."

Henry fetched the device and brought it to Lainie. She set it on the floor between she and Jeremy. The boy spotted it but continued his violent, almost angry tattoo. When she turned the winder at the side he seemed almost interested. She freed the pendulum from its mooring and the weighted stem rocked slowly, ticking as it reached the nadir of its swing to each side.

By sliding the weight up or down the stem Lainie adjusted the speed of the metronome until it matched Jeremy's banging precisely. Slowly at first, but then precipitously Jeremy quieted and then simply stopped his banging and watched the metronome as if entranced.

.Jeremy's parents seemed as transfixed as he was. Bringing a finger to her lips Lainie motioned Henry and Mary to follow her out into the hall

"I don't want to get your hopes up," she whispered. "More testing will have to be done. But I'm convinced your son does not suffer from autism."

"What?" Mary put a hand to her mouth, as if hardly daring to believe what she heard.

"What, then?" Henry asked.

"I think your son is suffering from a rare condition. So rare it doesn't even really have an official name. But in plain terms he suffers from a middle ear transmission delay."

"A what?" Henry said, looking horrified.

"It's a delay between when sounds reach your son's middle ear and when they reach his inner ear. This transmission is measured in microseconds."

"Microseconds?" Mary shook her head.

"One-one-thounsandth of a millisecond, or one-one-hundred-thousandth of a second. Never mind," Lainie said when they frowned at her. "The point is every sound comes to Jeremy just a tiny fraction of a second later than everyone else. This can distort sound, especially any concurrent sounds or echo effect at all, and is confusing when he tries to place the origins of sounds. It can be so distressing to him that he compensates by drowning out sounds around him as much as possible by making his own noise."

"Like banging," Henry said, his eyes clearing.

"Yes. It's also why some sorts of music sooth him, I'm guessing it's music with a steady, repeatable beat. The metronome calms him because I was able to set it to a frequency matching his delay, so he didn't experience the disconnect his condition makes him feel, giving him in effect the illusion of normalcy."

Mary looked at Henry, the worry lines on her face deeper than ever, and Henry brushed his hair back as if trying to clear away a rising panic.

"No, no, no, no," Lainie said, placing her hands on Mary's shoulders. "This is a good thing."

"How?" Mary asked.

"If that's what this is, and I'm ninety-nine percent positive, then your son's problems are not psychological, they are physical. That means he might be treated at the very least by medicine, and quite possibly by minimally invasive surgery. It's entirely possible that Jeremy can grow up to live a completely normal life."

"Is zis fact?" a stern female voice came from behind Lainie. She spun directly into the face from the promotional materials Lainie had studied before applying for a job at the clinic. The distinctly Germanic, iron-jawed, bulldog-jowled face of Dr. Ermina Reisen. In the flesh.

"Dr. Reisen, did you hear?" Mary said excitedly. "Jeremy isn't autistic after all. It's only this middle ear delay thing. Isn't it wonderful?"

When a pit-bull smiles, the expression never reaches its dead, shark-like eyes. Dr. Reisen smiled in just this way now. "It is zo vunderbar, Frau Jacobs."

"Jacobson," Henry said. "It's Jacobson."

"Just zo," Reisen said. "Vould you please to be vaiting for me in der music room. I must have der talk mit Dr. Parker, here."

Henry and Mary Jacobson returned to the music room to be with their son. Lainie beamed up at Dr. Reisen, however she didn't see admiration or praise on those rigid features, but mounting rage. Lainie felt herself withering under the unwavering gaze of the woman she'd hoped to ask for a job.

"Just vat did you sink you vere doink, *Dr.* Parker?" Reisen demanded, using the word 'doctor' as a whip to flog Lainie with. "Who do you sink you are? I haf four degrees from three universities, includink Johns-Hopkins. I am board certified in developmental psychology unt pathology, unt have served on twelve medical panels for ze AMCA *unt* ze AMA. I opened unt haf been operatink my own clinic here since you vere beink fingered by your high school football-playink boyfriend in ze back of his Volkswagon." She was advancing on Lainie, towering over her, forcing Lainie to stumble backward. "Vat makes you think you can valk in here unt diagnose a patient I haf been treating since birth?"

Lainie planted her feet and stood firm and tried to meet the sternness of that glare, but she was in the wrong and she knew it. Dr. Reisen's torpedo-shaped breasts came up against her shoulders and forced her to stumble back again. Lainie'd come into someone else's clinic and, without being asked for consultation, took it upon herself to diagnose after five minutes a patient Dr. Reisen had been working with for years. She didn't have a defense, and she knew it.

"I'll see myself out," Lainie finally said.

"Give me your resume," came the reply.

Lainie scrambled and reached into the satchel at her hip, pulled a copy of her resume from between her closed tablet. She tried to wait patiently while Reisen perused it, prune-wrinkled lips pursed in sour critique, but she was distracted by her phone which was buzzing persistently. A quick surreptitious glance showed Orin's app flashing red on screen. She was needed, and it was urgent.

"Top of your class, I zee," Reisen said. "Tell me, what made you apply to work with me?"

Buzz. "Well I. . ." *Buzz.* "It would have to be your work on. . ." *Buzz.* ". . .it's your focus on the application of juvenile. . ." *Buzz.* "Umm. . ."

"Is zere a problem, Doctor?"

"No, it's just I. . .I'm sorry. I need to get this, please. . ." Lainie held up a hand and activated her phone with the other. The app, when opened, was showing '911' across the front. One of the girls needed her, and it was an emergency. She looked up at Dr. Reisen, who was looking at something on a clipboard that a nearby nurse had handed her.

There was nothing, she realized, she could say to excuse what she was about to do. So she simply turned and left. It was raining, and she held her satchel on her head as if it would protect her as she ran across the parking lot. Tossing her erstwhile umbrella in first, Lainie dropped herself into the seat of her beat-up ten-year-old Toyota Camry. Cursing under her breath, she shook water out of her eyes and turned the ignition. A rapid clicking noise came from under the hood.

"Damn!" Lainie steeled herself, then got out again, ducking into the rain, and opened the hood. Nothing but a crimped wad of foil held one of the contacts on the starter in place. She reached down and squeezed this blob of tin as hard as she could, then went back to the driver's seat.

She turned the key again and the engine started. She patted the dash and blew a kiss in the general direction of the engine.

Both windshield wipers wiped, but only one made any headway against the fall Oakland downpour. Luckily it was on the driver's side. She pulled out of the parking lot and joined the late morning traffic headed toward the freeway back to San Francisco.

She could easily have afforded a new car, and paid cash, but whether through guilt or pride Lainie was reticent to spend any of the money she made as a digital pimp except on absolute necessities. Ridiculous, she supposed, but there it was.

Thirty minutes later she pulled into the parking lot outside the police station building and headed in. Ignoring the desk clerk at front, she knew where she was going and headed down a side hallway. There was a placard with which she was well familiar after 8 months:

Booking
Holding

Along the hall was a rank of benches, each fitted with brackets on the seat. Among those seated with their cuffs laced through these brackets was her girl, Lydia.

"Oh, Lainie," Lydia sighed, "thank God."

Lydia was a gorgeous blonde with a slight but tall frame, lithe and lengthy legs, and perky breasts. She was dressed in a midnight-blue evening gown and pearl choker. Lainie squatted in front of her. "Quickly, did you say anything, anything at all."

"Of course not," Lydia whispered back. "You told us to never say a word."

"And you didn't. . ."

It took a beat for Lydia to catch Lainie's meaning, then she shook her head. "No, you told us to never do that, either."

"Aw, shit!" The man's voice was also familiar to Lainie after eight months. "Not you again, Parker."

Lainie pivoted on her toes and met Detective Carlyle's rolling eyes. "Good *morning*, Detective. I see as always you've been keeping my friend on the benches all night long. This borders on harassment and abuse and you know it."

Vice Detective Carlyle stood by the booking window leaning on the small shelf there. He was a red-headed cop with a porn-star mustache and a constant, crooked sneer that looked as if he was always on the verge of telling a dirty joke. "We're undermanned, Parker. Makes for long waits for the interrogation room."

"Meanwhile, you ask her all the questions you want out here without charging her with anything, on the pretense booking is backed up, all the while starving her and not giving her anything to drink." Lainie pulled the neck-chain from under her collar from which depended a miniature cameo given to her by her father, and a handcuff key. She bent to unfasten Lydia's cuffs.

"Aw, don't do that," Carlyle whined, though not moving to stop her.

"Are you going to charge her?" When he didn't answer, Lainie said, "Soliciting? My girls don't solicit, and you know it. They are legitimate, above-board escorts. Nothing more."

"Yeah, and I'm America's next top model."

Lainie tossed him his cuffs and stood, helping Lydia up with her. "Unless you have any objections. . ."

It only happened once every few weeks that one of her girls was picked up and harassed like this, that Lainie had to come down and fetch them, but it was often enough that it finally made sense for Lainie to carry her own key. It expedited things, and since her girls were trained never to solicit, and never to speak when brought in, the cops never had anything to hold them on. Carlyle rarely interfered with her when she used her key like this. She knew he was playing a long-game with her, betting on cop's odds that sooner or later one of these escorts of Lainie's would talk. Until then he was content, Lainie suspected, to haul them in and make her come get them.

She led Lydia out.

*　　　*　　　*

From the top of the stairs – the elevator was impossibly slow – Lainie could tell the door to her apartment was ajar. Had she left it open? She doubted it.

In spite of the fact that in movies and television, whenever a door was left ajar something bad was lurking inside, Lainie would normally have shrugged this off as silly. But a year ago she'd experienced too much movie- and TV-style violence not to be very, very cautious.

She thought of calling the police, but likewise her experience with local cops was not positive – they were little more than overworked, under paid civil servants who resented being called upon for what they viewed as frivolous or inconsequential reasons.

She approached the door cautiously, stood to the side, reached out with her hand and pushed it the rest of the way open. Nothing slimy, undead, or murderous came leaping out, so she took the chance to lean and peer inside. There seemed to be no sign of intruders.

She walked into the apartment and commenced to take an inventory of her things. Nothing seemed to be missing.

"Lose something?"

Lainie jumped and spun around, aiming her keys, which she had laced one-by-one between the fingers of her right fist, at Leonid who sat in the wheelchair just outside her front door. "Leonid," she breathed relaxing.

"Easy kid. Little tightly wound?"

"Sorry," Lainie said. "My apartment door was open when I got home. I know I didn't leave it unlocked when I left. But nothing seems to be missing."

"Hmm," he said. "I haven't seen any suspicious characters around. Any reason to believe someone would target just your place?"

She thought about it.

"Really," he said, wheeling inside. "Do tell. Mind if I come in?"

"Yeah, sure," she said, closing the door behind him. He pushed his wheelchair around to face her. His legs leaned to one side as his feet rested on their pedals, but the arms that operated the oversized wheels bulged with muscle and popped with veins. He wore jeans and a Seahawks T-shirt. While his Vandyke beard was impeccably trimmed, his unruly mop of wavy hair hung about his ears.

Lainie still peered around her place, trying to spot any sign of anything out of place. She couldn't tell if it was just paranoia, but she thought the apartment felt...*violated* somehow.

"So?"

"What?" She looked at him. "Oh, my rudeness. You want some tea, or some soda?"

"Tea would be great," he said. "Earl Grey if you have it. But what I meant was what's the story? Why so freaked out? So you left the door open when you left, so what?"

"No, I didn't." She filled a kettle with water. "I wouldn't. I'm very careful about that sort of thing. Especially after..." She put the kettle on the stove and turned the heat to high.

"After..." Leonid prompted, his sharp eyes focused on her, though he smiled.

"Never mind." She set the pot on the stove and took a seat. He rolled up to the table and rested his arms on it. He wore gloves. His wheelchair was electric, operated by a small joystick bolted to one of the armrests, so he didn't need to push the wheels himself, but he did. He seemed to enjoy doing it that way more.

They sipped in unison for a few seconds.

"Oh," he said, as if just remembering to ask, "how'd the interview go?"

"It didn't."

"Why not?"

"You name it." Lainie shrugged. "Reason number one hundred ninety-four."

Leonid frowned. "C'mon."

Lainie sighed. "Got an emergency on the app, had to leave in the middle of it. But it doesn't even matter because I blew it before that just being me."

"Hmm. I don't even know why you're still job hunting."

"Where is my cell phone?" Lainie was eager to change the subject, something they've already talked about and it bored her. She stood, cast about her apartment, turning a complete circle. As if on cue the device rumbled atop the Formica of the breakfast bar. "There it is."

"You already have a very lucrative job," her neighbor from up the hall pressed.

"I have a degree in Special Education," Lainie told him, sitting and opening the app on her phone whose alert had caused it to go *burr*. "A doctorate degree. I'd like to think all that time and money wasn't wasted."

"How much does a doctor of education pull down these days," Leonid asked. "After taxes?"

"Enough. What does that matter?" Lainie asked.

Leonid's thick eyebrows like the fringe of a Persian rug, arched over brown eyes. "No matter how much it is, there's no way it can come close to what you're currently making."

Lainie huffed. "I'm surprised you approve of what I do. You used to be a cop. I would think you'd encourage me to get a respectable job." She was paging through the app on her phone, answering prompts.

"I've always been a pragmatist," Leonid said.

"When I worked for Capri Entertainment doing phone sex for lonely guys, it was okay for a young graduate student working her way through college," she said. "But I always thought I'd move beyond that sort of work with a PhD after my name."

Leonid chuckled. "I can see that. But kid, there's nothing wrong with what you do. It's a victimless crime, as they say."

"Leonid." Lainie thrust her phone at him so he could see the app on her screen. Orin's app. The one that was right now Lainie's sole source of income. The app through which men contracted for female companionship and were matched up from a stable of girls based on the customers' preferences. "I'm a pimp, for Christ's sake."

"I prefer 'Digital Madam.' You're an iMadam." He laughed.

She gave him a wry look and pocketed her phone. "UberWhores." They laughed, Lainie with rue.

"World's oldest profession," Leonid shrugged.

The app was disguised as a car gas consumption and mileage app, and served quite well as that alone. But through a secret entry, men could gain access to photos and vital statistics of a bevy of young women available for dates, including certain predilections and specialties. Conversely, the girls were alerted through the app, and if they accepted the date, his money was routed directly into her account, with a 20% cut routed to the company account.

It was Kate's job to screen potential girls, to field disputes between customers and their dates – of which there seemed an endless train – and facilitate any legal entanglements girls may encounter – of which there were surprisingly few. In the end the app only provided escort services for lonely men.

Whatever they and their escort got up to on that date was their own, purely adult arrangement.

The girls were under strict instructions never to solicited anything. If the man solicited them, they were permitted to accept with a yes or no, nothing else. An undercover cop couldn't solicit, that was entrapment. In the end the rare legal entanglement never resulted in a conviction for either party.

Apparently, the girls were creeped out by sweaty, socially awkward Orin, however harmless he was. He needed Lainie as liaison, as the face of the company. Sometimes she swore she was going to quit. Somehow, she never did.

"It isn't that," she said to Leonid. "It's just that no matter how voluntary these girls take the dates. . .and anything else, it still feels like female exploitation."

"Doesn't the word *voluntary* mean exactly the opposite?"

"They aren't forced by me or Orin. And we make sure the customers know any forced contact will meet with aggressive and unrelenting legal action."

"So there you go."

"No," Lainie persisted, "see, we don't have any daughters of one-percenters working for us. Not even girls with enough connections and academic backing to win full-ride scholarships. Our girls are all hard-working, blue-collar kids struggling to lift themselves above the circumstances of birth or the system, some already with kids to raise, who can't afford to work and attend school full-time."

"But that's just it," Leonid leaned forward. "You're giving these poor girls a chance they wouldn't have if it weren't for you and Orin."

Lainie stared at the table. "I just hate that they have to resort to exploiting themselves, while others get everything handed to them with a full tank of gas and a giant bow on top."

Leonid started to reply but Lainie held up her hand to stop him. "How are you doing?" she asked, determined to change the subject. "When are you going to let me see one of your paintings."

"Oh, god," he laughed. "If I had my way, never. I suppose I'm going to have to show someone someday, but not yet. I'm a cop...ex-cop...paralyzed from the chest down. Maybe trying to be an artist, now, after so many years, is stupid."

"Don't say that." There was a knock at the door. "You just need practice. I'll bet they're better than you think they are." Lainie went to answer the door.

She reached for the doorknob, but before she could turn it there was a thunderous crack and the door shuddered under her hand. She stepped back. "What the f..." The second blow flung the door open, whiffling past her nose by mere inches. Lainie cowered back under the shadow of the man who walked it.

Not that he was particularly tall, but he was broad, like a tank, built low to the ground and thick. He lunged at Lainie and pulled hard on her right wrist, drawing her to him while his other meaty paw encircled her throat, squeezing just enough to let her know what he was capable of but not enough to cut off her windpipe.

"Where is she?" He looked about him. "I'm not going to ask twice. Where is Eliza Andrews?"

"Who?" The name sounded familiar to Lainie, but with her throat in a vice her mind wasn't exactly focused on memory. It was focused on her fear, and a vague sense of déjà vu.

He squeezed ever so slightly, still not looking her in the eye.

"Eliza Andrews?" Lainie had her hands out to either side, as if trying to calm an enraged beast.

"Where is she?"

"I have no idea," Lainie said, her mind finally working. "I haven't seen Eliza in, what, three years?" It was a lie. As part of her master degree Lainie had worked for school credit at the university's free mental health clinic. Eliza was a junior, and she worked at Capris Entertainment, like Lainie. She had come in for one session a week for nearly a year. Lainie didn't see her again after that until she took over stewardship of Orin's escort app. She found Eliza on the payroll and the two had met several times since.

It was true, however, that Eliza had dropped off the app a few weeks ago with no sign, but that wasn't unusual. Girls came and went quite frequently. Was this one of Eliza's customers, demanding to know where she'd gone? And if so, how in hell had he gotten Lainie's address?

Lainie wondered why Leonid had said nothing so far. She craned her neck around but couldn't turn far enough to see him. The intruder took that to be a clue to the whereabouts of his prey and dragged Lainie around the chest-high bar separating the kitchen from the front room. At the table in the small dining nook was Leonid's wheelchair.

But the paraplegic was nowhere to be seen.

The intruder looked at the chair. Clearly making no sense of it, he looked around the nook, then looked at Lainie. "Where is she. I said I wasn't going to ask again. I've now asked nicely three times."

"Nicely?"

For that, Lainie got a squeeze to her neck that sent sparks swimming at the periphery of her vision. There was something wrong with Leonid's chair, but Lainie was too distracted to put her finger on just what. The intruder must've seen consciousness fading in her eyes because he let up the pressure on her neck. Her vision took almost a minute to reassert itself.

"Who are you?" she asked.

This time he shook her by her throat, which was almost worse than squeezing. She heard tendons and other connective tissue crackle like a bag of pork rinds and cried out with the pain. "I'm asking the questions. Is she here? Is Eliza Andrews in this apartment?

"Does it look like she's here?" Lainie said, her own voice sounding far away to her.

He glanced at the hallway. "What's in there?"

"Bedroom. Bathroom. Heliport."

He grunted. Letting go of her throat, he twisted her arm around behind her. Not to hurt her, this time, but to control her. She had no choice but to go where he steered her. Which was toward the hallway.

He first leaned into the bathroom and looked around the small space, using his free hand to yank the shower curtain aside. Then into the bedroom. She was forced to kneel and bend over with him as he searched under her bed, then stumble after him as he crossed the room and flung aside the sliding door of her closet.

"Told you she wasn't here."

He didn't seem to hear her. His brow furrowed, he was clearly thinking. She thought the act of using his brain looked painful to him, but kept her observation to herself. Through the loose lapel of his sport coat Lainie saw his gun resting in its shoulder holster. She tried to reach for it but he swatted her clumsy attempt away as easily as batting a moth.

Lainie understood why Leonid had ducked out of his chair – it would be much easier to hide himself than that bulky thing. She didn't know how well he could get around without the thing, pulling himself along on his arms alone, but she hoped he was even now making his escape out the front door and calling the police.

"Give me your cell phone," the man said.

"What? Why?"

"I want to see if she's called you."

Lainie handed over her cell phone readily enough – she knew she had no calls on it from Eliza. He discovered as much as he paged through her call and text history. Much to his surprise it vibrated in his hand. He pressed the alert on the screen and pulled up Orin's escort app.

Lainie wasn't worried. To the uninitiated it looked like a mundane interface for any run of the mill fuel monitor – mileage, consumption, efficiency, etc. Without knowing how, few could access the secret prompts that truly operated the app.

The brute grunted and shrugged much like a gorilla. Instead of returning her phone to her, he pocketed it. "Maybe she hasn't called you yet."

He let go Lainie's arm and as she grunted and massaged her shoulder he held up a finger in front of her nose. She didn't have to guess what that finger meant – don't call the police, don't even move from that spot, until I leave.

She nodded.

He walked back up the hallway toward the main room, at which point his head exploded back toward her in a shower of blood, skull fragments, and grey matter, splattering her face with warm gore.

CHAPTER 2

Lainie stood agape as the large man teetered, then collapsed. Beyond him, on the floor of the kitchen, lay Leonid aiming what looked like a shotgun right at her. Seeing her, he dropped the gun and peered at her, propping himself on strong, bulging arms.

Lainie stood, her hands inches from her face, as if she wanted to but didn't dare wipe the gore away. "Wha...what have you done?" She screamed.

Leonid looked from her to the body and back again. "I thought he was going to kill you," he yelled back at her.

Lainie walked forward, feeling like she was moving in a dream. "Where did you get a shotgun?"

He demurred lowering his voice. "Are you all right?"

"Yes, I am," she belted. "We should call the police."

"Wait now, just wait." He lifted a hand, cajoling. "Let's think this through. Ex-cop kills federal agent in the home of a woman once accused of arson and murder?"

Lainie blinked. "How do you know about that? Wait, how do you know he's a fed?" She was still yelling.

He shushed her, then, "He looks like one, doesn't he? Dealt with his type a thousand times on the force."

Lainie bent and with shaking hands, fished the man's wallet out of the inside pocket of his jacket. Sure enough, there was a badge inside and an ID. "Special Agent Angio Muntz of...The U.S. Secret Service?" She tossed it down on his chest like it was a scorpion. "What the fu..."

"As for the other thing," Leonid said, "c'mon, you were in all the local news for a while. Think I didn't recognize you from the papers when I moved in? I never brought it up because you never did. I figured you talk about it when you wanted to."

Lainie realized that was possible, though she hadn't realized the arson at Capris and the murders had made the news. As she quickly retrieved her cell phone from the corpse's outer pocket she asked, "But why did you shoot him?"

"As I said, I thought he was going to kill you."

"But if you knew he was an Agent..."

"C'mon, Lainie, cops can be bad guys, too."

When she poised to dial her phone, he pulled himself toward her a few hand-breadths. "Listen, listen, listen...we gotta get our stories straight before we call the cops, if someone else hasn't already called them. That shot will have been heard."

"Why can't we tell them the truth?"

"Lainie," he said, frustration edging his voice. "Me being an ex-cop...complicates things. There will be a lot more questions, a longer investigation, more press. Haven't you already had your fill of that?"

She had to admit she had.

He edged forward a few more inches. "Okay, so here's how it went down. There were two of them, see. They pushed their way in, demanded you turn over this Eliza chick. When they realized you didn't know where she was, they got into an argument. It escalated, then one shot the other and ran."

Leonid and Lainie both turned their heads toward the outer hall as they heard the slamming of doors and shouting. Sirens sounded in the distance, grew steadily nearer. Leonid looked back. "Lainie?"

There was no time to think. "Okay," she said, squeezing her eyes to shut out the corpse in front of her.

"Good," Leonid said, grunting as he strong-armed his way back into the kitchen toward the dining nook and his wheelchair, dragging his gun behind him. "Open the front door. I came rushing to check on you when I heard the shot. Got it?"

Lainie stood, lost for a moment, then turned and opened the front door. On legs that felt as shaky as a newborn foal's, she walked round the bar counter to watch him pull himself into his chair with bulging pectorals. She was shocked to watch him fiddle with the shotgun, and it came apart in his hands. He reassembled the barrel, magazine, and stock, and the parts became the backrest to his wheelchair. She had noticed earlier that there was something wrong with the chair, but had been too distracted by the man choking her to tell what. Now Leonid reattached the back to the seat and suddenly there was no sign of the shotgun to be seen.

He wheeled out into the living room and said loudly enough for anyone in the hall to hear, "Are you sure you're all right, Lainie?"

She could hear worried voices in the hall, neighbors wondering if they were safe. *Should we evacuate? Did you call the police? So did I. What could it have been? Did it sound like a gunshot to you? Yeah, me too.*

"Y-yes," she said, as loudly. "Just...just a little shaken up."

*   *   *

The police investigation was taken over by detectives when they arrived. Lainie was questioned quite thoroughly and repeatedly, Leonid by her side comforting her, a little too present. ME's had taken away the body and she felt shock draining from her, leaving her exhausted. She was only asked once if she thought this was related to that other case almost a year ago and she said she doubted it. She was told she couldn't stay in her apartment, which was now a crime scene, and Leonid said she could stay with him. She was told not to leave town.

The officer oversaw as she packed herself a couple of bags and stepped out, watching them place a big red adhesive tag across the jamb, then crisscross the threshold with bright yellow tape.

"Sorry for the mess," Leonid said as he unlocked his door and led her inside. He rolled quickly around scooping up discarded clothing and a couple of magazines, which he bore to the bedroom, tossed in, and slammed the door. "You'll want to sleep on the couch. I have an orthopedic bed and the position I have to sleep in wouldn't be comfortable for you."

"That's all right," she said, setting down her luggage, "I'll be fine after a shower."

"Sure," he said. "You know where it is."

His apartment was an almost exact mirror image of hers. Where her kitchen, bar-counter and dining nook had been on the left his was on the right, which put the hall, bathroom, and bedroom on the left. She opened one of her bags enough to pull out her shower kit and change of clothes.

She scrubbed herself thoroughly in the shower, only stopping once to lean out over the toilet and throw up. She'd seen a man's throat cut a year ago in the VIP lounge of the BWI airport, but that had been blood. Lots of blood.

This had been blood, but also bone and brains. This was worse.

In the shower she had time to think. Leonid had been right, she didn't want to get in the middle of another intrigue, like last year. Telling the lie to the police about what happened might shorten the whole affair and keep her clear. She'd shown negative for gunshot residue, the primary reason the detectives were even inclined to entertain the outlandish story Leonid had concocted for her.

Then there was Eliza Andrews. Eliza was a bright and cheerful girl. Parents dead, she'd been raised by a doting grandfather. Aside from residual issues with abandonment, a disconnection from her peers, and a spate of older lovers that suggested a bit of a father-complex, she seemed to Lainie to be a relatively well-adjusted young woman. Lainie liked her.

Lainie didn't find out till later that when her psych rotation had ended, Eliza showed up at the clinic looking for her. The girl had pitched quite a fit, made a real scene when she was not only told Lainie no longer worked there, but that the clinic couldn't give her Lainie's personal contact information for legal reasons.

It crushed Lainie to know that her leaving had left Eliza feeling abandoned, yet again, but was forbidden by the clinic to contact her for the same legal reasons. When Lainie took over Orin's escort app and saw Eliza on the payroll, she'd immediately contacted her, but Eliza feigned indifference. She was lying, protecting herself, Lainie knew, and only felt worse.

Now, clearly, gunmen or Feds or someone were looking for Eliza. Why they thought to look in Lainie's apartment she couldn't guess, but the girl was clearly in some kind of trouble. Much as Lainie had been before. She knew how frightening and lonely being hunted could feel.

Walking out into the living room again, still trying to get water out of her ear with a washcloth, Lainie said, "I have one more thing to do. I need to find and warn Eliza that someone is after her."

She expected Leonid to argue with her that the cops were probably already doing just that, and to stay clear of the situation, but instead he said, "I'll drive. Just let me hit the head first."

The bathroom door was too narrow for the wheelchair, so Leonid left it just outside and shut the door. Lainie's curiosity got the better of her. She examined the backrest and saw how it could come apart, recognized certain components of the shotgun, and was even able to unsnap the magazine, and then snap it back into place.

By the time he came out she was in the living room ready to leave.

$*$ $*$ $*$

Leonid's van was interesting, Lainie'd never seen anything like it. Instead of a slow-moving lift in the back or at the side, there was a ramp that extended rather rapidly, almost dangerously so, when the back doors were opened by remote control. There was a chain-conveyor that hooked somewhere under his wheelchair when he rolled up to the foot of the ramp, which hauled him up the ramp, again with speed and relative silence. He then rolled his himself, in his chair, up to the front of the van and into the empty space behind the steering wheel, where clamps trapped the wheels of his chair in place for the drive. There were squeeze levers for acceleration and braking on the steering wheel.

Lainie climbed into the passenger seat. "Sure have some fancy toys."

"Oh, yeah, it's great being paralyzed," he said with a dry smirk. "But you'd be surprised how many charities are out there for the handicapped. With a little diligence and the right amount of *woe-is-me* and you can get all kinds of free stuff and tax-exempt money."

"I don't like that word," Lainie said. "'Handicapped.'"

He started the van and snorted. "Please, spare me from political correctness. I broke my spine in an accident during a high-speed chase, and after years I'm still in physical therapy. Words or what someone calls me, that's the least of my problems." He tried to laugh the edge off this tirade, but Lainie didn't join him.

Lainie made a call. "Orin, how are you?"

"Lainie!" Orin had been the IT man at Capri Entertainment, the phone sex company that'd put Lainie through school, until a serial killer had firebombed the offices and killed the CEO in his hunt for Lainie. "What can I do for you?"

"I need an address of one of the girls. Can you get it for me?"

"Sure. Trouble?"

"No, she had asked me about a book and I told her I'd send her a copy." Lainie gave him Eliza's last name.

:Hmm, not here. You sure she works for us?"

"She did," Lainie said. "She stopped taking dates about two months ago."

"That explains it," he said. "The roster refreshes itself every month. Anyone who hasn't taken a date in six weeks drops off. It's easier that way, I mean we're not exactly the kind of job people give two weeks' notice, y'know?"

"What about the school? She's enrolled there."

After Capris fired him, before he published his app, Orin got a job at the university as Director of IT. He still kept the job for appearances. In a matter of seconds, he had an address for her.

But the address didn't get them far.

"Oh, the old man who used to live here?" said the woman who answered the door of the two-story faux-Victorian prefabricated home on the west side. "She said he died like a year ago, the granddaughter. We bought the house from her about, what was it, about two months ago now."

It wasn't lost on Lainie that this was about the time Eliza dropped off the app. "Was her name Eliza Andrews?"

"I'm sorry, I don't remember. But I might have her forwarding address. She left it in case any mail got delivered."

The note, scrawled on the torn corner of a manila envelope, was indeed Eliza's name and new address. The next apartment building was old stucco art deco. It sat across the street from a vacant lot taken over by weeds and bisected by a railroad track.

The girl who answered the door was on the chubby side, with short blond hair and forehead acne. "Eliza's my roommate," she said. "But she hasn't been here for a long time now. She used to spend the night at the lab sometimes, but never this long. Jeez it's been six weeks or so. I was about to call the police."

"About to?" Lainie demanded, then took a breath and forced the outrage down.

"Yeah, well, I didn't have to, did I? They came here looking for her."

"Did they say why?"

"No, just that she was wanted for questioning. Not even for what."

"You mentioned a lab?" Lainie asked.

"Yeah, it's at the college. She started working there for Professor Harkness in her Junior year and he hired her on permanently after she was accepted at grad school. She never talked much about what they were working on, but she's been working there ever since."

"Was the lab on campus?"

"Sort of. Just outside, I think. I only dropped her off or picked her up a few times but I think I can describe it to you."

The entire building she directed them to was vacant with a *For Sale* sign tacked to the front door. Lainie called the realtor's number from the placard and was told the building had been vacated by the university about six weeks ago and went on sale. No, they had no information on what it'd been used for before, or where those offices and facilities had been moved.

In a last-ditch lead, Lainie had Leonid drive her to the admin building of the University, where she spoke to the Human Resources manager, a Mrs. Gilligan with flawless ebony skin and a luxurious auburn weave that framed her round face in an up-do. "Well, I shouldn't say," she leaned forward with a conspiratorial tone, "but Dr. Harkness has been arrested. Embezzlement or something. Misappropriation of government grant money."

"Really," Lainie said, leaning in to encourage the woman's prurient nature. "Well, what happened to his research? Specimens? His staff?"

"Seized. Fired, as far as I know."

"That's rough for them."

Mrs. Gilligan nodded.

"Any idea what they were working on?"

Mrs. Gilligan looked around her empty office as if to make sure any nonexistent bystanders couldn't overhear, then whispered, "Nothing good. Something hush-hush for the government. Something they were hot to get their hands on."

Back in the van Lainie slapped her thighs in frustration. "Damn it. Trails run out. I have no idea where to look next."

"Home then," Leonid said.

Lainie was reluctant to give up, but shrugged. "I suppose." As he drove she speculated. "I wonder if Eliza got mixed up in Professor Harkness's troubles, that's why the feds are looking for her."

"Sounds likely," Leonid said. "But that guy in your apartment..."

"That guy you shot?"

Leonid frowned. "He didn't seem like he was there to arrest someone. He was there to hurt someone."

"Well he was pretty rough," Lainie said, rubbing her bruised neck. "But he was a Secret Service Agent. Aren't they supposed to protect the president?"

"The Secret Service is a branch of the Treasury Department. They also work closely with the FBI in investigating cases of fraud and malfeasance, especially when it comes to government grants and contractors."

"All this over money?" Lainie shook her head. "I know it was the heat of the moment and all, but I wish you hadn't shot the man. He was an asshole, but he was on his way out the door."

Leonid pressed his lips together but said nothing.

After a moment, Lainie mused, "Embezzlement. Doesn't sound like the Eliza I know."

"People Change," he said.

Back at the apartment building they both lived in, Lainie waited for Leonid to secure his van, then they went up the old and creaky, impossibly slow elevator together. Leonid's apartment was further along the hallway than Lainie's. As they passed her door Lainie noted that the bright yellow crime scene tape spider-webbing her threshold was no longer taught and rigid, but sagged a little.

She paused. "You go on ahead, Leonid. I'm going to get something out of my apartment."

"Cops aren't going to like you mucking up their crime scene."

"It's my apartment," she said. "It's already got my fingerprints and DNA all over it. Not like I can contaminate it any more than I already have."

He rolled on down the hallway.

On close inspection Lainie saw that the red seal on the door jamb had been sliced cleanly along the crease of the door. Turning the knob, she tried to open the door quietly, but it creaked as it opened. She tried to step through gaps in the crime scene tape, but it stuck to her pant leg, then her sleeve, and

27

before she knew it she was stumbling through the door, a-tangle in the sticky stuff, hopping on one leg and trying to pull it free of her clothes.

She froze as yet another intruder came out of the shadows of the hallway, moving slow and holding one of Lainie's bigger kitchen knives in shaking hands. She was thin, with tan skin and wide, dark eyes that receded into their sockets as if haunted. She was dressed quite fashionably – bright red knit mini dress, tan chunky-boots, and clutching what looked from here to be a designer handbag – but her clothing was rumpled as if it hadn't been washed in some time. But for the lines of fear and anxiety on her face, she was the very image of...

"Eliza," Lainie whispered.

"Who's with you?" The girl's voice was small and shaky. "It's just me."

"What happened here?" Eliza pointed at the blood splatter across the floor and on the walls.

"Runaway nose bleed," Lainie said. "Can I close the door?" Eliza gestured with the knife and Lainie, careful not to make any sudden moves, closed the door without a sound.

Then Eliza asked her a completely non-sequitur question: "Who do you work for?"

"What?"

"Are you one of them?" the girl demanded. "Do you work for the government?"

"Um...duh, nuh, n-no. of course not."

Seeming satisfied, the girl, peered around her as if afraid someone saw her through the walls, then lowered the knife, looking small and beaten down.

"Eliza?" Lainie tried to catch the girl's eye.

At mention of her name she abruptly focused on Lainie. "Ms. Parker," Eliza said. "I'm so sorry. It's all my fault."

"Is everything all right?" Lainie asked.

Eliza went to the couch and sat down, putting the knife on the coffee table. Lainie sat in the overstuffed and peered at Eliza. "Asking again, everything all right?"

The girl looked at her, finally smiled and let out a hollow laugh. "Ms. Parker. I'm so glad you're all right. I'm so sorry I sent them to you."

"Who? Are you in some kind of trouble?"

"I knew they were tapping my cell phone, so I threw it away. That was smart, right? I've been staying off the grid, basically living homeless on friends' couches. But I couldn't do that forever. I needed help. Someone smart who could help me. So, I came here. But when I was half way up the stairs I heard a gunshot and I ran. Ducked into a closed-up gas station across the street where I could see the entrance of your building until the cops came and went. But I didn't see any of *them*."

"Who? Eliza, what the hell's going on?"

"They arrested him. Professor Harkness. No wait, I didn't tell you, I've been working for Professor Harkness. At the university. Since before grad school. Government grant. Such a brilliant man."

"Go on."

"He came in one day a few months ago and started shredding folders. Told me to start shredding, too. There was banging on the door to his office. He sent me out through the records room. I saw them hauling him away in handcuffs. I didn't know what to do. They hauled everyone out in handcuffs. I went home but they were already there. I didn't know what to do, where to go. I went to a hotel. Next morning, I went to the lab but the entire building was sealed. They had a tent set up over the entrance and a long tunnel with big, like, exhaust fans attached to it. Men in containment suits were going in and out."

"Good god," Lainie said, taking Eliza's hands in hers. They were frigid and quivering like autumn leaves.

"I thought, fuck, there's been some sort of a containment breach. But we weren't working on that kind of stuff. I mean we were, but none of it was viable. That was the whole point of our work. None of our specimens had been activated yet. None of it could possibly be infectious."

Lainie wasn't sure what that meant, but didn't want to interrupt.

"Still," Eliza went on, "I was terrified. I went back to the motel. Kept expecting to get sick, but I didn't. I called Dr. Harkness's phone but it said the service was no longer available. I was running out of money. Just when I thought about turning myself in – it all had to be some big misunderstanding, didn't it? – I returned to the motel from getting something to eat and there was a man already inside sitting on the bed, aiming a gun at me."

Lainie gasped.

"I freaked and ran. He chased me but somehow I was able to lose him in the neighborhood – I was jumping fences, cutting through yards. Thought I was clear, knew I couldn't go back to the motel, so I took the bus to a...friend's house. Only I didn't get there. I was walking from the bus stop and two cars, SUVs, tinted windows, came at me, slow, y'know, from opposite ends of the block. How did they find me? Had to be my phone, right?"

Lainie moved to the couch next to Eliza and put her arm over the girl's shoulders.

"I ditched them again. Then I ditched my phone. I've been staying at friends' houses, never the same place twice. I think I already told you this part. Then I thought of you. Don't know what made me think of you. You just popped into my head. You were always so nice, at the school, then with the men's service. Only I didn't have your address or phone number because I ditched my phone. So, this morning I bought a prepaid phone and accessed my contacts using that."

Just hours later a Treasury Agent showed up to bully Lainie and get killed by Leonid. "You've been staying off the grid all this time?" Lainie asked.

Eliza nodded, a jittery movement. "I almost gave up and went home dozens of times, but I'm scared. When I heard the gun shot I thought for sure they'd killed you. But when I saw you from across the street, come out and get in that man's van, I was so relieved. But I couldn't do it anymore, hide, run. I needed help, human contact. So I snuck in here to wait for you. I didn't know what to think of the crime scene tape. But I figured they wouldn't look for me here, in an apartment sealed by police. Is that right? I can't tell, I'm not thinking clearly, I'm so tired. And I'm so sorry."

Eliza started to weep, a quiet drizzle of tears.

"It's okay," Lainie said. "You're safe now. We'll think it through. Just catch your breath. I'll get us some tea."

She picked up the knife and turned toward the kitchen, and stopped. The front door was open and just inside sat Leonid in his wheelchair. "Drop the knife, Lainie."

He was aiming his reassembled shotgun at her navel.

CHAPTER 3

"Wow, it's Leonid," Lainie said, but her tone was flat, overtly bored.

He cocked his head at her. "Funny, you don't sound surprised."

"No."

He reached behind his chair and flung the door shut behind him. "I said put the knife down."

Lainie looked at the knife, turned it around in her hand in a half-hearted flourish. "I wish I was wrong, but I knew I wasn't."

"Lainie..." Eliza said, voice shaking.

"It's all right, Eliza. Just stay behind me."

"Yes," Leonid said, "stay behind her so I don't have to shift my aim to kill you both."

"Kill us?"

"Yes, Eliza," Lainie said. "Leonid doesn't work for the government. He's being paid by someone else to eliminate loose ends."

"Very good," Leonid said. "How did you figure it out."

"It was in the shower at your place, the first moment I had to myself to calm down and think things through." Lainie remained casual but watched the barrel of his gun, kept herself between it and Eliza. "I realized you were no ex-cop. Cops're trained to de-escalated things before shooting. The man you shot had a gun, but it was in its holster, and he was clearly on his way out. As unnecessarily rough as he'd been, he wasn't threatening me anymore. At the very least you could've stayed out of sight and let him leave. You shot him when you didn't have to."

Leonid shrugged. He wheeled further into the apartment, over in front of the bar counter, operating the joystick with one hand while keeping the gun leveled at her with the other.

Lainie went on, "I went along with the lie you suggested because, still in shock, it made sense at the time. But on reflection I realized that you being an ex-cop would've simplified the investigation, not complicated it – cops tend to lend each other credence, they would've accepted your story without question. But they would've at least run you through the computer. Since you're *not* an ex-cop, you couldn't let them do that, they would've known you aren't who you say you are."

Leonid raised his eyebrows and nodded at her, faking polite golf-applause, still holding the gun on her.

"Then there was that collapsible shotgun of yours. What ex-cop has to conceal his weapon that way? If anything you'd carry a handgun, even if you kept it concealed. Who has a gun like that? I couldn't think of anyone but a professional killer."

"Bravo," he said. "I knew you were smart the first time we met."

"Only a month ago," Lainie nodded. "Seems like longer. I always thought making friends was my idea. But you were here to keep an eye on my apartment in case Eliza showed up here." Lainie wondered why he wasn't standing up, now that the charade was over.

"Well, yes, but I planned on keeping a low profile. Making friends *was* your idea. I didn't expect you to be so friendly. Most people aren't."

"What I don't get is why kill the agent? He was leaving. He hadn't yet seen you."

"If he was here at all it meant that they had reason to believe that *she* might come here," chucking his chin at Eliza. "Which meant my gambit in staking you out was about to pay off. I couldn't have him staking out the place himself and getting to her first. In the time it would take the police to identify him as an agent, notify his superiors, and for them to replace him with another agent, I hoped she might show up here. I was right."

"Who do you work for?" Lainie eyed the exit. "Why do they want Eliza dead?"

"Dead," Eliza repeated in a croak, followed by a very audible gulp.

He cocked his head as if considering telling Lainie, then shrugged. "Put down the knife, Lainie."

"Okay, a simpler question. You haven't gotten up out of the chair yet, which means you really are partially paralyzed. Who hires a paraplegic hitman?"

"You don't need legs to lie in a sniper's nest, and I can climb better than most people with four working limbs. As for close-up work, you'd be surprised how deferential people are to a man in a wheelchair. I'm helpless, don't you know? They make room for you in elevators, hold doors for you, even bend closer to hear you over the noise of traffic. You can get good and close to even a stranger and not arouse any fear in them. Close enough for blade work."

He grated his teeth. "Now drop the knife, Lainie."

"I don't think so." Lainie reaffirmed her grip and pointed it at him. "We're going to walk out of here. And if you try to stop us, well I can do a lot of damage with this thing while Eliza runs for the cops."

He frowned, pulled the trigger.

The firing pin came down on nothing – an empty chamber. He opened the breach and glared at the two empty holes, which in turn stared back at him.

Meanwhile, Lainie had taken Eliza by the wrist and led her toward the door in rapid strides. "While you were in the

34

bathroom," she explained. As he craned around and plunged his arm into the pouch behind his seat, she added, "All of them."

He pushed the joystick forward, lunging the chair toward them as they darted for the door. The two ladies sprinted up the hall to the stairs. They rounded the first flight down even as Lainie heard Leonid cursing, hammering the elevator button up above. The button to the impossibly slow elevator.

The women reached the ground level. Lainie looked out the door and craned her neck around. She then yanked Eliza after her into the parking lot, sprinting toward her car. They got in, Lainie behind the wheel. She inserted the key and cranked the ignition, only to be answered by a rapid ticking noise.

"Shit." When Lainie jumped out and ran to the front of the car, Eliza snapped, "What in hell are you doing?"

"She won't start," Lainie said. "I need to..."

Lainie flung the hood of the car up over her head and dove in, gripping the foil around the starter lead and crimping it hard. She closed the hood and ran to climb in again. Even as the engine roared to life, she heard Eliza's gasp.

She was peering out the side at the building above. "There's someone at the door. Drive. Now." After riding the elevator down, Leonid had gone to the window of the ground-floor landing at the foot of the stairs. Even now he knocked the glass out of the window with the butt of what looked like a revolver, which must've been stashed elsewhere on the wheelchair.

Lainie sped out of the parking slot just as she heard something pinging the body panels of her car: *plunk! Plunk! Plunk!* Bullet holes, she groaned to herself. Leonid was unlikely to be able to get into his van and start it in time to follow the women, so once she hit the main boulevard Lainie slowed down to ambient traffic speeds.

"I think now is a good time for you to tell me what the hell's *really* going on."

"What do you mean?" Eliza was still amped up from the escape, eyes wide, face shiny with a thin veneer of sweat.

"I mean, people are awfully damned determined to find you, some of them to kill you. I don't believe you're as clueless as you pretend to be. Remember: I know you."

Eliza shook her head. "Kill me? Jesus. What the fuck?" She looked cowed, as if she expected to be slapped or shot at any second. "All I know is they arrested Professor Harkness, like I told you. And now they're looking for me."

"All right," Lainie said, splitting her attention between the rearview mirror and the road ahead. "Start from the beginning."

"When I was accepted into the program. I was first assigned to Professor Denning, but once Judson . . . I mean Dr. Harkness saw what I was working on for my thesis he came to me and asked permission to have me transferred to him as his TA. The first thing he did was show me his pet project and I became his assistant in that."

"Let me guess," Lainie said, "a project funded by the government. Who? The CIA? Homeland Security? The Congressional Budget Office?"

"I never knew which specific agency," Eliza said.

"What was the research?"

"Something Professor Harkness and I had been working on for the last three years. He was already a good way down the road of his research when I joined him."

"What?"

"Um . . ."

Lainie swerved without slowing into the parking lot of a motel with a diner attached at one end and parked in front of the restaurant. "Don't think because we're stopping that I've forgotten you didn't answer my question."

"I'm not hungry."

"No, but this is a public place, and I need to leave you alone for five minutes while I make a telephone call."

The door banged into an old-fashioned bell as they walked in. "Who are you going to call?" Eliza's eyes were wide.

"Don't worry," Lainie said, leading her companion to a table directly in the center of the restaurant. "He's a friend. And he knows how to keep a secret."

"I hope," Lainie murmured to herself as she turned away and headed to the back of the diner. There was a hallway leading back to the restrooms, storerooms, and the kitchen where, she presumed, there was a back exit if needed. In the center of the hallway were two pay phones in waist-high cubicles. The last two restaurant payphones left in the city as far as Lainie knew. As it was, one stood maimed, it's handset and cord yanked off and missing. She went to the other one.

If whomever was after Eliza could track her cell call so easily, Lainie wasn't about to call Cord Steele from her own cell phone, assuming it, too, was compromised. She hadn't spoken to the CIA agent in nearly six months. After an initial torrid three months of sheet-scorching sex whenever he was in town, he became hard to reach by phone. At first, he returned her voicemails promptly, but that became more and more rare. After a month of no returned calls Lainie'd stopped calling.

She had no idea if he'd answer now, but...

"Steele."

Lainie was so stunned to hear his voice at first she couldn't speak.

"Cord Steele," he said, impatience creeping into his voice.

"It's me," she croaked. Clearing her throat she said, "It's me, Cord. Lainie."

After a beat, he said, "You changed your number."

Lainie needed a beat herself to register this greeting. "That's all you have to say after...what? Were you screening my calls?"

"No, I just..."

"If you were tired of me calling," she pressed, "all you had to do was say something. Tell me it was great, kiddo, but you're a maverick, a loner, who can't be tied down." Sarcasm radiated from her like a white-hot nova.

"Look I just..."

"I'm not some stalker." All evidence to the contrary, she thought with rue. "I'm not some teeny bopper with a crush. I know these things run their course. But the least you could've done, as an adult yourself, is let me know it was over so I didn't make an ass of myself calling and calling."

"Look I'm sorry, I just..."

"Whatever," she snapped. "I didn't call about that. I have a friend who's in trouble. Your kind of trouble. I thought I'd call and see what you could find out for us. You owe me at least that."

There was a moment of silence, during which Lainie wondered if Steele'd hung up. Then, "What's going on?"

"She worked for a college professor on a research project funded by the government."

"Which agency?" he asked.

"She never knew," Lainie said. "I get the impression she never bothered with that end of things. Her thing was the research."

"Either that," he said, "or she wasn't cleared to know. Go on."

"Anyway, they abruptly shut down the research. Arrested everyone. But not before the professor deleted some files off of the computers."

"Deleted." Steele's own sarcasm was audible over the line. What was he deleting?"

"Eliza doesn't know."

"All of it."

"Unknown."

"So she's in custody."

"Not exactly," Lainie said. "She slipped away but they've been looking for her."

"Lainie, the best thing your friend can do is go back. Return whatever it was she took and take the consequences."

"I didn't say she took anything."

"Don't be stupid Lainie. She wouldn't be running unless she had something she doesn't want to give up. She needs to turn herself in."

"It isn't that simple," Lainie said. "There is someone else after her, too. They've hired at least one hit man who has already taken pot shots at us. I have the bullet holes in my car to prove it. I don't think they're interested in a confession. Until we know who's who in this..."

He was silent.

"Steele?"

"Shit," he said. "All right, what was the scientist's name?"

"Harkness," Lainie said. "I think his first name was Judson, something like that. He was a professor at University of California, San Francisco, the Chemical Engineering department."

"Do you think this friend of yours and the prof were into something together?"

"If you mean romantically, I don't know but I'm pretty sure they were involved. Just from some of the things she has said, the way she said them. If you mean something illegal, I don't think so. He may have been, but I don't think she has it in her to do anything . . . criminal."

"Wouldn't be the first time a smart dashing professor led some young ingénue astray with the promise of romance and adventure."

To Lainie that was a distinctly chauvinistic view. Unfortunately, in this case she couldn't fault him. She knew Eliza to have a father complex and abandonment issues. "What's her name?" Steele interrupted her thoughts.

"Eliza Andrews," Lainie said. "She was his research assistant and TA. I don't know any more details. It's hard to get anything out of her. She's scared stiff right now."

"I'll see what I can find out. In the meantime, keep your head down. I assume this is a pay phone?"

"Yes."

"Good, Lainie, you always were smart."

"Fuck you," she said in a whisper.

"Call me back here in twenty-four hours."

Lainie hung up. She mentally berated herself for yelling at him. That wasn't how she wanted their next conversation to go. She was going to play it cool, maybe pretend to forget his name, act like their short time together was just one event in a life too full to pine over some man. Instead she'd screamed at him like a harridan.

Feeling foolish, she returned to the table where she'd left Eliza. The younger woman was such an obvious mark, looking around her, jumping at the slightest movement or sound, even someone who didn't know her could tell she was on the run from something.

"Jesus, chill," Lainie said, taking the coffee cup in front of Eliza and moving it as far from her as possible. Eliza made a half-hearted move to grab it, then sat looking at it with a forlorn look as she jiggled her knees under the table. "That's the last thing you need."

"Who did you call?" Eliza seemed ready to bolt. There was a small amber carafe in the center of the table with a candle in it. Someone had left a book of matches next to it. Eliza picked this up to fiddle with.

"Relax," Lainie said. "He's a friend of mine in the government. He's going to try to find out for us how much trouble you're really in. You may be paranoid for nothing. It could be all a big misunderstanding. Some questioning and they'll let you go. You'll be out of an internship, at worst."

"They're shooting at me, for God's sake," Eliza said. She was folding the matches down one by one, without ripping them free.

"Best case scenario."

"Worst case you'll be throwing rose petals over my grave this time tomorrow."

"Don't be morbid," Lainie said. Annoyed, she pulled the book of matches from Eliza's hands and put them in her pocket.

"When is he supposed to get back to you?"

"I'm to call him this time tomorrow. But we can't stay here till then."

"I sure can't," Eliza said. "I need to be somewhere."

"Where are you going to go, Eliza?" Lainie didn't expect her to have an answer.

"I need to go to Houston."

"Texas?"

"British Columbia."

"Canada? What the hell for?"

"There's a place there we're supposed to meet." Eliza kept a wary eye on their surroundings.

"Who?" Lainie asked.

Eliza looked at her.

"You said 'we're' supposed to meet there."

Eliza sighed. "Dr. Harkness and I agreed to regroup there if we got separated."

Steele was right, the two were into something together. "Why there?"

"Random place." Eliza shrugged. "Small lumber town, three thousand people or so. Last place they'll look, and if they do we'll see them coming."

"You guys thought this through."

"He did." Eliza seemed to realize she'd said too much and rushed to add, "I mean, just in case, y'know, anything happened. It was a classified project, after all. He's very thorough." She was such a bad liar, Lainie almost pitied her, if it wasn't so infuriating. "But I don't know how to get there. I don't have a car and I'm sure they have the airports and bus stations watched. I *have* to get there. He's depending on me."

"You're in love with him," Lainie said.

Eliza screwed up her face. "Gads, no! If anything, he reminds me of my grandfather."

Lainie, of course, saw right through this denial. "But Harkness's been arrested. He's not going to be there."

"Doesn't matter, I have to go. If he doesn't show up, I promise to do whatever you say."

It seemed unlikely to Lainie that she was going to convince Eliza to turn herself in at least until she was sure Harkness wasn't coming to rescue her. Even if he did somehow appear and managed to offer some plausible, acceptable explanation, this whole mess would finally be over.

Lainie asked, "How were you planning to get there?"

Eliza colored. "I . . . was going to ask you."

Lainie frowned at her.

"I know it's a big favor," Eliza said. "I'm sorry."

"So you were going to drive," Lainie said. "That's got to be like . . . I don't know . . ."

"Little over fifteen hundred miles," Eliza said. "About a 24-hour drive, accounting for stops for food and gas. If we leave now, we'll get there just in time for you to call your friend back."

"We," Lainie laughed. "I can't go to Canada."

"Why not?"

Lainie stopped to think. God knew she couldn't go back to her place, not with Feds and assassins watching the place. Not, at least, until this was over. She had plenty for a weekend road trip if she dipped into the pimp-stash, as she had come to call it, the money paid her through Orin's app.

Eliza stiffened. She was watching a grey nondescript sedan troll slowly through the parking lot outside. "We have to go now."

Lainie didn't notice anything outstanding or suspicious about the car. The driver was pretty, a girl of some Asian ancestry. The passenger was African-American, with glasses and a tablet computer held up as if reading from it. They were speaking to each other and smiling, and gave no sign they'd noticed Eliza and Lainie inside, nor gave their car any special attention.

"I don't think..." Lainie started.

"Now," Eliza snapped. She grabbed Lainie's arm and headed for the door. Lainie followed, willing enough. She supposed those looking for Eliza would choose as unassuming an appearance as possible.

The couple had parked and were climbing out of their vehicle. They seemed to take no note of them as Eliza yanked Lainie out of the entryway and onto the parking lot.

"Eliza." Lainie pulled free of the younger woman's grasp. "Even if they were from the people after you, you're acting suspicious enough to draw everyone's attention in a mile's radius."

Eliza didn't answer. Once the couple was inside and she and Lainie out, she seemed to relax visibly. "You never can tell," she said, but without much conviction. "Let's get moving."

Lainie followed Eliza to the car, they got in and Lainie turned the key.

Tickticktickticktick...

Lainie sighed, got out again, went through the ritual of crimping the foil over the starter's contact, got back in and started the car in earnest. She steered the Camry toward the 101 onramp and joined the stream of traffic. Just past the final exit before the Golden Gate bridge, and the sign warning there were no more exits nor U-turns until the far side of the bridge, Lainie let up on the gas and cursed.

"What's the matter," Eliza demanded.

Lainie pointed up. The electronic road sign spanning the northbound lanes blinked, "Accident ahead. Expect delays."

"What does that mean?"

"It means," Lainie explained, "that we're going to be sitting in traffic for the next hour or more. Accidents are notoriously hard to clear on the bridge, especially near rush hour like this when the traffic backs up. People have trouble knowing how to make room for emergency vehicles in such tight quarters."

Eliza looked as if she were making a conscious effort to relax.

"See," Lainie said. They were well onto the bridge when they finally came up to the stationary bumper of an RV ahead of them. Traffic around them stacked up quickly and soon they were at a dead stop in gridlock.

Eliza's body language was that of a caged wildcat, casting about her wild-eyed, looking for attack from any direction. Her fingers flipped the door handle as if she was unaware of it, not far enough to release the latch, but enough to make a *thump, thump, thump* noise that was sure to drive Lainie bat-shit if she didn't stop.

"Relax," Lainie said, "how could they possibly know..."

There was the soft *tinkle* of glass and a shard of the rear-view mirror fell onto the back of Lainie's hand as it rested on the gear shift, balancing there like a bright, shiny dagger. Her eyes met Eliza's, then together they looked at the mirror, now splashed with cracks radiating outward from a single, tiny black hole.

Lainie looked back at the rear window to see a matching tiny hole perfectly level with the first. Meanwhile, Eliza had tried to open her door. It struck the large semi-tractor next to them and would not open far enough for her to squeeze out. Eliza slammed the door and tried to squeeze out the window, but no matter how she contorted her body there was still no room.

"Sit down," Lainie said.

"Your side," Eliza said, trying to climb over Lainie. "We can get out on your side."

"Siddown," Lainie shouted, using her forearm to slam the smaller woman back into her seat. "Put on your seatbelt."

Eliza did as she was told while Lainie revved the engine, hands squeezing the steering wheel at ten-and-two, face a 3D relief of determination. She'd seen Cord Steel drive a Lexus convertible like it was a dragonfly, flitting and floating among traffic like it was little more than marsh weeds and cattails.

With automatic transmissions predominant, few people still bother with the gear shift settings past drive, to the point where some automobile factories have ceased putting in low gears. But Lainie's Camri still had the little numerals 2 for second gear and 1 for first to the right of the D. These lower gears, she knew, were for when a driver needed power over speed.

She popped the shifter into second and the car moved forward with a solid rumble. Lainie pulled the steering wheel to the right. Her efforts to squeeze into the space between lanes met with mixed results. The Camry moved but not without scraping both side panels against the RV in front of them and the trailer of the semi on the right.

Lainie hesitated as she looked around at the stunned faces of other drivers around her and wondered if this had been the smartest course of action. There was a double-*pop* sound behind and in front of them in rapid succession and another tiny hole appeared, this time in the windshield. Lainie didn't doubt the entry of the bullet left another matching one in the rear window.

"Keep down," she said, applying her foot to the gas pedal with renewed determination. The grinding of metal on either side was nothing to her now compared to the relatively smaller yet deadlier bullets flying at them from who knew where. The Camri's tires squealed in protest, smoke and the acrid smell of overheated rubber rising around them. But the little car crept ever onward despite the tight fit.

They were abreast of the trailer attached to the semi-tractor on Eliza's side. Beyond was the accident causing all of this commotion. A bus had been driven into the guardrail separating the roadway from the pedestrian sidewalk on the right and flipped over on its left side. Rescuers had borrowed a long, heavy plank of wood from the semi past which Lainie was trying to squeeze and had placed it as a ramp to gain access to the top of the bus, thereby to help survivors climb out and down to safety. Even now two EMTs were stepping off the bottom of the ramp, a woman laid out on a backboard held between them.

Traffic was being directed to merge on the left by a patrolman in order to get by the accident, thus causing the traffic jam. This gave Lainie the room she needed. She heard more *popping* noises of bullets peppering her own poor machine, fired from what was obviously a silenced rifle. In spite of the traffic cop, even now waving his hands at her to stop, she revved the engine.

Seeing what Lainie intended, Eliza said, "No. Oh fuck no," even as she tightened her seatbelt.

"Bullets or water," Lainie said, to Eliza. "How do you want to die?"

Being rush hour the ferries were out in force, traversing the bay from terminal to terminal with their cargo of cars and people. The Pier 39 ferry to Sausalito on the north shore was only just pulling up alongside the Golden Gate Bridge to give passengers a fish-eye view of the majestic crimson span.

With no idea of how far it was down, and no frame of reference for timing such a stunt, Lainie waited until the ferry was only just pulling even with them. With one last prayer – which went something like this: "Oh God. Oh God. Oh God oh God oh God oh God..." – Lainie clamped her eyes shut and gunned the gas pedal.

The little beat-up Camry roared like the lion it wasn't, charged up the ramp, across the bus askew on its side and flung itself bravely out over the San Francisco bay.

CHAPTER 4

"Well, at least we're not being shot at any more," Lainie whispered.

"No," Eliza said with sarcasm-laced tone, "but at this rate we're still not going to make my rendezvous with Professor Harkness."

They sat on a bench in an ante-room outside the command center and bridge of the ferry *Miwok*. A man introduced to them as the deck mate stood against the wall by the only other exit out onto the upper deck of the boat. He had prodigious muscles, which were well defined by crossing his arms like he did now. He glared at them with incredulous eyes.

"What the fuck were you thinking?" he asked in a thick accent Lainie couldn't place.

"Honestly," she said, "I was just thinking of getting away from the bullets."

She flashed on the brief feeling of weightlessness as the car flew off the bridge; the sudden panic that screamed in her mind, "What have you done?"; clamping her eyes shut as she expected any moment the impact and splash of water all around them, swallowing them rapidly as they sank into the dark olive-green bay like a cinder block.

The car pitched forward and she thought they might flip entirely, when they impacted the roof of the ferry, directly over the upper carport. The *Miwok* was an older, smaller ferry, two parking decks topped by a fiberglass carport-like roof. This portion of the boat, being mostly aluminum girders with a fiberglass skin, collapsed under them, absorbing the greater part of the impact, and depositing them right down on the roofs of the cars that were parked there.

Then all she remembered was she and Eliza sitting in the vehicle, stunned and gasping for breath, until they were pulled from the car and virtually carried up to the command deck of the ferry boat. The captain questioned them briefly, questions they answered honestly until asked *why* someone was shooting at them. To this they professed ignorance. The Captain left them here under guard and stepped behind the closed door of the bridge, which only muffled their voices as he, the boson, and the captain's mate argued about whether to turn back or push on to Sausalito..

"One foot to one side or the other," the deck mate said now, motioning with the flat of his hand a car pitching into an abyss. "And the damage," he said, ending with an ominous whistle.

The sliding door to the bridge banged open and the boson leaned out. "Go check for any other injuries, and be sure the crew is at their posts. Put up some kind of rope perimeter around the wreckage to keep the passengers from getting too close. We can't afford anyone getting injured."

"And them," the mate cocked his head toward the two women sitting on the bench.

"Where're they gonna go, Dutch? We're at sea."

"Aye," the deck mate, Dutch, nodded. He and the boson ducked out their respective doors and shut them behind them, leaving Lainie and Eliza alone on their little bench against the bulkhead.

"We haven't really gotten away," Eliza said. "All the shooter has to do is drive around to the ferry terminal when he gets off the bridge and be there when the cops cart us off."

"You saw that traffic on the bridge," Lainie said. "The shooter's going to be stuck there for a while. Much more if someone spotted them taking potshots at us and called the cops, which is pretty likely - there was a cop right there already, he had to see something. Meanwhile, a ferry takes roughly thirty minutes to cross the bay, and we hitched our ride half-way across." She glanced through the round windows in each of the two doors, the bridge and the exit to the deck. "You could be right about the cops, though. Probably be there to meet us when we arrive."

"Then why don't you look as trapped as I feel?"

Lainie smiled back at her – really less of a smile than a set sneer of determination. "Because we aren't going to be found when the cops come to get us." She went back to peering out each window.

"Where can we hide?"

"The very last place they'll look."

*　　　*　　　*

They each watched from their hiding place as crew members came into view, peered around, then moved on, clearly searching for the two fugitive women who'd flown their compact car from the Golden Gate Bridge onto a passing ferry, and then vanished from custody.

Lainie found that even in this supposed enlightened age, men continued to underestimate the will and resourcefulness of women. It was a mistake to leave she and Eliza alone, unrestrained and in an unlocked anteroom to the bridge. Lainie had only to pick her moment, when everyone on the other side of the bridge door was busy and distracted, to lead Eliza by the wrist out the other exit and onto the upper causeway. Walking casually, so as not to draw attention, Lainie led the way down to lower decks and, when no one was looking, up and into their current hiding place.

Lainie could see shore approaching, but as the boat veered away from the docks, the captain's voice came over the public-address speakers, "Ladies and gentlemen, this is Captain Coridan. We apologize for restricting all passengers to the observation deck and trust your trip has not been uncomfortable because of it. Due to the accident we experienced, it is safest.

"Unfortunately, now we appear to be missing two passengers, so we must impose upon your patience one more time as we have been diverted away from the Sausalito terminus to another docking station further up-channel where police will be able to join our search. This is for your safety, if not necessarily your convenience.

"The good news is you will be permitted to debark as soon as we dock. We only ask that you be patient while each vehicle is searched before debarking. In the meantime, coffee will continue to be served by the crew free of charge. Again, we apologize for the inconvenience and hope to have you on your way to your homes and other destinations just as soon as we can possibly manage it. Thank you."

"Great," Eliza said. "Cops'll be swarming all over this place as soon as we dock."

Lainie felt worried, too, but saw nothing to be gained by kvetching about it. Instead she continued to watch the activities outside their hidey-hole, biding her time, hoping to recognize her window of opportunity when it came and exploit it. Search efforts continued but none of the crew thought to look up into their concealed nest.

As they neared the dock, Lainie read the banner-like sign above it – *United States Coast Guard Pier 4A* – and felt panic rise in her blood. Eliza gave voice to that panic, "Ah shit! The Coast Guard. Lainie, we're screwed."

But were they, Lainie wondered. Coast Guard were still just cops when it came to apprehending people. Sure, they had gunships, but they weren't likely to employ those in the pursuit of two women whose great crime wave consisted of crashing their car onto a ferry boat.

The boat finally pulled up to the end of the pier. There was more activity as the gangway dropped and what looked like about fifty – but was more likely no more than twenty-five – sailors trotted onto the deck and took up positions.

"Now or never," Lainie said.

"What?" Eliza said.

Lainie reached for the key, still in the ignition of the beaten Toyota Camri in which they'd hidden. It'd been tricky climbing the wreckage to get back inside her without being seen, and once here Eliza kept grilling Lainie about what good it was to hide here, until Lainie finally had to tell her to shush, lest they be heard.

As Lainie turned the key, Eliza's eyes went wide and she hurried to put her seatbelt on. But the engine merely went *tick-tick-tick-tick* again in defiance. Sighing, Lainie reached for the door handle.

"They're going to see you," Eliza warned.

"Then I guess I better move fast."

When Lainie popped the hood-release lever under the dash it made a loud *k'thunk*. She and Eliza slumped low in their seats. But while the crew and the sailors nearby looked around, not one looked up at them.

Lainie opened the car door as slowly and quietly as she could. It creaked slightly and she froze, but no one outside down on the deck below them seemed to take notice. She got out carefully and crept on the dented and bent fiberglass carport roof that'd collapsed underneath the car when it'd landed. It was slippery with sea spray but her sneakers held traction. She reached the front of the car without being noticed but when she lifted the hood a few inches it emitted the familiar rusty grind of hinges. Lainie froze.

She knew from long association with this Camri that there was no way to raise the hood without it making a god-awful racket. She steeled herself, then threw the hood up over her head. The squeal of hinges whose lubrication had long since worn away by age and grit seemed to Lainie the loudest sound she'd ever heard. Reaching for the foil blob crimped around the starter lead, she waited for shouts of alarm to descend about her, but they didn't actually come until she was reaching to close the hood again.

Crew and Coast Guard alike shouted. She heard commands of, "What are you doing up there?" and, "Who are you?" and the more threatening, "Freeze! Put your hands over your head!"

She ignored these and rushed back to the driver's side. She doubted any armed sailors were going to shoot at an unarmed woman, and she was right. She was able to get back into the car without interference. Only then did she look at the people gathering around the parked cars on which the roof of the car port had collapsed under the Camry. Shore patrol had pulled guns and were aiming them, others were waving at her to get out of the car. One man, bless his heart, even shouted to them, "It isn't safe up there ma'am. Please come down before you get yourselves hurt."

Eliza was watching the men as well, eyes wide in trepidation.

The car started with no more stubbornness. Lainie met Eliza's permanently saucer-sized gaze and tried to grin, but her mouth was dry and her lips stuck to her teeth. Putting the shifter on Drive, she popped the brake. As soon as the car jumped forward the fiberglass roof popped and crackled and pitched under them. Sailors rushed in front of the ranks of cars.

"Lainie," Eliza screamed, putting her hands on the dash.

Lainie hit the brakes, not wanting to run over anyone. The car stopped...but the roof under them did not. Like a sled, the entire platform broke loose of its resting place, slid along the roofs of the cars on which it rested. With gathering speed the roof, with the Camri on it and the women in that, rushed forward like a luge on high-test rocket fuel, right toward the rank of blocking sailors.

The entire thing pitched forward as it reached the end of the parked cars, tipping over the parallel front fenders, metal and paint crying out in protest. Sailors scattered, and Lainie watched the faces rushing past them, each expressing some variety of shock or amazement, as the erstwhile giant sled bore down the ramp to the lower deck. She raised her hands as if to show them she was no longer under control of their forward momentum. She turned the other way and Eliza looked as if she wanted to scream but couldn't manage to take a breath to do so.

Pitching again, the roof and the Camri and the women sluiced down the upper-deck ramp toward the gangway. More Coast Guard sailors scattered as the roof leveled out and slammed down onto the main deck and Lainie saw that the entire sliding roof on which they rode was too wide to make it through the gap in the outer bulwark to the gangway beyond.

Thinking fast, Lainie let go the brake pedal. The roof slammed into both sides of the exit and stopped abruptly, but not the Camri. The car leapt forward, hit the upward-curving, bent and mangled end of the fiberglass and smashed through it like tinder. Suddenly they were on the dock.

Lainie floored the gas pedal and the little car took control of its own destiny once more. It rushed along the wooden deck, scattering cops and Coast Guard alike, some even leaping into the water to avoid being steamrolled by this madly careening automobile. Immediately, four vehicles with spinning police lights, Shore Patrol and Police, fell in behind and gave chase.

At the end of the dock, hard-barrier pylons had been activated, rising up from their hiding places beneath to block the path of any vehicle like this one. Lainie took careful aim with the steering wheel, then clinched her eyes.

"No," Eliza screamed, hair nails creaking in the vinyl of the dashboard.

The compact Camri only just slipped between two of the pylons, paint and plastic panels on both sides grinding loudly in pain as her passengers were jolted left, then right, then left again in rapid succession. Jostled and bruised, they were free. The police cruisers, too large for such a squeeze, applied brakes with a tortured scream of tires on pavement. The front vehicle stopped in time, but the third did not and piled into the second, which in turn pushed the first into the pylons, bringing steam like a geyser from a ruptured radiator.

Someone screamed like a bull, "Lower the god damn pylons!"

Lainie applied the gas again and steered them through a series of loading areas and covered warehouses resembling hangars. No one appeared to follow them. She suspected they'd not been prepared to have to give chase. They'd not been told the two fugitive women were liable to pull the stunt they'd just survived. Lainie herself could hardly believe it, and couldn't tell if she wanted to laugh or scream.

She found herself on roads again surrounded by buildings, uniformed personnel, and other cars. It was Eliza who spotted the gate with the guard shack in the center of it and pointed. As Lainie veered toward it she slowed down. The guards in the shack watched them as they cruised out of the compound. Lainie guessed they were mere seconds ahead of a call from the pier to lock down the base.

She slowed to legal speeds so as not to draw attention as she merged with traffic on the surface streets. The two kept their eyes open for any pursuit, and while they heard fading sirens, they saw none. "Still," Lainie said, "it won't be long before every cop in the state is on the lookout for this car. Not to mention whoever was shooting at us."

"Oh my god," Eliza huffed. "What the hell did we just do?"

Lainie felt equally gob-smacked by the audacity of what they'd just been through. "Jesus. We should've turned ourselves in."

After a moment to catch her breath, the resolute clench to Eliza's jaw returned and she said, "No. They would've turned us over to whomever is trying to kill me."

"Kill us," Lainie corrected her.

Eliza looked at her lap, clearly feeling guilty. "Because of me. Why are you doing this, Lainie? I mean, you don't owe me anything. Now you're banging up your car, going on the run, risking your *life*...for me. Why?"

Lainie thought about it. Over a year ago she'd had the audacity to impersonate a spy, break into hiding places, steal classified intelligence, and even confront a cell of hardened terrorists. Had it all been from an inflated sense of her own competence? Had it been nothing more than hubris and overreaching ego?

No. If she was to be honest with herself, she had to acknowledge that she'd gotten in over her head a year ago through little fault of her own. Most of the events had dictated her role in them, not the other way around. She'd been swept up by currents greater than herself, and she'd only done what she had to in order to survive.

Today she saw an old friend, an ex-patient in distress, one over whom Lainie already felt great guilt over abandoning when her psych rotation had ended. Lainie offered Eliza shelter and a sympathetic ear. That they'd been chased by bullets ever since had not been expected, nor Lainie's doing. Last year's adventure, she'd come to care about Simi and her brother and father, and now as then she could not bring herself to abandon someone who needed her help, even if it meant putting her freedom on the line.

Or even her life.

To Eliza she said, "You can't do this alone. I'm all you have, at least until you meet Professor Harkness. The least I can do is get you that far."

Eliza looked at Lainie with gratitude. Then her face went hard again. "We need to go north. And don't stop until we've reached Houston."

"Houston, British Columbia," Lainie said in a wry tone.

*　　　*　　　*

It was almost 365 miles from the bay area to the Oregon boarder via US 101 along the coast. When Lainie first bought the car in high school, almost eight years ago, like any first-time car owner her intentions were noble. She always got the fluids changed every three thousand miles, she washed it religiously, and she tracked the gas mileage. This lasted about six months before, again like most car owners, she got busy with other things and let her diligence slack. But not before she clocked the Camri's mileage at a rock-steady 20 MPG. But while both she and the Camri were younger then, that was city driving. She hoped to make more on the highway.

Lainie drove exactly the speed limit and stuck to the center or right lane as if it had grooves. She always slowed when someone signaled to cut in front of them, and always waited until there was at least a two car-lengths opening before changing lanes herself. In other words, she drove like a blind pastor. And it seemed to work – even though they saw one or two Highway Patrol cruisers, none of them took any notice.

Lainie chanced that, BOLO or no, the cops probably had their hands full enough with speeders, drunk drivers, and traffic accidents to worry about a be-on-the-lookout for two women in a Camri. She'd been right.

During the drive, as the sun set out over the ocean and cast a crimson glare over the sky, Lainie tried to draw Eliza out about more details into the research she and the professor had been doing.

"We were doing experiments on latent dead cultures from actual viruses," Eliza said.

"What kinds of viruses? What kinds of experiments?"

"I don't know how much I can tell you. I mean, it *was* government work and we did have to go through clearance checks to work on the project. Not exactly top secret, but not for public consumption, either."

"Who am I going to tell?" Lainie pressed.

Eliza seemed to think. "We were experimenting with some pretty nasty stuff. Hantavirus, dengue, Ebola..."

"E-fucking-bola?"

"Like I said, it was all latent, mostly dead."

"*Mostly* dead."

"Sure." Eliza sounded matter of fact. "I mean you'd virtually have to inject the stuff into your vein for it to have any effect, if then. What kind of person would do that?" The girl fell silent, her brow darkening, until Lainie called her name.

"Eliza? You were saying?"

The haunted expression faded and she seemed to pull out of whatever dark corner of her mind she'd retreated to. "Anyway, we were doing experiments. Genetic-level stuff. Genome mapping and such."

"Tell me you were trying to find better cures, vaccines," Lainie said. "Tell me you weren't looking for ways to weaponize, to make even scarier shit."

Eliza held her tongue and just looked forward.

"Shit." Lainie punched the steering wheel. "Eliza, how could you?"

"No," Eliza said. "I don't know."

"Yes, you do," Lainie snapped. "You let your feelings for Harkness blind you. But you suspected, didn't you? Didn't you?"

Eliza said nothing, just stared at her shoes.

"Eliza."

Eliza nodded.

"Something happened, and the government pulled the plug," Lainie speculated. "Not a containment breach - aside from the tents and hazmat suits you saw there doesn't seem to be any indications of any breakout. There would have been something in the news, some cockamamie cover story. And you say you never got sick."

Eliza looked at Lainie.

Lainie pursed her lips. "You said Harkness was deleting files and shredding documents just before the feds showed up. He was trying to hide something, something he didn't want them to see."

"Yeah."

"Something off-book. Something unauthorized. Something he didn't want them to get their hands on. Maybe he was working on one thing and telling them something else."

"Maybe," Eliza said, "he decided that what they were paying him to work on was too dangerous to hand over to the government."

"A sudden conscience?" Lainie scoffed. "No, he would've agreed at some point. To suddenly change his mind, it just doesn't seem likely. More likely is he found a higher bidder in the private sector and was selling his secrets to them. Maybe even a foreign government."

"Harkness would never do that," Eliza said.

"How do you know?"

"You don't know him. He's a patriot. He would rail against open borders and terrorism and Democrats who seemed

57

determined to sell this country to Socialism and some shadow global government. He was kooky on the subject sometimes, but he loves America and all it stands for. He could never betray it."

Lainie simply had to take Eliza's word for it. "And nothing else happened? He didn't say anything? Do anything else before he rushed you out the back way?"

Eliza turned to look out the passenger side window. "No."

There wasn't a doubt in Lainie's mind that Eliza was still keeping something from her, it was obvious, but she couldn't guess at what.

For her part, Eliza sat back in her seat and seemed to descend into a black depression for the rest of the trip. It was almost midnight when they pulled into a truck stop just over the Oregon border. From there Lainie and Eliza breathed easier with each mile they put between themselves and California. By now, Lainie was sure that if anyone had taken down her license plate number – and why wouldn't they have – the authorities knew who she was, and patrolmen had probably already been dispatched to her apartment.

She was a fugitive again. Last time it'd been arson, murder, and espionage. What would it be now? Driving recklessly? Endangering the public? Violating the peace and tranquility of the People's Republic of California?

In spite of their urgency, after the initial shock and adrenaline flow of the last few hours wore off, Lainie's eyes felt heavy in her head, and her lids wanted nothing more than to close. Though she hadn't slept, Eliza swore she was okay to drive, and she certainly seemed entirely awake and alert. So Lainie let the younger woman take the wheel as she, herself, reclined the passenger seat and went to sleep.

She woke up to the sound of crying. "Eliza?"

The girl was silhouetted against the driver's side window past which the headlights of cars passing the other direction strobed. Her lower lip quivered and her cheek glistened. She turned away.

"Are you okay?"

"I'm all right," Eliza said. "I'm not crying."

"No one said you were. Would you like me to drive?"

"No."

"Then could you slow down?" The speedometer was pegged halfway between 90 and 95.

Eliza let up on the pedal and they slowed to a more reasonable speed. "Sorry. I'm not crying. I'm pissed off."

"Okay," Lainie kept her voice level. "Why?"

Eliza pressed her lips together. "Never mind. We're here."

The road was still flanked by forest as they passed a large sign painted with pine trees and fish and reading, *Welcome to Houston, Population 2300. Home of the world's largest fly fishing rod!*

"When did we cross the border?" Lainie asked.

"You've been out for like six hours," Eliza said, slowing as the forest gave way to houses, the highway melding into an unlit surface road. "You slept through the checkpoint. Hope you don't mind, I found your passport in your purse."

Lainie opened her window a crack. Chill air flavored faintly of pine came in and she shut it again. "That's fine."

"There," Eliza said, pulling into the parking lot of a motel with a large lodge-pole sign, *Bulkley River Lodge.*

"This is where Harkness told you to meet him?" Lainie asked as Eliza parked and turned off the engine.

Eliza looked at her and then away and opened her door. "Yes." She climbed out and shut the door. She was obviously lying, but Lainie said nothing. She'd wait to see more before she pressed Eliza for the truth.

When Lainie got out Eliza said, "We'll get a room here and wait to hear from him. Shouldn't be long."

They checked into a room about halfway down the long strip of accommodations. There were two twin beds, a flat screen television, a telephone and a bathroom. It was cozy and clean and smelled of Pine Sol and laundry detergent. Lainie looked at a digital clock on the nightstand: 9:00.

"You made good time," Lainie said. When Eliza, who was just standing glaring out the large front window, didn't answer, Lainie said, "I'm going to go call my friend."

"Why don't you call him from here?" Eliza turned.

"I need to find a pay phone. Whoever is tracing your cell phone has resources. I don't want to risk them intercepting a call leading them straight to this hotel. I'll be right back."

Eliza watched Lainie leave. Lainie once again crimped the ball of foil on the starter-lead under the hood, then drove the Camri to the other side of the small hamlet to a gas station outside of which was a phone booth. Lainie hadn't seen a phone booth in years.

She dialed Cord's number.

"Lainie?"

"How'd you know it was me?"

"I don't get many calls from Canada exchanges," he said. "Where are you? Is Eliza with you?"

"We're in Houston. She's back at the motel. I'm on a pay phone on the other side of what I'll loosely call a town. More of a fishing village, really."

"Good," Cord said. Lainie was just picking up on the edge to his voce. "Listen, your friend, Eliza Andrews, isn't just hot, she's radioactive. You need to leave there right now and don't look back. Leave her behind and don't get any more involved than you already are. I might even be able to cover for you, if you don't get in any deeper."

"What do you mean radioactive? What's going on?"

"I don't have many details, but they are looking for her and I mean some serious looking. We're talking nationwide communications net sweeps, satellite targeting, hell they've sent out everything but the bloodhounds. Someone wants her and they want her bad. I've only seen this once or twice my whole career. She's tweaked some very important noses of some very important people and when they find her..."

He left his last sentence unfinished.

"You don't mean they'll kill her," Lainie said in a reasonable tone.

She'd never heard Steele himself sound scared. "Let's just say it'll be hard to find evidence she ever existed in the first place."

"Geez, Cord, all she did was flee the scene of a raid," Lainie said. "I mean, she didn't even know what agency she was working for."

"It's more than that," Steele said.

"What, then?"

"I don't know," he said. "This level of scrambled eggs only happens in response to a national security threat. She's done something a damn sight more substantial than rabbit. Or she's got something they want very, very badly."

Lainie was beginning to feel his panic and shook it off. "Come on, Cord, there has to be some mistake. I know this girl. She's pretty vanilla. I mean, the worst I can see her doing is stealing a pen off of one of those chains at the bank."

"Lainie, I know that tone. There's no mistake. I'm telling you...no, I'm ordering you not to get involved."

"Ordering me?"

"As an officer of the law, yes."

"You're a CIA agent, Cord. You have no authority inside United States borders."

"You're not in the US."

"You're right," Lainie chuckled. "I sometimes forget Canada's a different country. It's like USA lite. Same great taste, fewer assholes."

She hung up, knowing he'd take her point.

And immediately regretted it. Why was it every time she spoke to him she acted like some jilted teenager, when she swore to herself to never show him he'd hurt her? This time, he was only showing genuine concern for her welfare, exaggerating the threat to make her heed him.

If he wasn't exaggerating then someone had made a big mistake. It was just too far a leap for Lainie to believe that little Eliza was a threat to anyone's national security, much less the United States. She needed to get back to the motel and talk to Eliza. Things had definitely gotten out of hand. It was time Eliza turned herself in and explained everything. Surely they wouldn't execute her, as Cord implied. This was a civilized country, for God's sake.

She drove back to the Bulkley River Lodge and let herself into their room with her key. The room was dark, though late morning light filtered in through the curtains. At first Lainie expected to find Eliza in bed – she'd been awake driving all night. But both beds were undisturbed. She looked in the bathroom but there was no sign of her companion.

Eliza was gone.

CHAPTER 5

There was no note, Lainie checked everywhere – the bathroom mirror, the dresser, the nightstand, on either bed. Had she maybe gone for some snacks? Make a call of her own? Had someone come, god forbid, and taken her away against her will?

Lainie didn't know whether waiting here for Eliza's return was a good idea, or if she, Lainie, should leave in search of her. If Eliza left of her own volition she had to be on foot, Lainie had the car with her, so the girl couldn't have gotten far. But the longer Lainie waited the further Eliza would get, and if Steele had the line she'd called from traced, which he most certainly would have, then the government agents after Eliza now knew where to look. The longer she was out and about the more danger she was in.

Lainie regretted making the call. She knew from experience Steele couldn't be trusted. Yet somehow, she kept making that mistake. Standing here berating herself now wasn't going to solve anything.

She decided to go after Eliza.

The first thing she did was check the motel office. The bored teenaged girl behind the counter waved vaguely north, saying she'd seen Eliza walking in that direction when a pickup truck came and she'd gotten in.

"Did you get a license plate number?"

The teenager snorted.

"Damn," Lainie said under her breath. "How am I going to find her now?"

"Just go to the Donelly place," the girl said.

"Where?"

"The Donelly place, up the highway a few miles. Big ole broken mill wheel. Can't miss it."

"Why there?"

The girl rolled her eyes. "It was Von Donelly's dad's truck picked her up. Duh."

"Oh."

Lainie drove north on Highway 16 and saw the big broken mill wheel, as promised, about two hundred yards off the road on the left leaning against a dilapidated two-story millhouse. Another, newer two-story house stood closer to the road with a huge garage behind it. The garage was full of heavy equipment Lainie didn't recognize but guessed had something to do with either lumber milling or construction.

Even as she neared the driveway a convoy of vehicles was circling the yard and pouring out single file onto the highway. Lainie had to stop to wait as they swerved in front of her and headed north, the direction she was already pointed. Lainie watched the windows and sure enough as a big tan dually pickup with extended cab and floodlights on the roof bumped over the culvert at the break in the fence and turned north Lainie saw her.

Eliza sat, small and scrunched, between two bearded men in the front seat. The girl spotted Lainie and glared at her with wide eyes as the caravan continued to file out of the enclosure and strike up the highway.

Clearly Eliza's expression was a call for help, and as the last vehicle trundled onto the blacktop – a little 1970's style dune buggy, of all things, with one passenger standing, gripping the roll-bars for stability – Lainie fell in behind and followed what she thought was about twelve vehicles, but she'd forgotten to count.

Who were these people, and why had they taken Eliza? They certainly didn't seem like government agents. But then this was Canada, for all she knew secret agents looked like lumberjacks here. But if they were agents, why were they taking

Eliza north? An airport maybe, or jailhouse? And why so many men and vehicles to escort one young woman?

No, Lainie was relatively sure these were not the Canadian equivalent of the FBI, whatever that was. But if not, then who? And what did they want with Eliza?

The clerk at the motel said the truck had picked Eliza up, and while she may be no more likely than any other teenager to show interest in anything, Lainie was relatively sure she'd have used a different term if there'd been any kind of a struggle. Did Eliza know these men? Did these men know Professor Harkness? Were they taking Eliza to the rendezvous now? If so, why would Eliza have left without Lainie, and no note saying she was okay?

The file of follow-the-leader was moving at a pretty good clip. Lainie was afraid if they drove any faster the poor, beaten old Camri wouldn't be able to keep up. Lainie didn't know where they were going, but she knew at some point she was going to have to peel-off or the group might grow suspicious that she was following them. Her hope was to do so somewhere near their destination so she could creep in with a little more stealth after they'd landed. At least until she knew whether they were friend or foe.

W.C. Fields supposedly once said, "I want to spend my last penny the day before I die." While the quote is almost assuredly apocryphal, the obvious problem with such an aspiration is that one can never know when the day one is to die is going to be. Likewise, Lainie had no way of knowing where these men headed, and so did not know where to pull away from them. So, when they slowed and turned off on a dirt track, narrow and overgrown, little better than a game trail, Lainie kept going, lest she draw their suspicion.

At the first wide shoulder, she pulled the Camri off and nosed it into the brush. It wasn't entirely hidden from the road, but enough that she hoped cars passing by at speed would be moving too fast for anyone to notice the little blue car in the bushes.

She was not dressed for a hike, but in jeans and athletic shoes, it could've been worse. Still, as she crept through underbrush and shrubbery, between rocks and trees, through draws and over knolls, she was none too stealthy. Nowhere near as much as she would've liked. Twigs crunched underfoot, rocks rattled against each other, and over it all she found herself huffing for air like a steam locomotive.

She hoped they hadn't driven too far off the road, that the distance wouldn't be measured in miles, but in yards, otherwise they'd left her far behind by now and this excursion was a waste of time and energy. Mostly energy, she reflected as she paused to rest for the twentieth time. She was an academic, not an athlete. But as long as she could offer Eliza any help at all she couldn't give up. So she pushed herself away from the boulder on which she sat and headed west again, further away from the road.

She used the GPS on the cell phone to keep track of where she was. While it didn't tell her where she was headed, it did keep her oriented in relation to the highway behind her and give her some idea of landmarks in the area. They were currently in public hunting lands, according to the geo-app she had on her phone. She knew in most locales in the US hunting seasons didn't start until later in the fall, but she had no idea about Canada. Still, she thought she was relatively safe from being mistaken for a deer and shot.

She reached a point about a mile off the road before she felt safe turning south again and heading back toward the side road the trucks had taken. She knew she hadn't driven far after passing it before ranging out on foot, but god knew what turns that trail took once it left the highway. She might have just a few yards to go, and then again it might be more miles. And it was entirely possible she'd miss them entirely.

But she doubted it. In satellite view, her app showed a collection of nondescript cabins and outbuildings not far from here, and she strongly suspected this is where they headed. This, then, was the location of Eliza's rendezvous with Harkness. Or it was some hillbilly rape camp and Eliza had just fallen into the wrong hands.

Lainie heard voices ahead and peered through the thick brush, and something glinted ahead. Looking through the brush she noticed one tree standing taller and straighter than all the rest, only it wasn't a tree because its boughs flashed in the sunlight. Using the magnifier app on her phone she got a closer look at it: it was in truth instead a high-reaching man-made pole, and angling out from it in tiers that only emulated an evergreen tree were broad, flat solar panels.

She followed the pole down with her phone, its screen filled with a telescopic image of the erstwhile tree, down to its base, which ended at a shack. Beyond that shack was a clearing ringed by cabins. Some of the cars she'd seen pull out of the house back in Houston were visible, as well as people milling about, intent upon various tasks that were indecipherable from this distance.

Until the image went blank, showing nothing but a mostly black shadow.

Lainie lowered her phone to look into the barrel-chest of a man. Tilting her head up she got an impression of a beard and a floppy-brimmed hat of some sort, but the rest was backlit by the sun. He grabbed her and she dropped her phone. She reached for it, scrabbling in the dirt and fallen pine needles, but it slipped through her fingers as he dragged her away, toward the cluster of buildings.

He had a fist full of the front of her sweater twisted in his grip and was dragging her by that. It forced the fabric to bunch up under her arms, and that hurt, but she wasn't going to give him the satisfaction of crying out. She just kicked her heels frantically, trying to regain her feet.

She heard the sounds of conversation die away as he dragged her out into the open area amidst the buildings before letting her go. She rolled from one side to the other, looking around her to see multiple faces looking down at her, both men and women. Some were the gruff, bearded faces of rugged men, and these also bore weapons, more than one of which trained on her. But the majority were young, clean-shaven men and pretty women seemingly in their twenties or younger, none of them much younger than Lainie herself.

She spotted Eliza among the faces. The girl gave Lainie a brief shake of her head, so Lainie refrained from showing any sign that they knew each other. Instead, she tried to speak with the strong voice of authority. "What the hell is this?"

"I found her out there," the man who'd dragged her out said, waving an arm in the direction they'd come from.

"I said..." Lainie started to repeat herself.

Another man's face came into view. He was grizzled, with a full beard and a tree-trunk neck. "Who sent you?"

"Harkness," he asked, though he didn't look like a college professor.

"Professor Harkness?" He seemed incredulous. "Are you asking me or telling me?"

Clearly, he wasn't the professor, and now he assumed she was telling him that Harkness had sent her. "I'm telling you. Harkness sent me."

"Okay, what's the password?"

Oops. She wasn't going to be able to bluff her way through this one. "You got me. Harkness didn't send me."

"There is no password, stupid. Are you with the ACMA?" he asked. "You're with the ACMA, aren't you?"

Lainie had no clue what the ACMA was. "I'm not with anyone. No one sent me. I saw the tower and the buildings and I was curious. That's all."

"She's lying, Zeke," her captor said.

"You think, Dorn?" the bearded man – Zeke – said to him. "Of course, she's lying. She knows Judson's name."

"Look at her," he went on, addressing the rest of the crowd. "She's not dressed for survival and she's clearly not an RCMPig. I don't know who she is. Dorn, take two men, take the girl to the galley. Tie her up. Everyone else to the mess hall. We have a decision to make."

Three men, including Dorn, her captor, lifted Lainie and carried her toward one of the cabins. Everyone else in the camp – at quick guess as many as twenty-five men and women of all ages – followed inside. Her bearers carried Lainie across a mess hall with tables and chairs while everyone else paused to talk amongst themselves, many taking seats. Lainie found herself carried through two swinging doors at the back of the mess into a kitchen. There were two large refrigerators, wood and propane stoves, prep areas, etc. She could hear the guys in the next room through a large serving window that separated the kitchen from the dining room.

Dorn and his helpers hoisted Lainie onto a stainless-steel table in the center of the room and tied her with nylon climbing rope to the table. She was spread-eagle and feeling vulnerable. She was afraid the men would try something, helpless as she was, but they seemed to forget her as soon as she was secured and sauntered out of the kitchen, chatting between them and joining the rest of the crowd.

It'd been futile to struggle while they carried her, there were just too many of them and even if she did manage to get away they'd run her down again. But the moment they left the room she tested her bonds.

When Lainie was seven years old her family moved across town. Lainie's father, a dear and loving man, was determined to take the one furnishing his harpy wife had allowed him in the entire house, his backyard hammock. But years of the stress of he and his daughters laying and playing on it had stretched the nylon cords with which it'd been hung to the point that the knots were seized as tight as little granite stones. After one entire Saturday of little Lainie handing him tool after tool to work at those knots, grunting and sweating and pretend-cursing – "Ratchin-fratchit! Carn-sarn poo-thing! Shim-shammle-pammle it!" – he turned to her and said, "Pooh-bear, go get Daddy his Bowie knife!"

Lainie knew it was useless to try to break her nylon binding – struggling to do so would only pull these knots as tight as those on her father's hammock. She flopped to the table in despair as Zeke called the meeting to order in the next room.

"Okay, pipe down," Zeke shouted from the dining room. Lainie heard chairs scraping on the wooden floor as the mob took seats and the hubbub subsided. "One of the things I respect most about Professor Harkness is transparency. There are no leadership meetings behind closed doors. We all get to hear the plan, and we all get to ask questions and make suggestions. That's how it was from the beginning, unlike when I was in the military, and that's what makes me trust him.

"We need to bug-out," another man said, young, nervous. "We've been compromised."

Zeke said, "Von's not wrong." He was speaking about Von Donelly, the boy whose dad's truck, according to the clerk at the motel, had picked up Eliza. And from the softening of Zeke's voice Lainie guessed Zeke was Von's father, the elder Donelly. But that was a guess.

"Go where?" someone, a woman, asked.

"Phase three." Von's voice again.

"But Dr. Harkness's not here."

"This new girl," Zeke said. "Lainie Parker. She says that Harkness's been taken by the authorities, which is why we couldn't reach him for the last few weeks. Can we afford to wait for him?"

Lainie puzzled over this. He could not be talking about her, she'd said nothing of the sort. She could only guess that for some reason Eliza had used her name when joining these people. But why? If she was a friend of Harkness, and they were friends of Harkness, what reason could she possibly have to lie to them.

"Phase three means nothing without Harkness," the woman said. "Phase three is moot if they can make him talk."

"Harkness would never talk," Von cried out, indignant.

"Even if he doesn't talk," the woman pressed on, "he's got everything: the formulas, the serums, everything."

"So what are you saying, Ruth?" Zeke asked.

"Harkness's been arrested," Ruth answered. "Then suddenly a woman sneaks into our camp, knows Harkness's name but not the password. I agree with Von, we're compromised. But I don't agree that we accelerate phase three. I say we wait, find out how much this woman knows, who she works for."

"Does it matter who she works for?" Von again. "I guarantee you if she's here more are coming. If we leave now, move on to phase three, we're still a step ahead of them. Whoever *they* are."

There were murmurs of agreement about this.

"Von's right," Zeke said. "We leave, go off the grid, take care of phase three. If Harkness can get himself released he'll know where to find us. If not, we revisit the question. The time for talk's over. All in favor of moving on to phase three?"

The room reverberated with "Ayes."

"Okay," Zeke said. "Bed rolls and tent poles, ladies and gentlemen. Hop to. We bug-out in one hour."

The room filled with loud conversation as the group filed out of the mess hall. The cabin fell virtually silent but for the sounds outside of shouting, engines and people striking camp in preparations to leave. Lainie lay on her table and wondered how long it would take for someone to find her here after the people left. She heard soft footsteps cross the dining room and the swinging doors to the kitchen creaked. She strained to lift her head, looking down her body at who'd come in.

"Eliza," she said. "Or should I call you Lainie."

Eliza crept to Lainie's right side and peered down at her. The younger woman's face bore sympathy.

"You lied to me," Lainie said. "You and Harkness are working together. Working on some *thing*, something you don't want the government to get their hands on. And these people are, what, mercenaries, paid by Harkness?"

"I don't think they're mercenaries," Eliza said.

"No," Lainie conceded, applying her psychology expertise to the problem. "They have many of the hallmarks of true believers."

"In what?"

Eliza was keeping her voice low, as if afraid of being overheard, so for now Lainie followed her lead.

"What do you mean, what cause? You're one of them, aren't you?"

"No," Eliza whispered. "I don't even know who they are."

"But you knew their password."

"Long story."

"I have all the time in the world," Lainie hissed, shaking her right wrist, bound with nylon rope.

"But I don't. I shouldn't even be in here. They're going to miss me soon."

"If you aren't one of them, then what's going on."

Eliza sighed and looked over her shoulder, seemed to be struggling with how to make her long story short.

"When the feds came to raid the office, before they got anyone to let them into the secure lab, which was at the back of the suite, Judson was deleting files from the server, as I said. He handed me a stack of files and told me to shred them. When I turned away to do that, he grabbed me from behind, covering my mouth. I fought him, then I felt a burning sensation at the side of my neck. He let me loose. He was holding a syringe."

"He'd injected you with something?"

"I demanded to know what he'd done. Why? He told me to leave out the back way. That this was the only way to get his most important research out of the lab. He told me if I didn't get away, that I'd be dead in three months. He told me where to go. . ."

"The Donelly place," Lainie said.

Eliza nodded. "He gave me a password to give them. Told me he'd find me before it was too late. He'd draw my blood in order to replicate the research, then he'd give me the antidote."

"Jesus, Eliza!"

Eliza's eyes were welling up. "I felt so betrayed. I felt so afraid. I felt so pissed. I trusted him. I loved him."

No wonder this one small woman was able to elude the authorities so well till now, nothing is more motivating than running to save one's own life. It could make one capable of extraordinary things. Lainie knew from experience.

"How do you feel?" Lainie asked.

"Aside from some minor flu symptoms the first day or so I've felt fine," Eliza said. "Jesus, Lainie, I only have three or four weeks left. I don't want to die."

Lainie felt sympathy for the girl, but needed to keep her focused. "But why the alias," she said. "Why give them a false name? My name?"

"I'm sorry," Eliza said, "It was the first one that came to mind. I'm not sure why, but it suddenly seemed unsafe for me to give them my real name. In case. . ."

"In case," Lainie finished for her, "they managed to speak to Harkness and he was to ask about you."

Eliza nodded.

"Eliza, you need to turn yourself in."

Eliza shook her head so that her hair flared out.

"Well at least untie me," Lainie said.

"No," Eliza said.

"Eliza, I won't call anyone. But if you vouch for me with these people I can come along. You can't do this alone. You're going to need help."

"No," Eliza said again. "I have to do this. It means my life. But I've already asked too much of you. I shouldn't have gotten you involved in the first place. After we're away I'll find a chance to call, get someone to come get you.'

"Eliza, no."

"Thank you, Lainie," Eliza said. She gave Lainie a kiss on her forehead and smoothed her air out of her eyes.

"Eliza!" Lainie stage-whispered. The girl paused at the exit to the kitchen.

"What's phase three?"

"I don't know," Eliza said. "But whatever it is, it's happening in Yellowstone. That's where we're going."

"Yellowstone, Wyoming?" Lainie asked, but Eliza was gone.

"Damnit!" In spite of her father's hammock, Lainie fought her bonds, but they were un-slippable. If anything, the bonds seemed to tighten, if that was possible, instead of getting looser. "Ah, Cord Steele, where are you when I need you?" she murmured out loud.

"Not far."

The familiar voice from deep shadows at the back of the kitchen, just inside the back door, startled Lainie and she nearly cried out. She strained her eyes to penetrate the gloom.

Cord Steele emerged into the dim light.

CHAPTER 6

Lainie stared in shock. Invoking Steele's name, she'd had no real expectation that he'd hear her and appear, as if from nowhere. Her relief at seeing him was tempered by sudden fear. In their last conversation he'd all but threatened to arrest her for aiding and abetting a fugitive.

"How in the world...?" she started.

He slipped forward on silent feet and set to untying the rope holding her to the table. "Sneaky son of a bitch," he said.

"No I know that," Lainie huffed. "I mean how did you find us?"

"I've been tracking your cellphone just as soon as we hung up the first time you called. I was already as far as Canada when you called the last time, a few hours ago. It didn't take long to get here."

She rubbed her wrists and sat up on the table, stretching her back. He placed her cell phone on the table next to her. "Here, you left this in the woods."

"How long were you standing there?" She pocketed her phone.

"Long enough," he said. "Pretty much heard it all."

"Why didn't you arrest her?"

"Because I'm not supposed to be here." His glare was angry. In fact there was something altogether different about him from the last time she saw him. His hair was somehow unkempt, even shaggy around the edges. His eyes seemed steeped in shadows, and he had a scruff of beard where before he'd been impeccably shaven. He seemed withdrawn and guarded.

"I'm supposed to be on leave," he said. "But I had to come get you out of this mess. I know you, Lainie. I knew you weren't going to take my advice. Not while you thought you could help your friend. You weren't about to do what I told you. I don't know why I even bother warning you. If my department head finds out I'm here instead of..."

"I'm not leaving Eliza," Lainie snapped in a harsh whisper. "She's in over her head. She has no idea the kind of danger she's in."

"I can make you." He bore a serious, no-nonsense glare. "But you won't."

Steele sighed, stepped back and ran a non-manicured hand over his eyes. "No, I won't."

She grinned back at him. "Cheer up, Cord. You get to play the..."

She wasn't able to finish when a gunshot cut the silence outside, and a woman screamed. Lainie recognized the voice. "Eliza!"

Lainie ran through the dining room and out the front door onto the boardwalk porch, Steele close behind. The compound was alive with movement as people ran to their vehicles to arm themselves with long rifles and shotguns from gun racks and duck for cover. On the other side of the compound Eliza knelt over a supine form. Zeke, his yellow shirt orange with blood.

"Dad!" Von Donelly cried and Lainie saw a young man running toward Eliza and Zeke. Another shot rang out and a rooster-tail of dirt kicked up just inches from where Eliza squatted.

"Eliza," Lainie cried again, and bolted across the quad toward her friend. Gunshots rang out and the dirt by Lainie's feet spouted little dust geysers. She found herself tackled by

Steele, who shielded her with his body, while urging her behind the giant wheel of a monster SUV.

Two ricochets rang out before the firing stopped again. Von Donelly reached his father and examined him. They had no cover.

Steele held Lainie back from running to them. When she struggled with him he slammed her hard against the wheel, winding her. "Sniper," he snapped, holding her there until she met his gaze and nodded.

"S'that you, Lainie?" A voice from the woods to the west.

"Fuck you, Leo," Lainie called back.

"Friend of yours?" Steele asked.

"Not hardly," Lainie said. "But yes, it's Leonid, the killer I told you about."

"The crip neighbor?" Steele asked.

"I don't have time to correct your language," Lainie said, "but yes, that's him."

Clearly recognizing her voice, Eliza strained around to spot Lainie, but Von struggled to pull his dad into the passenger seat of the truck, so Eliza turned to help him.

"For god's sake, Eliza," Lainie shouted, "Stay down! It's you he's aiming for." Even as another shot rang out, a lock of Eliza's hair sprung away from her head, catching the breeze of the bullet and floating away, but there was no blood. Still, Eliza yelped and jumped into the truck behind Von and his father, slamming the door behind her.

Other trucks and jeeps and cars peeled out of the compound, and Von's dad's truck fell in with the fleeing vehicles. Just like that, Lainie's and Steeles cover left them as its driver kicked gravel into their faces and fishtailed out of the clearing with the others, back toward the road.

Gunfire erupted around them as Steele pulled Lainie back toward the mess hall, ducking behind the skirting below the porch. The compound fell silent as the roar of fleeing engines faded to the east. Steele put a finger to his lips, and they waited.

Lainie's crouching legs had just begun to cramp when Steele held up a palm for her to stay as he slowly crept forward out of cover. He crouched there a moment, then stood with a slow rise and eyed the woods to the west. After nearly a full minute her motioned for Lainie to come out of cover.

"He's not there anymore," he said. "He's not strictly after you. It's Eliza he's been contracted to kill. He probably just shot at you because you got the better of him at the apartment. But he's a pro, he's not going to risk losing her to hunt you."

"Damn it," Lainie said, wiping the dirt from her hands and knees.

"Come on," Steele said, turning back up the road.

"Where to now?"

"Back to the cars."

They hiked in silence. Lainie couldn't deny the obvious, Steele was angry with her – he pulled several paces ahead of her, back straight and rigid, judging her. She could even think of several reasons why. But she also couldn't shake the surety that this wasn't Cord Steele. It was him, of course, but something about him had changed, hardened. The Cord Steele she knew was a cocky, energetic, Devil-may-care rogue with a crooked grin and jaunty demeanor.

This scruffier, stiffer, angrier Cord Steele was a side to him she'd never seen before. Something had changed him in the months since she'd last seen him. Was it the same thing that'd kept him from calling her in that time, or showing up unannounced on her doorstep with flowers and a bottle of scotch, as he'd been wont to do?

It seemed like a longer walk back to where she'd left her car than it'd been walking in.

"I parked about a half-mile back," he said, walking to the passenger side. "Give me a ride."

They climbed into the car.

She put the key in the ignition, then dropped her hand. "Cord," she said.

"What."

"Is everything okay? Are you all right?"

He studied the view out the window on his side as if to avoid looking at her. "Just drive."

She reached up and turned the key in the ignition. The car roared instantly to life.

"Get out!" she screamed, diving out her side and sprinting straight into the woods on the other side of the road. She didn't get far, only just tumbling into a ditch when the impending explosion sent a hot blast over her. Pine needles, dirt and plastic car parts flew overhead, and her ears rang so vociferously that for long moments it was all she could hear.

"Cord!" she called, scrambling up the embankment and peering through the trees at the blaze beyond. Her voice sounded dim, muffled to her. "Cord!"

She attained her feet again, though shaky, and stumbled out onto the highway pavement, screaming at the burning wreckage of her little red Camry, "Cord Steele, are you all right?"

Someone grabbed her from the right side and spun her around. It was Cord Steele, none the worse for wear. He, too, was calling her name, but she could barely hear him even this close. They embraced each other hard and held each other for long moments, both seeking and giving comfort.

*   *   *

Several fire and rescue vehicles zoomed past them as they drove in Cord's rental car back toward town, away from the explosion. Lainie couldn't afford to be detained and questioned by authorities at the moment and Cord didn't seem in the mood to argue with her, so they'd walked the half mile back to his car. Understandably it'd taken first responders longer than usual to respond, since no one was around to report the explosion, giving Lainie and Cord time to make a clean getaway.

"I don't understand," Steele said. Their voices were still muffled to Lainie, though not as much. "How did you know the car was rigged to explode?"

She told him about the blob of foil crimped around the starter-lead on her Camry. "She hasn't started on the first try in almost a year," she finished.

Steele nodded. "Your friend Leonid must've inadvertently fixed that when he wired the bomb to the starter. Good thing he put it on a delay, probably wanted you and Eliza, if you were able to get away, to think you were home free before you died. Quick thinking on your part, I must say."

It occurred to her that Steele had to have jumped the instant she said so in order to get away in time, not pausing to ask why or what she was talking about. His reflex, to act instantly without questioning her, had most likely saved his life. He'd always trusted her implicitly, treating her like an equal from the day they'd met. It was one of the things that made her like him.

He pulled in to the Bulkley River Lodge and put the car in park.

"I'll get my things," Lainie said, reaching for the door handle.

"No," Steele said.

"But we need to go to Yellowstone," Lainie said. "Eliza's with those people, and they're in with Harkness, the man who injected her against her will with God knows what. And Leo's still out there, too. She needs our help."

"I'm going to Yellowstone," Steele said. "You are not."

"But. . ."

Steele startled her by slapping a hand roughly on the back of her neck and pulling her in, so close they were nearly nose to nose. The intensity in his eyes *did* scare her.

"This is not a fucking game, Lainie Parker. Those were real bullets. Your friend, Eliza, is infected with a real virus, for all we know one of the deadliest ones. Have you ever seen anyone bleed out from Ebola, twisted and writhing, crying out in pain as their guts liquify, their last moments on Earth tortured and blackened by agony? Or not even that, have you ever tried to recover from a gunshot wound, not even a fatal one? A bullet doesn't just pierce your flesh, it shocks the muscle and tissue around its path, burst blood vessels, bone-deep contusions, a disruption to organs and marrow. A fired bullet is hotter than blazes, it cooks you on the inside, if it doesn't pass through. Healing from that, the weeks of antibiotics, and physical therapy, and more than one surgery if you're lucky, if the bullet doesn't hit any organs on its way through."

Frightened, she tried to punch him, but he dodged the hit and grabbed her wrist. "Let go of me," she growled but he didn't.

"Go the fuck home, Lainie," he said. She saw for the first time the moisture in his eyes. He wasn't being cruel, he was genuinely afraid for her. "This is not the life for you. It's not the life for any decent person."

He abruptly let her go. He leaned across her and opened her door. "Get out," he said firmly. When she didn't immediately comply, he bellowed at her, "Get out of the car, Lainie!"

She did so with alacrity, more from alarm than any intent to obey him.

He sped away, letting the momentum of the car slam her door shut with the loud report of a gunshot. She watched him fishtail in the gravel drive and out onto the road, where he sped away and out of sight.

Her neck was stiff, her wrist bruised, and she rubbed them alternately as she turned and went back to her motel room. It was the first time Cord Steele had ever lost hist temper in front of her, the first time she'd ever been the target of those steely blue eyes. He'd scared her. But she didn't resent Steele, not really. He was clearly laboring under some heavy trauma, and from all appearances not dealing very well.

After a moment to breathe and slow her heart rate, Lainie dialed her phone. "Orin?"

"Lainie, how're things going?"

"You said you didn't have any details on the project Dr. Harkness was working on, that it's all classified, right?"

"Yeah, sorry."

"What about any administrative details? Those wouldn't be classified, would they?"

"What kind of administrative stuff?" he asked.

"Like what facilities they held," she said. "Real estate. Where any other labs may have been located, backup sites, storage facilities, things like that?"

"Let me look." She heard him typing on a keyboard. "No, sorry, it only shows the one you mentioned just off campus here."

"Nothing in, say Wyoming? Yellowstone?"

"Nope," he said. "Sorry again."

Lainie sighed. "No, it was a longshot. Thanks anyway, Orin."

"Although now that you mention Yellowstone and backup facilities. . ."

Lainie clutched her phone tighter. "What?"

It's just that there's a company the university uses as a failback facility."

"Failback?"

"Sure," Orin said. "Disaster recovery. In case of catastrophic failure of the systems here in San Francisco, everything is backed-up in its entirety to servers at the company, Summit Data Solutions."

"Let me guess," Lainie said. "Their facility is based in Yellowstone, Wyoming."

"If the bay area suddenly fell off the continental shelf right now, the university could pick up exactly where it left off within an hour, with only miniscule data loss, from the Yellowstone facility."

"I'm guessing it's a secure facility?" Lainie asked.

"Has to be. They have all sorts of joint university-government research data in there, and the university isn't their only client. It's got to be one of the most secure facilities in the country."

Lainie entered the address of the SDS failback facility into her phone as he dictated it.

"Thanks, Orin," Lainie said.

"Was that helpful?"

She hung up. You have no idea, she thought. In addition to preserving his research in Eliza's body, Harkness had been intent on deleting everything from his research and development from the servers there at the facility in Oakland. But everything would have also been backed up.

Phase three: wipe the data from the servers in Yellowstone as well. She bet her life on it.

She dialed again, a number she'd been given by very complex and secret channels, a number never to be used unless she really needed to.

*   *   *

Lainie waited at the curb just outside the little airport of Jackson Hole, Wyoming leaning against her rental car, a cobalt blue Jeep Wrangler. The airport was all done in a light wood, probably pine, and glass and was a very charming blend of rustic and modern. She'd arrived in plenty of time to pick up the car and be in place to meet her traveling companion, also arriving from Canada.

As the dark, diminutive, and beautiful woman emerged from the sliding doors Lainie ran to her. They embraced warmly.

"Lainie, my sister. It is so good to see you."

"Simi," Lainie sighed. "I've missed you. I'm so glad you could come."

As they separated Simi flashed Lainie her red Canadian passport. "It is a forgery, of course. But a good one." Her name was apparently now Shima Ateem.

Simi was of Iranian decent, born and raised mostly in Kuwait and the UAE. Lainie had met her and her brother, Ibrahim, in Baltimore when they'd kidnapped her, mistaking her for a CIA agent who could tell them where their father was. The misunderstanding had led to adventure and an unbreakable bond between them as Lainie eventually aided all of them in leaving the country to escape terrorists and agents alike.

"I was so sorry to hear about Faisal," Lainie said.

"Father died in peace," Simi said. "In his bed and with his family around him. And that is all thanks to you."

"Surely not just me," Lainie blushed.

"Certainly entirely," Simi smiled. She'd developed some lines on her face but was otherwise unchanged from when Lainie had last seen her a year ago.

"I'm sorry I had to use the contact number you gave me," Lainie said as she helped Simi put her minimal luggage in the back of the jeep.

"Not at all," Simi said. "I'm glad you did. That's what it's for."

Lainie waited until they were in the front seat and headed north before she filled Simi in – they had a solid 2-hour drive yet to Yellowstone.

"I called you because I had a suspicion, have had for a while now, that you can help in a crisis like this. I don't want to pry, but on retrospect you showed some pretty impressive fighting skills during the whole mess a year ago. There never seemed a good time to ask you, then, but it's my understanding women from your part of the world are only just beginning to achieve freedoms most of the rest of us take for granted. Education, jobs, fashion. Never mind learning to fight better than most men I know."

Trees, cliffs, and canyon walls sped past the windows as they drove along; the gradual bend of rivers; broad, blue, still lakes; and standing majestically over all, great snowcapped peaks overhead and on the horizon. When Simi didn't answer right away, Lainie pressed her, "Simi?"

"Krav Maga," Simi said quietly, "and some Kung Fu. I was still just learning then."

"Whatever for?" Lainie asked. "You couldn't've known what was going to happen then. What made you train in Kung Fu and. . .that other one, of all things?"

Simi shifted in her seat. "Please don't ask me questions I cannot answer," she said.

Of the answers her friend could have given, Lainie expected anything like this the least. It only served to deepen her curiosity, and she realized, as she had only suspected before, that there was much more to Simi than met the eye.

Which is why Lainie had felt compelled to call her for help in such a dangerous situation.

The town of Yellowstone, as they crossed the city limits, wasn't as premeditatedly rustic and quaint as Jackson Hole, but perhaps more authentically so. Yellowstone, the town, was actually in Montana, that odd little finger of border that reaches down from the north as if trying to come between Wyoming and Idaho. There were long tracts of shops with log-beams and rails and wooden boardwalks. Souvenir shops aplenty to be sure, but also wood furniture stores, western art galleries, cafes, rock stores, restaurants, candy stores, etc.

Lainie drove straight through town and continued East, because the highway had turned that way. At nearly the far end of town, she eschewed the West entrance road to Yellowstone National Park and turned instead North again on US 267, known locally as Gallatin Road. Not far up this road they passed West Yellowstone Airport, only served by one major airline, Delta, with no direct flights from British Columbia, Canada, which was why Lainie had had to fly in to Jackson instead. She could have probably afforded a seat on a private airline, but again she wanted to minimize her use of the pimp stash as much as possible.

Further up the highway they came to Madison Arm Road, leading back West toward Hebgen Lake. Another hour of twisting mountain roads and they emerged on a ridge overlooking a sharp drop toward the vast, beautiful lake itself. On its shore below stood a modern-looking building, built in green-shaded sheet-glass reflecting the lake and the green scenery around it. The grounds were modest, with some outbuildings. The main complex itself was only three, maybe four stories high, sprawling for a mere 400 or 500 yards at its longest. It came right up to the edge of the lake itself, overlooking with balconies and walkways, but nevertheless a sheer drop to the mirror surface of the deep aquamarine water.

"Summit Data Systems," Lainie whispered, consulting the GPS map on her phone.

From here it didn't seem like Orin's "one of the most secure facilities in the country," but Lainie suspected appearances were deceiving in this case.

"And you are sure your friend and those people came here," Simi said.

"I'd bet my life on it. It won't be easy for them to get in. But I figure they wouldn't try if they didn't have a plan. Which is something I don't have."

"They have had a pretty good head start on us even from the time you called me," Simi said. "Perhaps they are already underway"

"They were loaded up for a long road trip when they left the compound in Houston, tents, sleeping bags, RVs, etc. They're driving. I'm hoping by flying ahead we've hop-frogged them and gotten here ahead of them."

"Maybe we just drive up and warn these people."

"Who?" Lainie shrugged.

"Whoever is in charge down there."

Lainie thought for a moment and then shook her head. "If this facility is as secure as I've been told, with government data to protect as well as universities and God knows what else, I don't think they'll welcome such a warning with a gracious thank you. More than likely they'll take us into custody and question us. Thoroughly. Given what happened in San Francisco, and your less than legal status here in our country, it's unlikely an interrogation would go well for either one of us."

Simi sat back in her seat and sighed. She was an impetuous sort, Lainie recalled, the kind to rush in first and figure out tactics as she went. "What do you suggest?" Simi asked. "Maybe an anonymous call?

"I could've done that from Canada. These days calls aren't as anonymous as we would wish. Even calling from a payphone, it would only serve to lock the facility down. Besides, that wouldn't get me any closer to finding Eliza, which in the end is all I care about. The data can get deleted or not get deleted. I don't care."

"What if it is as deadly as it may be?"

"Then let Cord Steele worry about that. But Eliza has been injected with whatever it is against her will. She needs to get to a doctor, get an antidote or a cure or whatever."

"What if there is no cure?" When Lainie looked at her Simi put up her hands. "You said it was new research. No hospital is likely to have a cure. If it is possible a cure was being developed by this professor along with the thing he injected, is not Eliza's best chance with these people?"

"I don't trust them, least of all Harkness, a man so desperate that he injected her with something deadly just to preserve it and keep it away from the government. I'm not comfortable with that man having a say over whether Eliza lives or dies, especially since she's now a witness, a very direct witness, to what he's done. He's more likely to use her to revive his research and then just let her die, or kill her outright."

Suddenly, the back door to the Jeep opened and they both turned in alarm to watch Cord Steele climb into the back seat, closing the door behind him.

"How did you. . .?' Lainie started.

Steele held up his hand to stop her. "Let's not do that again. I never doubted for a second I'd find you somewhere around here, no matter what I said. But I am, surprised to see this one." He glared at Simi.

"Hello, Agent Steele," Simi said.

"Never expected to see you again, Simi Al-Sehremni."

"My name is Shima Ateem."

"Of course it is. I guess now that I think about it, it was inevitable that you two would stay in touch. That you'd call her for help when I pushed you away. Do you even know who Simi, excuse me, Shima works for?"

Lainie looked at Simi, who continued to smile cordially at Steele.

"She can't tell you," Steele pressed on, "but I can." He paused to give Simi time to stop him, but she said nothing. "She's a covert for Mossad."

"Israeli intelligence?" Lainie said.

"Very good."

Finally, Simi turned and looked at Lainie. "They recruited me when I was still in college at NYU. They approached me in Paris when I went to visit father."

"Did they know who he was working for?" Lainie asked.

"It was how they recruited me, the chance to protect my father and get him away from that cell of terrorists he was being forced to work for."

"So they knew about Sayed and the New Jersey cell?"

"Simi was supposed to use her cousin Sayed to infiltrate that cell," Steele said. "Meanwhile the CIA, at cross-purposes, had set Sean Brandt on Faisal to kill him. Brandt fucked everyone up when he helped Faisal escape and disappear."

"He saved my father's life," Simi said, defensive of Brandt, with whom she'd had an inchoate romance.

"And Simi went rogue from Mossad trying to find her father," Steele finished.

"Ibrahim?' Lainie asked.

"My brother is an innocent," Simi said. "He knows nothing of any of this."

Lainie sat back in her seat, metaphorically winded. The tangled web of international intrigue never ceased to intimidate her since her ordeal last year. She had been in the midst of more than she could know even then. "That's where you learned to fight."

Simi nodded.

"So what's Mossad's interest in Harkness and his research?" Steele asked.

"None," Simi said. "They do not know I am here. Lainie called, and I came, as any sister would."

"Sister?'

"For her service to my family in a dark time, Lainie Parker will forever be my sister. I will never fail to come when she calls."

"Right," Steele said, his voice dripping with sarcastic doubt. "And I suppose it'll do me no good to tell you two to stay here and keep out of this. You're going to try to get to Eliza no matter what just as soon as I go. I suppose I could tie you up."

"You could try," Simi said.

Steele raised his hands in surrender. "No, no, no, I don't want to waste time fighting, maybe drawing attention."

"Wise."

"Okay," he said, opening the car door again, "stay close, do what I say, and bring comfortable shoes."

*   *   *

Steele led them on foot through brush, shrubbery, and trees, then at a crouch down an embankment across the lone road leading to the gate to the compound. The gate was bifurcated by a guard shack, from which appeared an unarmed guard from time to time. He then led them at a crouch around the compound away from the guard shack. At one point the road began to turn away from the compound. Here Steele led them across, then up an ever-rising slope, moving deeper and deeper into the woods. Finally they came to a shallow bluff overlooking the compound, screened by pines and shrubs.

Steele pointed, "There, that culvert. I've studied the layout of this place and that's the most likely place for a breach."

"Great," Lainie said. She started down the slope but Steele pulled her back. "What?"

"We wait."

"For what?"

"To see if Donelly and his crew even show up."

"Why wouldn't they?"

Steele reclined on his haunches, the slope keeping him upright so he could view the scene below. He was clearly socked in for a stakeout. "Maybe this isn't where they're headed after all. Or maybe, after taking sniper fire at their compound they lost their religion, changed their minds, decided whatever they're up to, it's not worth bloodshed."

Lainie snorted and Steele shrugged.

"I will take first watch," Simi said. She spread her jacket down and lay on it a short distance away from them.

"What does she mean?" Lainie asked.

Steele folded his arms under the back of his head. "She means get your sleep when you can. You never know when you're going to get another chance."

Lainie studied Steele. His posture bespoke of relaxation, but the ropes in his neck, the way his sunken eyes seemed nevertheless to bulge from their sockets, as if seeking escape, the tear in the left knee of his jeans, the slightly matted look of the fur at the collar of his bomber jacket. . .this was not a man at peace.

"What happened to you, Steele?"

"You mean why didn't I call you back?"

"No," Lainie said, dropping to her butt next to him. "I don't care about that. I mean, you're not yourself. I can see it. Something's happened to you. You're cold, like we don't know each other as. . .intimately as we do."

His eyes flickered away every time she tried to engage them. Finally he sighed, signaling impatience. He turned away from her to his side. "Get some rest if you can. You can't have gotten much sleep in the past couple of days."

Lainie looked from him to Simi's back silhouetted against the lake as it turned translucent before giving in to the falling night. Lainie sat on her butt, knees pulled up to her chin, arms around them. Steele had changed, and now it had been revealed that she didn't know Simi like she thought she did. Flanked as she was by two erstwhile friends, two capable and resourceful professionals, Lainie never felt so vulnerable, so alone.

She awoke to the sound of Steele mumbling. Her neck was stiff as she turned to see him on his back, face twisted as if in agony, legs kicking, hands balled into fists.

"Lainie, no!" But Simi's warning came too late as Lainie went to him on her knees and shook him. In a flash he was on her, pinning her to the ground, growling in rage. His eyes were alight with such hatred she'd never seen and he bared his teeth as if prepared to rip out her throat with them. On instinct she brought her knee up into his groin, but this only seemed to infuriate him further. He reared back and cold-cocked her across the cheekbone.

Lainie's vision went dark but for the bright embers dancing and winking in and out in the blackness. As she struggled to remain conscious she was only vaguely aware that his weight had been quite abruptly cast from her. She heard shouting and the impact of more than one fist before all fell silent again.

Then someone was pulling at her wrists, not strongly but insistently. It was Simi: "Lainie, let me see. Move your hands."

Lainie took her hands away from her face and felt gentle fingers probing her cheek and eye on the side that she'd been hit. The skin felt hot. She hissed and pulled away when she felt pain there again. "Stop it."

"Nothing broken," Simi said. "Going to bruise pretty bad, I'm afraid."

She helped Lainie sit up again. When she opened her eyes Lainie cast about her for Steele. He sat further down the slope looking up at them, but in the dark she couldn't make out his face. His voice sounded strained, scarred: "Lainie I. . .I'm sorry, I didn't. . ."

"What the fuck, Cord!" Heedless of the need to stay hidden she was screaming at him. Simi hushed her.

Steele fell silent, then turned away from them and dropped to sitting again, his face in his hands. Lainie rose to a squat and started toward him, pushing Simi's hands away as the other woman tried to forestall her. She moved down the slope slowly, set herself down a distance from him.

They sat in silence for a while. Then she said, voice hard, "You were having a nightmare."

He looked up at the moon, wet cheeks glistening in the silver light. "I'm sorry. I shouldn't have come."

"What the fuck, Cord," she said again, this time her voice softer. Her cheekbone throbbed. She knew as much about PTSD as any graduate student, which was to stay she read case studies in text books. She'd never seen it in vivid life before. "Who were you seeing just now, when you hit me?" She kept her voice hard, neutral, not forgiving, which according to the textbooks would only cause him to withdraw again.

He tried to turn away, then he chuckled. "The company shrink says I should tell someone, someone close, not a professional." He spoke in a barely audible whisper.

"I'd say it's about goddamn time, wouldn't you?"

The harsh language did what it was supposed to – kept him sharp, present. At length he spoke to the dirt at his feet. "I was in Afghanistan. I was embedded with. . .well, embedded with a Special Ops team. I was in a building with my body guard, Whirls. Sgt. Joe Worley, we called him Whirls. I was talking to an asset when a sniper got him, right in the left ear, right in front of me, I felt the heat of the bullet as it came. Whirls grabbed me and we tried to make it back to the vehicles waiting for us outside. There was an RPG, one of the vehicles went up, heavy suppression fire. We got separated from the unit, and were captured."

Lainie said nothing, lest she spark his silence again.

"I knew we were in for a rough time of it. They held us for a few days in the back of a truck, no food, heat, always driving during the hottest hours of the day. They gave us their urine expecting us to drink it. Finally we got to an encampment and thrown into a hut. I knew they were going to torture us for information.

"First rule of being taken hostage, tell your captors everything they want to know. Protocol. By the time they can act on any intel – frequencies, signals, codes – everything will have been changed as soon as you are captured. Right off the bat I made it clear I was CIA, Whirls was not. I thought they'd leave Whirls alone, torture me instead. But they're smarter than that, meaner. They figured out it would be worse for me watching them torture him than being tortured myself. So they used him, tortured him to make me talk."

As Steele talked his hands wrung themselves together, turning the knuckles red with friction. "I don't know, but I'm willing to bet you've never seen a man's eyelids torn off with pliers. The skin doesn't split nicely, it tears up through the eyebrow, up the forehead, taking hair and scalp with it. . ."

"Stop," Lainie gasped, swallowing back bile. "I'm sorry, please."

Steel looked at her. "I'm sorry, I didn't mean to. . ."

Lainie reached out to touch him, but he pulled away.

"Whirls was alive when they finally rescued us," Steele said, "but he wasn't conscious. He died somewhere on the helicopter ride back to base. I never returned your calls because. . ."

"No," Lainie said. "Stop. I get it. I've been an ass. A stupid, jealous, self-centered ass." She felt childish, ashamed.

"I've been on administrative leave ever since," Steele said. "I just can't seem to shake it. I keep trying to get back to the old Cord Steele, but I'm not sure I know who that is any more. I didn't want you to see me, not like this."

He fell silent and they sat in the deep wooded dark.

Simi let out a loud hiss. When they turned upslope to her she motioned down to the building below. "They come," she whispered.

Looking down, Lainie saw nothing, not near the fence nor around the culvert. "Where?"

"There," Steele said, pointing. In the distance five shadows strode boldly across the parking lot from the main gate toward the building's front entrance. Among them Lainie recognized one by her silhouette.

"Eliza," Lainie whispered to herself. Then louder, though still at a whispered, she asked, "How did they get in the gate? They don't appear to be trying to hide or sneak."

"They have someone on the inside," Steele said. "Probably on the security team. The one at the gate for sure. Maybe others, too. Stay close."

He led them down the slope, sometimes walking at a crouch, sliding on their butts where the slope was too steep. The ground grew swampy as it leveled out. They came to the culvert and Lainie bent low to look inside. "It's dark in there. Not very inviting."

"We aren't going in that way," Steele said. That's too easy. It's most definitely grated off with some pretty heavy-duty iron." He climbed up the slope over the culvert and peered at the fence post at its very apex. There were in fact two poles here adjacent to each other, pretty much side by side.

"Ground's too wet here for electrification," Steele said. "There's a seam in the fence here, a break in the perimeter. There're no sensors between these two poles."

"I don't know about you, but I'll have to go on some extreme diet to fit through there," Lainie whispered.

At ground level, below the ragged tops of the wild grass, two metal sleeves were buried in the ground, into which each of the poles were set, held in place by crimping screws. Steele extended the screwdriver from a knife he produced from a zippered sleeve pouch and went to work on the pole footings. First one pole, then the other came free. Simi lifted one out of its mooring and Steele pulled the other. They each leaned these aside making a wide gap in the fence.

"That's what happens when some CEO is hell bent on pitching his tent in a picturesque setting," Steele remarked as he climbed through first, "landscape challenges be damned." Lainie went through next, Simi taking up the rear. "Good to assume, though, that this weak spot is monitored by video." Steele led them across a perimeter drive at a run toward the building.

Even as they reached the low hedge at the base of the wall, a black electric golf cart came trundling around the corner at a snail's pace. The trio pressed themselves to the ground behind the hedge. The brakes squeaked a little as the cart came to an abrupt stop. Two men stepped from the cart and parted ways, the driver toward the break in the fence, brightly illuminated by his torch, the other toward the low hedge and Lainie's small party, the intense blue LED beam of his light searching.

Lainie popped up suddenly and as the halo of his light flashed to her face, he smiled and waved. "Howdy." Before he could recover enough to raise an alarm, Simi sprung up behind him and gave him a solid blow to the base of the skull. His eyes rolled back, his knees coupled, and Lainie caught him and he fell forward.

"Help," Lainie yelped as she was born backwards. "Help." As she went to her knees. Simi grabbed the man by the scruff and shunted him to the side, off of Lainie, and let him slump face-forward over the hedge.

"Put your hands up." The driver had returned. He had a Glock semi-automatic aimed at the two women, braced by his left hand underneath. He wisely kept the golf cart between he and Simi. "Don't move." He reached for the mouthpiece of his two-way, clipped to his left lapel, and keyed the mic.

Instead of raising the alarm, however, he let out a low wail of surprise. The lasso of black monofilament wire that'd dropped over his head and pinned his raised arm to his throat would have been invisible in the night but for the thin crease it caused in the flesh of his wrist and neck. A crease that was even now being lined with the smallest trickle of crimson blood.

"Don't move," Lainie heard Steele whisper as he came into sight behind the man. "Monofilament'll cut through skin like a hot knife through Jello if you wiggle too much." Steel reached around and took the man's gun, putting it to the back of it's owner's head. He then reached around and pulled the cord connecting the mic to the two-way at the man's waist. Only then did he loosen the garotte and set the man free.

The guard rubbed his hand and neck where they'd been cut, looked at the blood on his fingers, but didn't turn. "Look," he said," my shift's over anyway. I'm on my way out. I won't say anything, I swear it."

Steele's face was stony, his eyes dead of any light or life. He took ne step back to give himself room to straight his gun arm.

"Cord, no," Lainie hissed.

Steele cocked the gun.

"Please, Cord," Lainie said. "Not like this."

Finally, Steele's eyes blinked over to meet hers, softened. When they hardened again, it was only as he raised the weapon and give the man a sharp wrap across the back of the head. The guard crumpled at Steele's feet.

Lainie nodded as Steele put the gun in the waistband of his pants. Then he bent briefly to remove the man's two-way and clip it to his own belt. Checking the volume knob, he returned her nod.

"Do you see the patch on the sleeve of his windbreaker?" Lainie whispered. "'Donelly Private Security.' Should've known." To their blank stares she said, "Donelly's the name of the leader of the group in Houston that Eliza hooked up with. He said something about being ex-military."

"He owns the security firm contracted by SDS," Steele said.

"So, calling SDS with a warning would have done nothing anyway," Simi said, "except alert them we are onto them."

"Explains how they got past the gate," Steele said. "They're still trying to avoid cameras, which SDS could check later, but it should be easy for them since his firm most likely installed those, too."

"No longer three against five," Simi said, referring to the five shadows they saw crossing from the gate to the building earlier.

Steele motioned them to follow and crept to the front corner of the building. Lainie waited for him to signal the all clear and followed him around the corner and along the front of the building, Simi on her heels.

"I don't get it," Lainie whispered. "If they're here to erase Harkness's research data, but they already control the security guards, then why come at all? Why not have one of the security guards do their dirty work?"

"I'm guessing it's not a simple matter of hitting a delete key," Steele said. "It's going to be more complicated than that. Gatekeepers aren't necessarily going to be trained in and versed on the complexities of IT security."

"Still, someone with skills could come in wearing a guard's jacket," Lainie said.

"Even if they had their own info tech geek, these days no one person has the keys, metaphorically speaking, to the entire databank."

"They were not ready," Simi said from behind Lainie.

"What do you mean?"

"You said that Harkness's lab was raided, and that he was forced to shred documents and delete files in a hurry. The group's plan, whatever it is, was not in place yet. They had to accelerate it. This, too, is happening in a hurry."

That made sense to Lainie. She remembered the vote to move on to the next phase, whatever that meant.

Steele reached the front doors, a bank of glass inset by two regular swing doors on either side and four revolving doors across the center. "Wait here while I slip the lock on the door."

As he slid along the glass to the first swing door, he craned his neck up and down to study the locks. Lainie, who'd ignored his instructions to wait and came up behind him, reached out to the door handle.

"No," he hissed, but she'd already pulled. The door swung open silently.

"Worth a try," Lainie shrugged.

Steele gave her a crooked smile, shaking his head, and entered the building. Lainie and Simi followed.

The lobby was broader than it was deep. There was a circular security desk directly in front, deserted, and a bank of doors to the right of that, including a set of his and hers restrooms. To the left was a rank of four turnstiles, each with a tall transparent tube standing by. Each tube had a single pale-yellow light, a line down its core.

"Essodyne 940, series EsEf," Steele recited quietly. "Security gates. More than they appear. Not just metal detector, but motion detector, with limited ultrasound and chemical sniffers."

"No," Lainie said in disbelief, but Steele gave her a steady glare. "Well how do we get past those?"

"Easy," Steele said. Keeping a wary eye up the passageway beyond, he pushed through one turnstile and turned to look at them. "Yellow indicates maintenance standby."

"They aren't on?" Lainie asked, following him if a bit more cautiously, as if she expected the turnstile to start blaring an alarm any second. Simi came through another of the turnstiles.

"Unlocked front door," Steele said, "disabled security gates. Looks like all security systems have been disarmed."

"The better to sneak in," Simi said.

"And back out again," Steele said, "reactivating everything behind them as they leave. No one will ever know they were here."

"Well, it's a sure bet they don't know anyone's on to them," Lainie said. "You stopped the guard outside from calling in, worth hoping they aren't really looking out for anyone."

Steele nodded as he led them deeper into the building. "They don't know we're here."

The next hall was empty, and then they were in the elevator vestibule. Steele walked to the touch-screen office index on the wall above the call buttons and swiped through the digital list. "All of the office space in on the ground floor. Server bays are on the top three floors."

"Three whole floors of servers?" Lainie asked.

"You have to suppose they keep the servers for many of their higher profile clients in bays by themselves, based on the specific needs and requirements of each client. For example I happen to know something about government data security compliance, and they would require that sort of isolation for their servers."

"Is it possible to delete files from the servers from an office terminal on this floor?" Lainie asked.

"Yes," Simi said. "But you need passwords, and you need to know where the files are that you are looking for, which means you need to know something about the server architectures."

"But if you had all that," Steele said, "you could do the deletions from offsite, you wouldn't need to come here to do it. There's a more direct, brute-force way past the security of a server."

"Dongle," Simi said.

"A what?" Lainie looked from one to the other.

"A device plugged directly into the server hardware, sometimes into an external port, but most likely in this case either into a bus slot inside or directly onto the motherboard itself."

"To do that they would go directly to the servers storing the failback data for the university," Lainie said. She gestured to the touchscreen on the wall. "Which server bank does that?"

"Doesn't say," Steele said, swiping through it again as if to show her. "That would be pretty classified, even from those with enough clearance to get this far. That's probably stored somewhere else."

"Somewhere we'd have to hack into."

"Yup."

"So we're back to square one: how do we find the servers they are deleting?"

Steele shrugged. "We're going to have to go floor by floor, stay quiet, and hope we catch them in the act."

"That will take some time," Simi said. "They could finish and be gone again by the time we find them."

"We're going to have to split up," Lainie said. "There are three server floors and three of us."

Steele chortled as if he thought she were joking, but when he met her determined glare he looked back at her in alarm.

*   *   *

As the elevator ascended with them aboard, Steele took Lainie by the shoulders. "Now remember what we agreed."

"Do not be seen," she recited back to him in a whisper, "do not engage, text you if I find them and stay out of sight."

He still looked worried, but the elevator doors chose that moment to open and they were running out of time. With one last admonishing look, he stepped out onto the second floor and let the doors slide closed between him.

Lainie and Simi held hands as the elevator rose another floor. When the doors opened they looked at each other and Simi gave Lainie's hand a single squeeze before letting it go and stepping out. She turned to meet Lainie's eyes as the doors closed again.

The last floor up Lainie concentrated on evening out her breathing, on trying to quell her pounding heart. Splitting up like this was quicker, but it wasn't safe. All depended on their ability to regroup again when the others were found, to confront them as a group and rescuing Eliza from them, whether she wanted to be rescued or not.

Just as the doors opened her cell phone vibrated. She was pulling it out of her pocket when someone called out in surprise:

"You?"

Lainie looked up. A group of men and women stood a good distance up the hallway. They were looking right at her. It was Eliza, among them, who'd called her out.

Two of the men launched themselves up the hallway toward her at speed. Lainie fumbled at the elevator buttons, hitting several without seeing which ones. The doors began to slide closed and she pressed her back up against the far wall.

The doors were going to close, she was sure of it. She was going to make it.

As the doors came together in the middle, four strong fingers appeared between them. She heard a manly grunt and slowly the doors were pried open again.

CHAPTER 7

Lainie guessed that the neck was convenient leverage for a stronger adversary to steer weaker prey, but this was the umpteenth time in the last year that someone had taken her by the back of the neck and forced her to go where he wanted her to go and Lainie was getting tired of it.

She only allowed herself to slump as if resigned under his yoke for just a few steps up the hall back toward the others before she lashed out suddenly, flinging her left arm out and to the side, grabbing as big a fistful of his khakis at the crotch as she could get and gave it a considerable shove, then yank.

The young brute holding her cried out and let her neck go as he slouched over, thumping against the wall to keep himself from going down. Not wasting any time, Lainie turned and bolted back toward the elevator. Realizing that was itself a dead end, she veered to one side where the hallway split around the bank of elevators and continued deeper into the building.

She almost made it, too, but her other pursuer was on her in a flash. He grabbed both of her elbows from behind, pulling them back like chicken wings. Lainie cried out in pain as she felt herself turned and led back again.

"Don't hurt her, Von," Eliza blurted out.

"What do you care, Lainie?" the man leading Lainie asked. Donelly the younger.

"I just don't think it's necessary," Eliza said, holding Lainie's gaze, trying to convey some message without letting on to the others.

"It was her people shot my dad," Von snapped, shaking Lainie.

"I told you that's not true," Eliza said," I saw. Whoever shot your dad was shooting at her, too."

"Bullshit."

"It's not, Von," Eliza said.

"Is he all right?" Lainie asked, "your dad?"

Von let her go but stayed between her and escape. "And what do you care? Man, we're just bubbling over with compassion for each other here, aren't we?"

Von was a tall, strapping young man of about Lainie's age, mid- to late-twenties, though not quite as bulging and over-defined muscularly as his father. Still, he had the same blond hair, ruddy complexion, and strong, broad Nordic features.

"She's right," Lainie said. "The sniper was targeting everyone in the compound, not just your father. Is he okay."

Von eyed her. "He'll live. Take more than a dot-fifty to take down my da. Now who the fuck are you, once and for all?"

Lainie just looked back, flexing her arms to get the circulation going again. Besides Eliza, Von, and the first man who'd grabbed Lainie, another muscular youth like Von but with brown hair, there was another woman in her thirties wearing khaki shorts and a utility vest with nothing underneath it, and another man with glasses and holding a computer tablet in the crook of his elbow.

"Fine, hold her.," Von instructed.

The first man to grab her by the neck had recovered from Lainie's assault on his jewels and now wrapped arms like anacondas around her, trapping her own arms across her chest. Von searched her and found her phone.

He tapped the screen, then turned it to show Lainie. "Who the fuck is Steele?"

The text window identified Steele as the sender at the top. The first text on the screen was in all caps, "STAY IN

ELEVATOR! COME BACK DOWN! NEED TO LEAVE NOW!!"

The next text no less urgent: "NOT DELETING! WIRING FOR EXPLOSIVES! THEY R GOING TO BLOW THE WHOLE PLACE!"

Lainie flashed on a memory of the dim figures they saw crossing the parking lot. They weren't hunched to stay unobserved, all the security systems were shut off. They were carrying explosives in their knapsacks. Even now Lainie spotted a black device mounted to a nearby support pylon, a single sinister red light blinking eagerly to one side of it. She didn't doubt it was just such similar devices that Steele had spotted down on the second floor, sparking his urgency.

She knew if she didn't respond Steele wouldn't leave, save himself. He'd come looking for her. But she had no way of warning him that she'd been taken prisoner. And what about Simi? Like Steele, she'd come looking for Lainie.

"How long are those bombs timed for?" she asked Donelly.

Von looked at his watch, then showed it to her. "No timer." It was a smart watch with one red dot glowing in the middle. "Detonator, once we're clear. In fact, it's time to leave now."

He led the way, Lainie still being held like a mummy, back toward the elevators. In response to the call button both elevators opened. The one on the left was empty. On the right Simi emerged. It took her less time to register the threat than it took Von's crew to respond, and she propelled herself into the woman in the vest, who happened to be nearest. The woman went down under Simi's assault and she turned her attention to Von.

But Von was ready and engaged her. Even as he took the worst of the flurry of kicks and fists that had once been a diminutive brown girl, he shouted, "Get them out of here!"

The man holding Lainie shouted, "Into the elevator."

He dragged Lainie into the empty elevator, Eliza and the bespectacled man following. Even as the doors slid closed

Lainie saw the woman on the floor get up and turn to join the fight. Now out of sight, Lainie wondered if Simi could take them both.

She was alarmed to see the bespectacled man press the top button on the elevator panel instead of the ground floor. Eliza was apparently equally uninformed. "Wait Roy, where are we going?" Eliza demanded. "This place is wired to blow. Don't we need to get out of here?"

"We are," the man in glasses, Roy, said.

But the elevator carriage went up, not down.

Lainie tried to struggle only once and got such a tremendous squeeze as reward her vision swam amid bursting stars. as she gasped to regain her breath she caught Eliza's eye, but saw only worry and regret. The girl was barely holding it together, Lainie could tell. She'd seen the same look of desperation in her own eyes in the mirror almost a year ago.

The doors slid open on a small, cramped landing just big enough for the four of them. A set of iron stairs led up but not down. Roy led the way up the stairs to a utilitarian door at the top. He paused to consult his tablet.

"They're on approach. Do we wait for Von and Rose?"

"Let the man figure that out," Lainie's captor said. "We follow the plan."

Roy looked doubtful but nodded. He tapped the screen in the crook of his arm a couple of times, there was a mechanical click at the door and he pushed the push-bar. The door swung open on a dark starry sky and they all climbed out onto a rooftop lit by amber floods. Air ducts and exhaust fans stood cold sentry about the place, but out near the edge was an open expanse.

The air thrummed with tornado-like dervishes as a large helicopter, hovering above them, even now descended to land on the cleared space of the roof. All of its lights were dowsed, and Lainie spotted a swatch of tarpaulin covering the call-letters on the tail section, held in place by duct tape.

Even as the four, Lainie in tow, ran in hunched posture toward the vehicle the roof-access door banged open again. Von came limping out, supporting the vested woman as they, too, headed for the elevator. Lainie's heart quailed for Simi, whom she imagined on the hard floor of an elevator vestibule, bleeding, injured or dead. And where was Steele?

Then two strong arms released Lainie, only to shove her up and through the open door to the rear of the copter. The others piled in behind her. Inside there were jump-seats, aluminum frames with canvas straps that folded down from the walls of the craft, but not enough for all of them. Lainie found herself on the floor next to Eliza.

Even as the thumps of the chopper's blades intensified, Von shouted, "Look out!"

Steele appeared, crouched in the open door. The burly man who'd held Lainie kicked out, connecting squarely with Steele's face. The CIA agent cried out and disappeared once again.

The helicopter suddenly pitched and Lainie felt sick as the craft made an emergency horizontal departure from the roof, swinging perilously out over the lake. The chopper turned as it pitched left and right, so that Lainie caught fleeting glimpses of the roof of the building as Steele picked himself up from the tarmac and ran to the parapet, looking out after the fleeing aircraft.

When the explosion came it didn't sound distant at all. The whole panorama on that side lit up orange and the next swing of the helicopter gave Lainie a clear view of the building engulfed in red and blue fire and billows of black smoke. The next swing showed the structure collapsing in on itself.

She felt sick as Steele's fate worked hard to blacken what little hope she had of rescue. Simi's, too. It was all her fault. It was she who'd gotten them involved. She'd had no idea the immensity of what she was plunging them into, but once again, as before, she'd leapt in feet first anyway, leaving her head with thoughts of self-preservation and common sense entirely out of it.

But it struck her that she didn't have time to wallow in guilt. She knew she had one small window to escape now and she had to take it before it closed. She gripped Eliza's wrist. The girl looked at her in confusion, and Lainie hoped her own return gaze conveyed, "Trust me."

She yanked Eliza after her as she threw herself at the still-open door. Having taken a horizontal departure, the chopper was still fairly low over the lake. At most, 50 or 60 feet, Lainie reasoned. It wouldn't be a soft landing, she admitted to herself, but their chances of living were worth freedom.

The reaction as Lainie cleared the door and felt herself slipping past the threshold, was immediate. There were shouts and screams, and she felt hands scrabbling at her torso and legs. They caught her and she found herself dangling upside down outside, head pointed directly at the surface of the serene mountain lake.

But even as she felt her captors struggle to haul her back in, Lainie saw something that left her utterly nonplussed, something that shouldn't have been, and yet was. Simi lay atop the landing skid under the helicopter on the far side from where Lainie hung, hugging the thing like a lifeline. And Lainie swore the girl was grinning at her like it was all such grand fun.

Before she could give any sort of signal or communicate in any way, the men inside the copter got a good grip on her jeans and she was bodily lifted, then slammed so hard back against the bulkhead of the aircraft that she slid to the floor again beside Eliza, unable to catch her breath.

The woman in the vest, face hard and cold, bent down and produced a set of handcuffs. She shackled Lainie's wrists. Then she reached for a roll of duct tape in a nearby cubbyhole and used that to bind Lainie's ankles. Then for good measure she ran a short length of tape between the cuffs and Lainie's ankles, crumpling it to make a wrinkled cable, trussing her like a calf.

Then to Eliza's obvious surprise, the woman turned and reached for the girl's arms. Eliza fought back. "What the fuck are you doing? I'm one of you."

She got a very hard slap across the face for her trouble and Lainie could tell by the way Eliza blinked her eyes that she had been well and truly stunned by the hit. Enough so that she was unable to struggle until her ankles had been bound. By then it was too late.

"I don't understand," Eliza shouted. "Why the hell are you tying *me* up?"

The woman simply nodded at the back of the copilot's chair. As if on cue a man leaned and turned so he could see them past it. He was in his fifties with a full head of gray hair and a distinguished van dyke beard. His bright, nearly manic hazel eyes wrinkled at the corners as he smiled at them.

"Hello, Eliza," he yelled over the *thwop* of the chopper blades.

Her face froze, her cheeks drooping as if she'd just had a stroke. Her pallor turned ghostly and she swallowed hard. "Judson. . .I mean, Professor Harkness."

*   *   *

Lainie had blundered into this mess in an attempt to look out for a friend and former patient. But even though now Eliza was clearly crushed by the realization that her former lover now held her captive, with some deadly something coursing through her veins, doing God knew what, something *he* himself had injected into her against her will, Lainie was at the moment unable to offer her succor.

Because Lainie, herself, was dealing with a despair that threatened to engulf her usual resilience in the blackest of depression. Once again, she'd plunged headlong into a deadly game the scope of which she had no conception until it was too late. However, this time, unlike a year ago, she'd deliberately drawn two friends in with her, Steele and Simi.

Simi in particular, who'd shown Lainie nothing but devoted loyalty and gratitude, did not deserve this suffering in return. Even now Lainie thought of her clinging to the helicopter runner beneath them, most likely freezing and trembling under the assault of high-altitude wind and condensation.

Steele, who was under the emotional and mental strain of survivor's guilt, had undoubtedly come to Lainie's aid as some sort of misguided bid for redemption for what he blamed himself for, living while his friend died. Now engulfed in smoke and flame and buried under God knew how many tons of rubble.

A loud sob like the bark of a clubbed baby seal erupted from Lainie's throat before she could clamp her lips around it. Others in the chopper looked at her and she buried her chin in her chest, allowing the tears to flow freely in tribute to the fallen CIA agent.

Overhearing the conversation of the others during their flight, which she could only grasp in bits and pieces because of the way the beaten air thrummed in response to the pounding of the rotors, Lainie was able to grasp the names of the people around her.

There was Judson Harkness and Von Donelly, of course, and the bespectacled man with dark hair and pretty eyes named Roy. The pilot's name, or nickname at least, seemed to be Dutch, and the middle-aged woman in the utility vest with the face as hard as glacial ice was Irma.

The man who seemed to delight so completely in restraining Lainie and compelling her to go and do what he demanded was Conrad, first or last name she couldn't tell. Every time he caught her looking at him he'd grin a cruel grin, showing missing teeth in front like a hockey player.

This was, of course, not the entire group Lainie'd seen at the compound in Houston but must be Harkness's most trusted. Upon first seeing Eliza with the group crossing the parking lot earlier tonight Lainie was a little puzzled why they'd bring a girl who'd only just joined them, about whom they knew little but that she knew Harkness's password. The answer was, of course, that they'd somehow been alerted by Harkness to keep an eye out for her long before she'd appeared. They'd known who she was all along. Harkness would have wanted her in the chopper with him – given that she carried the secret to his research within her veins he'd want that precious cargo under his scrutiny as soon as possible.

They weren't talking about anything in particular, Harkness's crew, at least as far as Lainie could tell. They each had been given a headset with boom-mike so they didn't need to shout to be heard by each other, so Lainie had to go by what little she could hear aided by her very amateur lip-reading skills. Von and Conrad were talking about hockey. Roy's attempts to draw Irma into conversation were being met with one-word answers, and while Harkness himself was clearly chiming in, Lainie could only see his jaw working from behind and not his lips.

She glanced over to Eliza occasionally. The girl had lapsed into silence, all indications from her facial expressions and body language were that she was entirely consumed by terror. Lainie nudged her with a shoulder and got a wan look in return, but she couldn't manage to give Eliza the smile of encouragement she'd meant to. Instead they only met one another's gaze for a moment, then looked away again, each cocooned within her own chrysalis of shame, guilt, and grief.

As the pitch of the engine and the yaw of the craft itself changed Lainie guessed they were landing. That and the body language of the crew, who became more animated and looking out the windows. Lainie reflected that they hadn't been aloft long. They couldn't have gone far.

There was a bank of small windows along the bottom of the door opposite which Lainie and Eliza sat, presumably for external ground crew and whatnot to peer inside before opening the doors. Lainie couldn't see much out these window except sky.

Then they descended enough that a jagged rocky cliff sprung up outside these windows. That alarmed Lainie, especially when its rim rose too high for Lainie to see any more than its craggy face, clearly taller than the altitude at which the copter now flew.

And still they descended. The cliffs in view scanned up pass the windows, and now a mist or haze of sorts blurred them, then blocked them from view entirely. The crew donned breathing apparatus, like gas masks but much more streamlined and form-fitting to the face. Lainie supposed the haze outside was toxic. Already she smelt the strong and decidedly unpleasant sting of rotting eggs.

Sulfur gas.

At first she felt a panic as it seemed no one was going to provide she or Eliza with a mask, when Harkness himself turned and tossed one each into their laps. Hobbled as they were it was a nearly impossible task to put their masks on until Irma leaned over with a very large knife she'd drawn from a scabbard strapped to her hip and cut only the strap that linked their wrists to their ankles.

Even with that limited freedom they found difficulty adjusting the masks correctly until they turned to doing it for one another. The air they breathed now was pure and untainted by any odor at all. Lainie reflected that this also meant Harkness wanted them alive. . .at least for the time being.

Von opened the sliding door and he and Roy hopped out. Roy disappeared at a trot but Von turned to watch as Irma cut the tape at Eliza's feet and led her by the arm to stand and debark. Conrad took Lainie roughly by the bicep and did the same. The first thing Lainie did was look under the chopper, beneath the guise of ducking the pounding of the rotors, but she saw no sign of Simi. Had she fallen off along the way?

Lainie scanned the area around them but saw no sign of her friend. The yellowish smoke around them swirled wildly as the rotors of the helicopter still spun, but Lainie looked out over a landscape that was at once nightmarish and beautiful.

The chopper rested on a ledge about a hundred feet up the wall of the cliff, which as Lainie turned appeared not to be a cliff at all but a ring, a tall circular ridge surrounding them. The face of the ridge was uniform with blackened crags and almost symmetrical vertical crags.

Below, the bottom of the crater, for it could be nothing else, was a yellow desert, a sulfur flat that was really little more than a maze of endless curving, interconnecting, and back-switching trails between innumerable pools of boiling tainted liquid of various degrees of viscosity. Sulfur pools, none of which larger in circumference than ten feet.

"Don't try to run that way," Harkness shouted. He'd leaned forward to insert his head between Eliza and Lainie so that they could both hear him through the mask. "Those pools are boiling at upwards of 510 Kelvins."

To Lainie's blank stare Eliza yelled to be heard, "Over 455 degrees Fahrenheit. They are also highly acidic. Sulfuric acid." Lainie supposed Eliza, a Chemical Engineering PhD candidate, would know.

"Yes," Harkness said, "and many much deeper than they look. You fall in, you die before you climb out again." He turned away.

If Simi had made the trip, had somehow managed to slip away unseen as they landed, how was she able to breathe? Was she wise enough to give the acid pools a wide berth? And what could she possibly do alone and unequipped for this alien, toxic terrain to help Lainie and Eliza?

What could anyone do?

Conrad turned her and shoved her toward a hewn trail leading up the crater's face at an angle. They took up the rear, with Eliza and Irma ahead of them. Everyone else had hurried on ahead and were out of sight behind a razorback line of rocks hiding the stairway from the air.

It was a steep stair cut into the rock itself, narrow and with her arms bound Lainie didn't feel very safe climbing them, unable to catch herself should she teeter to one side or the other. As if to further warn her a sharp fang of obsidian caught her pants at the knee and cut through the heavy denim there like it was taffeta.

At a landing some fifty feet up, the stair switched back and led the other direction. Lainie could see the top, and as they neared the cover of rock above fell back and exposed, by stages as they approached, a house. No, a mansion. In the style of a swiss chalet, as if this were some high-end ski resort, the huge building came into view, a large gravel courtyard below, circular, filled with all sort of incongruous vehicles.

There were old beaten pickups and brand-new ones, dune buggies and panel vans of every color and degree of rust, and outnumbering them all line after line of RVs. These were not just the vehicles from the Houston compound. The entire mob had clearly driven here, joined by many others from God knew where, and here they waited for their prodigal five to return.

Lainie could see near the steps leading to one of the house entrances Von and his father embracing. The elder Donelly winced and Von stopped, placing a hand on his father's chest and asking him something inaudible to Lainie. Donelly only smiled and pushed his son away, as if to say not to worry.

More people were emerging from the chalet to greet the group. All clapped in informal applause as Harkness moved among them, shaking hands and accepting slaps on the back. They treated him with a familiar sort of deference, like a baseball team congratulating their star hitter for a well-run grand slam.

The haze had been clearing as they ascended the stairway and up here it was virtually clear, such that most of the crew of the helicopter had removed their masks and none of the others wore any. So when Conrad rapped on her windshield, making her blink, Lainie pulled her mask free. The atmosphere still stank of sulfur, but it no longer stung her nostrils and she could breathe the air, such as it was. Conrad took her mask away from her, holding it with his in his free hand – the one not clasped tightly to her arm.

"How can we breathe here but not down there?' she asked.

"Inversion drafts," Eliza said as they were forced to walk toward the chalet entrance. "Just like when you pour a glass of wine, that gurgling is air rushing in to replace the evacuated fluid. As the heated gasses below rise, there are certain channels, crevasses around the volcano's rim down which fresh air rushes to replace them. Protected as it is from the inner air by that ridge, this shelf is clearly one such channel."

"Volcano?" Lainie said.

Eliza nodded. "Inert, obviously, but yes, this is a volcanic crater. The area around Yellowstone is a hotbed of volcanic activity." From the haunted look in her eyes, the girl was not talking as much for Lainie's edification as she was to keep herself from screaming in mad panic. How much was left of the time Harkness had given her to live when he'd injected her? Lainie didn't know, but she was sure Eliza did, right down to the minute.

Conrad and Irma led Lainie and Eliza across the courtyard toward the front steps, but hung back as the people who were not prisoners filed in ahead of them. They got several pointed looks and not a few whispers as the people passed them. When finally they were led inside, the doors closed behind them with a hiss. Vacuum sealed, Lainie reflected. Inside it was cool, the air pure and fresh, the décor in keeping with the whole Swiss motif. Heavy influences of polished wood, both planked and beams, cobbled river stones on two enormous fireplaces, and plush furniture.

The foyer was large, but the great-room into which it led was huge. People filled the room, lined both stairways to right and left, and along the loft above facing the entrance. Fully 100 plus people, from the Houston compound and elsewhere, were here. There were no children, otherwise the mix of ages seemed entirely random, from twenties to fifties at least.

Harkness stood in the center of the room addressing the crowd, turning slowly to take them all in, speaking with the cadence of a Baptist minister:

"The culmination of our goals is at hand." The crowd cheered. "Phases one, two, and three are completed, plan A of each. I told you at the beginning no plan comes off exactly as laid, but it appears fortune has been with us. We have only experienced a single wrinkle – the raid of the San Francisco laboratory."

For some reason Lainie's gaze settled on a fortyish man dressed in a cowl-neck sweater and khaki slacks, standing at the exact center of the banister of the loft above. While he bore a sort of beatific smile, unlike the others he didn't shout or cheer at the pauses in Harkness's sermon.

"Thanks for some quick thinking," Harkness continued, "that raid only set us back a small half-step in one sense, but also unexpectedly advanced us half-way on to phase four and beta test. Once I regain that little lost ground, we will actually be ahead of schedule."

Lainie watched the man at the bannister. Scanning the crowd, when he saw Lainie looking at him he paused and looked back. When she didn't look away he cocked his head slightly at her, as if her boldness intrigued him. For a second it almost seemed as if he might wink at her in a moment of cheek, but instead he just scanned away from her and kept looking at the crowd as if nothing had passed between them.

"It won't be long now," Harkness concluded. "Please stay, attend the workshops that many of our members have put together for you, eat, drink, and above all. . .be prepared for the future!"

The applause was thunderous, especially for a mere 100 people. They continued applauding as Harkness worked his way through the crowd toward the double doors at the back of the room. Conrad and Irma forced Lainie and Eliza forward a few paces behind him. Offering and accepting greetings, it took longer than it should have for Harkness to reach the exit. Once he did, the five of them emerged into a broad corridor leading back deeper into the mansion.

Harkness led them down the carpeted center, doors on either side leading to meeting rooms, a massive banquet room with a dais and podium and giant flat-screen at the front, and a kitchen teaming with cooks and the clack and clatter of food preparation. The corridor ended in a T-intersection, where Harkness turned left.

This corridor wasn't as decorated as the prior one, being a little more utilitarian, with plasterboard walls and tile floor. Coming to a secure door, Harkness applied a keycard to a flat security pad and there was a beep and a click. He pushed through, and Lainie and Eliza were shoved through behind him.

Here was a set of stairs leading down to a landing, at which another flight switched back and further down. Through another security door was another corridor, this one entirely empty of décor. Doors to right and left led initially into what appeared to be machine rooms, storage rooms for food and others for dry or chemical supplies. These gave way to locked and secured doors, then what appeared to be an infirmary where one or two white-clad people appeared to be at work. Upon seeing Harkness they gave a spattering of applause.

At the end of this corridor was a pair of double doors through which they were only permitted after Harkness applied his card again. This opened onto an ante-room with lab coats on hooks. Harkness paused to don one, then through an inner set of double doors plated with metal into an extremely large room This room was filled with work tables, lab equipment, cabinets, machinery at whose function Lainie could only guess, etc.

She looked at Eliza who certainly recognized more than Lainie did. But Eliza was focused on something at the far end of the room, her eyes wide in what was unmistakable terror. At that end a section of the lab was cordoned off by a glass wall. This chamber was accessible by what could only be a form of airlock vestibule to the right. Inside was more lab equipment and sealed glass storage bins along the back wall.

Overall there was the whoosh of air-exchange machinery working behind the walls and in the ceiling. The smell was odd, tangy and dusty together, the smell of ozone and purified air.

"Excellent," Harkness murmured. "Excellent." He roamed among the equipment, gazing at it in admiration, touching things, squinting to read the labels on containers, the avaricious half-smile of a shark on his face. "He was able to get it all. Excellent." This was clearly the first time he'd seen this room, or seen it all fitted out as it was.

Finally he turned to the four still standing by the door. "I'm going to need you to put on a gown, my dear." He addressed Eliza. "Please disrobe first." When Eliza refused to move. Harkness sighed. "Irma, please."

116

Irma shoved Eliza toward the indicated exam tables on the far right. When she approached the girl and started pulling at her clothing Eliza tried to fight her off, bound-wrists and all. Irma grabbed her from behind. A well-placed and sudden fist up into Eliza's kidney caused the girl to cry out and fall to her knees.

"Leave her alone," Lainie shouted. Conrad shook her.

Ignoring Lainie, Irma bent to take Eliza's clothes off. Clearly weak, Eliza managed to shake her off. "Get your hands off me. I'll do it myself." Then, clearly favoring the pain in her flank, Eliza removed her clothes piece by piece, down to bra and G-string.

"Everything," Harkness said.

Eliza was clearly unwilling, but did strip down to nothing. Lainie looked at Harkness, but the professor was not watching. He was tapping on the keys of a laptop. Conrad showed interest in the nudity before him, but made no salacious remark. If he had Lainie was prepared to apply both bound fists with force on his nose.

Eliza donned the turquoise gown Irma brought to her, then accepted the woman's help onto the exam table. Irma bound Eliza's ankles to straps attached to the table. Only then did she use a knife from her belt to cut the girls bonds, thereby freeing them to be strapped to the table as well.

"How'd you escape Federal custody," Lainie asked.

Harkness looked up at her as if seeing her for the first time. He sauntered over to her, putting his face so close to hers that she felt the urge to recoil. She resisted with difficulty, not wanted to give ground. "They told me, the Donellys, that you appeared only minutes after Eliza turned herself over," he said. "We still don't know who the hell you are, but that alone told us you have some connection."

"I'm. . .I'm nobody," Lainie said, on the defensive. "My name's Lainie Parker. I'm just a friend."

"Mmm, perhaps. But there's more to you than just that. I see it in your eyes. Something bold, something irrepressible. No, you're much more than Lainie Parker, friend. Cop? No, I think not. Federal agent? Perhaps. But no matter." He turned away as if done with her, going back to his laptop. "There'll be plenty of time to find that out shortly. For now, Conrad, put her over there. Make sure she can't move."

Conrad pushed Lainie over by a bank of sealed cabinets in the corner on the right, a few paces from where Eliza was strapped down. He produced a roll of duct tape he must've carried from the chopper and strapped the short length of chain linking Lainie's cuffs together to the handle of one of the drawers stacked behind her and up over her head. She exchanged looks with Eliza. The girl looked petrified.

"Give her something to drink," Harkness told Irma, holding up a popular brand of energy juice. He'd already removed the cap for her. Irma took it. She propped Eliza up enough to let her drink. Eliza held her lips clamped shut at first, but when the liquid touched them she must've realized how parched she was and began to drink, deeply and with relish, only pausing to gasp for air twice, until the juice was entirely gone.

"Good girl," Harkness said. "That'll also help hydrate you, make it easier to find a vein to draw blood from. Retrieve my research."

He walked with no hurry to stand over Eliza. "In answer to your query, Ms. Parker," he spoke while regarding Eliza, not looking at Lainie, "they let me go, the FBI, as soon as my lawyer invoked *habeas corpus*. They had no physical proof. At least nothing they could tie directly to me. It's all been bleached from the servers at the lab. And now that SDS is so much slag by the shore of a lake, they never will."

He turned to a tall tray next to the head of the examination table. A tourniquet, a needle, and three evacuated collection tubes later he moved back to his workstation.

"All right," Lainie said. "You have what you want. You can recreate your virus or whatever it is. Now give her the antidote."

Harkness looked up at her with a perplexed furrow to his brow. Then, as if only now realizing something, his brow cleared and he chuckled.

"You promised. If she turned herself over to your group, whoever they are, you'd give her the antidote to what you injected her with."

Harkness continued to chuckle.

"What's so goddamn funny?" Lainie demanded.

"In point of fact, the point is moot," he said, clearly enjoying her reactions. "Eliza was never in any real danger. Not from the virus, at any rate."

"What are you talking about," Eliza snapped, finally finding her voice. "You told me. . ."

"The stuff you injected her with was inert," Lainie said. "Just like the samples you were working on at the lab."

"Oh no," Harkness said. "The virus is quite viable. But it is of no danger to her. Not to anyone, really, not as yet."

"But you told me," Eliza said. "If I didn't get the antivirus, it would kill me within twenty-one days."

"I lied. The virus is in you, no doubt about that. But you have been perfectly safe all along, because it was never meant for you."

"Wait," Lainie said. "How is that possible?"

"The holy grail of virology," Harkness said, his tone that of a professor lecturing before a gallery of rapt students. "The genetically programmed virus. Targeted to a specific DNA profile, any DNA profile you wish to program it with."

"Is that possible?" Lainie looked to Eliza and could tell from the shame in her eyes that it was.

"Has been really for many years now," Harkness said. "But way too expensive to produce in any quantities that would make it a viable weapon. And too unstable, unreliable. Until now."

"You knew this is what that lab was working on?" Lainie asked Eliza.

"No," Eliza protested, her eyes earnest.

Lainie addressed Harkness again, "So since the virus isn't programmed to her DNA, the virus is harmless to her."

Harkness tilted his head. "Not exactly. The virus is harmless to anyone right now. It can be passed from person to person regardless of their cellular makeup, without any ill effects. Oh, they might feel feverish and have a scratchy throat for a day, otherwise nothing. It dies off in their system in a few weeks with no ill effects."

Lainie shook her head. "So, what's the point? I don't get it."

"The virus Eliza carries is merely the catalyst, the carrier wave, as it were. Think of it like a pizza. What she carries is the crust, with none of the toppings. It is the avatar, the unprogrammed template onto which we can impose any specific form we like."

"You aren't making any sense," Lainie said. "How can you program it once it's in her bloodstream?"

"It isn't easy," he said. He lifted an empty test tube and shook it as if there were something in it. "Meticulously, painstakingly, precisely controlled mutation. We introduce a mutagen so carefully and exactingly designed as to program our little virus to target any range of DNA markers we have programmed it with. An activator, as it were."

Lainie looked at Eliza again and this was clearly all news to her, as well. "My apologies my dear," Harkness said, clearly seeing in Eliza's shocked expression what Lainie saw. "I found it, hmm, expedient to keep certain details from you. If you had known there was no danger to you, you would have hardly made such a mad dash to Houston to get my cure, would you?"

"So, wait," Lainie said. "From what you're saying, the virus should have died off in Eliza weeks ago."

He chortled, clearly in such rapture at this exchange, as if she were asking each question he wished her to ask, in just the order he wished her to ask them, giving him the chance to expound his own genius while seeming to merely enlighten a thirsty protégé.

"That was the original plan, yes. But then I developed an even more ingenious thing. Why inject a host with a virus, then a mutagen to program it, only to have that programmed virus die off in so short a time? If we can use DNA to program the virus to target specific victims, why could we not program the virus to attach itself permanently to a host's DNA?"

Eliza shook her head. "What?"

"I have found a way to adhere the virus to a person's very nucleotides. In effect, the host doesn't just spread a virus for a short time, but their own bodies continue to produce it indefinitely." Harkness's eyes were bright as he glared at Lainie, and he even nodded, encouraging her to make the connection on her own.

And she did. "She's a. . .Eliza's a carrier."

"Precisely."

Eliza began to weep uncontrollably. In an effort to comfort her, Lainie hurried to say, "But it hasn't been programmed yet, right. It's harmless unless programmed." Eliza looked from her to Harkness, the tiniest spark of hope trying to relight her darkening eyes.

Harkness was all but glowing. "Aw Ms. Parker, how very Pollyanna of you. Don't you know? The drink Eliza drank just a moment ago, why that was laced to the brim with the mutagen we have chosen for our beta test. In only a few short hours she will be the grenade with the pin pulled. She will be the full-fledged carrier of our beta test plague."

Lainie expected Eliza to start crying again but the girl's face seemed to have gone limp. She stared at Harkness with haunted eyes but evinced no other emotion. What was she thinking? Had she gone catatonic?

"Why?" Lainie's voice had fallen to a whisper. "Why activate it in her? She did what you asked. She came to you of her own free will. Why not do this to one of your own people?"

"Oh they'd gladly take the burden," Harkness said. "All of them. And in fact they will, after the beta test. If successful, they will all line up for this, to help spread the plague across the globe. But Eliza was chosen, even before the raid in San Francisco. She was chosen, but was never to know. She's the beta test I mentioned earlier."

"Then. . ."

"It's called beta test for a reason. We don't actually know for sure the long-term effects of carrying the virus, especially once activated. We don't even know if it will actually spread the way we think it will. She will need to be exposed to test subjects. People who meet the genetic profile we've chosen for our first test. They will have to be monitored and studied."

"You're a sick man," Lainie said, still whispering.

Harkness ignored that. "This is our proprietary brand, how we were able to do inexpensively what others failed to. Bonus: we can inject a subject against their will, and even the most studious exam will turn up nothing but a mild version of a cold. Then we can later activate the virus at a time and place of our choosing with nothing more than orange juice. Or coffee. Or soda pop. Even if they are able to isolate the proverbial *patient zero*, how could they ever trace the infection back to us?"

"With your research gone, you needed Eliza's blood to reproduce your carrier virus." Lainie looked at her friend, but Eliza had let her head fall back on the pillow and was currently turned away from Lainie.

"Exactly," Harkness said. "The carrier virus is the difficult, the expensive part to produce. The activator is comparatively simple."

"One is useless without the other."

"Yes. And unfortunately with all of the data destroyed, a necessary step to evade the government, only I possess the necessary knowledge to reproduce the carrier, until I can transcribe it once again here. You may go."

At first his last command disoriented Lainie. Non-sequitur as it was, it also seemed unlikely to apply to her, handcuffed as she was. Irma and Conrad turned and left the room unceremoniously, the command had of course been directed at them.

Lainie fell silent. She was thinking. Harkness worked on in silence, tapping on his laptop. Then something occurred to her. "What target?"

"Pardon?" Harkness was clearly only half-listening.

"The mutagen you just had Eliza drink. Who is it programmed for?"

"I think I can answer that." A new voice in the room. Lainie craned herself around to see a man standing just inside the entryway. It was the man she'd seen at the center of the banister during Harkness's rally, as it were, earlier.

"Ms. Parker," Harkness said with a grin, "please meet my pride and joy, my protégé for many years, John Dreck."

"Hi," Lainie said. "I'd shake your hand, but obviously. . ." She rattled her handcuffs.

"Yes," Dreck said. "Have we found out who she is, yet?"

"Says her name's Lainie Parker," Harkness answered. "No ID, and the cell phone they took off her was locked, wiped itself after the fifth time we tried to break the password."

It was an NSA-grade security program Steele had put on her phone for her, on the chance the police got hold of it and tried to penetrate her escort app. It was overkill for something so mundane, of course, which had amused him no end.

"How much did she know?"

"I don't know," Harkness said. "I didn't ask. I just told her everything."

"Why? Now there's no way to know how much the government knows."

"Please, John, they know pretty much all of it, too, or have guessed as much by now. It doesn't matter. We're too far along, no one can stop us now."

"Said every Bond villain ever," Lainie said, "right before he blows up their secret lair and kills them."

Harkness laughed. Dreck didn't.

"Is that how you see me," Dreck asked. "Some movie villain?"

"I don't even know who you are," Lainie said. "I was talking to the professor."

"I'm not interested in credit," Harkness said. "He can have it. I'm here for the science."

"My name is John Dreck," Dreck said to Lainie, taking a step toward her, "*Jr.*" To her shrug, he said, "Of course, why would you remember? There have been so many events, more every day. How could you remember the names of the fallen?"

There was such a mix of sadness and rage on his face as he spoke Lainie fell silent. "Just nine years ago. Burundi, Africa. A clinic built and primarily funded by my family's foundation, 'seeking to counter terrorism through humanitarian and philanthropic aid.' My father's philosophy: 'Show them love and it weakens their hate.'"

He took slow steps toward her, his eyes turning inward as he spoke. "They hit midday. My father, Dr. John Dreck Sr., was in the middle of doing surgery. They slaughtered as they came, room by room, floor by floor. They asked if each person were Christian or Jew. Those who said *yes* were shot.

"My father managed to stabilize his patient and evacuate thirty people into a supply room on the third floor. His back was turned when the patient drew an M16 from his athletic bag stashed on the shelf under the operating table for safe keeping. This cockroach had permitted his own people to shoot him in the stomach in order to get inside the hospital before the attack. He shot his own surgeon, my father, in the back like a coward."

He fell silent and Lainie looked at Harkness, who tapped serenely away at his laptop, as if he'd heard this story a hundred times before and had grown bored with it. Eliza, on the other hand, had turned her face toward them again, watching Dreck with a wan sort of horror on her face.

"He didn't ask," Dreck went on. "Not this man. He lined them up, on their knees, and executed them indiscriminately, one at a time. In the chest. In the heart." His eyes came back into focus. "The sickest thing is he died anyway. They found him dead on the table in the supply room, surrounded by his victims, my father among them."

Dreck looked into Lainie's eyes, boring into them with an intensity that made her want to look away, but she didn't. "Only one survived that day. A young graduate student on

Spring break, assisting his father in the field, learning from the greatest surgeon, the greatest man he'd ever known."

Dreck looked away and paced. "No one knew why the killer let him live. But I do. It wasn't mercy, it was cruelty. Letting him. . .letting me. . .live with the memory, helpless to see anything but the sight of those men and women dying every time I close my eyes. The same question in each of *their* eyes as they died. . .why?"

"So this is revenge," Lainie said. "Programming this virus for what? African DNA? Middle Eastern? To randomly kill them, just like they killed your father and his people."

Dreck growled like a feral dog. "No. Vengeance is such a petty, small thing. An eye for an eye only leaves both sides blind. No, this is a much greater cause." He turned and looked at Lainie again, this time cunning and focus sharpened his gaze. This wasn't grief, this was something even more dangerous. This was cold, calculating reason. This was zealotry.

"I watched over the years. I waited to see the Western world finally once and for all deal with these hate-mongers, these wastes of human flesh, these sacks of human sewage. Yet year after year, one event after the other, the response was always rhetoric, punitive sanctions, weakness, even appeasement."

He was spitting his words like a pit viper. "No one ever took the action necessary to put these gutter-dogs down once and for all. And the terrorism events only increased. London, Paris, Miami, Boston, Santa Monica for Christ's sake. And still only talk, and posturing, political scorekeeping."

"But my old college Chemistry professor." Dreck turned to look at Harkness. "He had something. Something that would put a punch in the gut of the extremist Muslim community, something that would not only make them question their faith, but the very purpose of their own existence."

"This virus," Lainie said.

"It wasn't what the government was paying me to do," Harkness said, "but it was while working on their nasty little weaponization scheme that I stumbled on the idea. I had pitched it to them, but the proposal was bogged down in red tape. So I went ahead anyway with the grant money they were giving me."

"But it was only a matter of time before they were onto him," Dreck said. "And that's where I and my family's foundation comes in. I offered to set him up in his own lab, move everything there before the government caught on."

"Only they caught on before you expected them to," Lainie said. "Which is why your lab was raided."

"They didn't find out," Dreck said. "They were tipped off." He looked pointedly at Eliza.

"Anonymously," Eliza protested.

"If we could figure it out, it was nothing for the Feds to."

"So that's why they were after me." She seemed bemused.

"Leonid is your man," Lainie said, making a leap of logic.

Dreck turned to her, looked as if he were considering denying it, then nodded.

"Who?" Harkness asked.

"Your benefactor set a hit man on Eliza."

"He what? Jesus, John."

"All I knew then was she was the rat," Dreck protested. "No one knew yet that you'd injected her with the only surviving carrier virus. I didn't know how much she knew. I couldn't afford exposure."

"What if he'd killed her?"

"He didn't."

"What if. . .?"

"She's here, Jud," Dreck snapped.

"And did you call off your man?"

Dreck demurred. "I haven't been able to reach him. Hit men tend to go off the grid when they're on a hunt."

"So he's still after her," Lainie said.

Harkness didn't answer, didn't have to.

"Well it appears we owe you a debt, Ms. Parker," Harkness nodded to her in way of a bow. "You kept our little petri dish here safe."

Lainie wanted to tell him to go fuck himself, but held her tongue. "You plan to release this virus into a Middle Eastern community. Kill off what, Hundreds? Thousands?"

"He thought that small, too," Harkness said, chucking his chin at Dreck. "I was the one who pointed out to him the potential we're dealing with."

"Yes," Dreck said. "There were others out there who felt like I did. Some families of the fallen. Some just patriots of the world. People who see the need, as I do, for a definitive stroke. Something that will shake, literally, the entire world."

Dreck's eyes had turned inward again. "After beta test, after we expose a single community to or little Bloody Mary here, and make sure the results are what we want, each and every person here in this building, and another hundred or so with whom we have communicated, will step up to be injected with our carrier virus. Each one will be activated for Middle Eastern DNA. And each one will take an all-expenses paid, whirlwind tour of some of the world's most active hotspots of extremist Muslim activity."

"The death toll, Ms. Parker," Harkness chimed in, "won't be in the thousands. By the time this virus spreads from person to person across the globe, we are hopeful of demographics in the *millions*."

CHAPTER 8

He savored the word *millions* like one did a sip of fine wine.

"My. . .God," Eliza whispered.

"I suppose it's to much to expect a total extermination," Dreck said almost to himself, and with genuine regret. "But with any luck, that garbage DNA, that racial taint on humanity will never recover."

Lainie felt her skin crawl. "But not every Muslim is an extremist. Hell, not every person of Middle Eastern descent is Muslim, and vice versa. How about the tens of thousands of people who don't even know they have any Middle Eastern blood in them? You'll be killing countless innocent people."

"So much stronger the statement made," Dreck said. "That we would gladly sacrifice those in order to scrape the other dog-shit off our genetic shoe." He turned somewhat defensive. "Nothing short of an action of this scope, like a punch to their collective gut, will be enough to take the wind out of the terrorist's sails once and for all."

Lainie fell speechless. It was obvious there no reaching the man's sense of morality, his humanity. If there was any left in him. She was having trouble wrapping her mind around the enormity of the thing. The government raided Harkness's lab at the university because they found out he was planning to take the research they paid for private – even they had no idea what these men truly planned. And unless she and Eliza could escape, they never would, not until it was too late.

A soft *bong*, like a gong stuck by a child's fist, sounded from above. Harkness looked around, plainly confused. But Dreck's face lit up. "Ah, the lunch is ready." When Harkness moaned and winced and rolled his head like a stubborn three-year-old Dreck addressed him sternly, "You need to put in an appearance, Jud. The folks are going to want to see you there."

All but dragging his feet like that same recalcitrant child, Harkness went with Dreck to the door. Neither even looked at Lainie or Eliza again, as if they'd already forgotten about them, and left. Lainie listened carefully until she heard the outer door closed, then counted to fifty.

"Finally," Lainie exclaimed. First she stepped forward, then pulled hard on the drawer-handle above her head. As she suspected, in a newly furnished lab like this one the cabinets were likely to still be empty. The entire cabinet teetered toward her and yawed against her shoulders, bringing her hands down to the level of her neck. Just a little fumbling and she lowered her arms to her sides and rubbed her shoulders with a grunt after pushing the cabinet back to its own footing.

Eliza did a doubletake. "Hey, how did you get out of the cuffs?"

As Lainie lifted the silver chain around her neck, about to put it back under her collar, she paused to wave it at Eliza. Both her grandmother's cameo and the handcuff key danced at the end of the necklace. Moving to undo Eliza's restraints, Lainie said, "When Conrad searched me he never gave my jewelry a second glance."

And now Eliza was liberated.

Lainie moved around the perimeter of the room looking at the walls. They were in a basement level, she knew, but she was hoping they were at garden level, meaning there would be windows high up in the walls. But there were none that she could see, nor any sign that windows had been there and sealed or covered up.

"Don't waste your time," Eliza said. She was sitting at the edge of the examination table, but had made no move to get off it, not even to get dressed. "Professor Harkness said Dreck designed this lab to his specifications. That means there won't be any windows, and the walls will be lined with hermetically sealed steal. No seam big enough for a microorganism to fit through. The only way out is the way we came in."

Lainie stood in the center of the room, turning slowly, examining things around her. "We can't go that way. Too many people between us and the exit."

"And where would we go once we got out," Eliza asked. "The whole crater is full of sulfuric gas and they took our masks."

"One problem at a time," Lainie said. "What's in there?" She indicated the glass room at the back of the lab with the airlock.

Eliza blanched again when she looked at it. "See the red band painted along it at chest height, interspersed with that biohazard symbol? Level 5 containment. Those glass cubbies along the back wall? That's where he would keep all the true nasties."

"But I doubt if he has anything in there just yet," Lainie said. "I get the feeling he's only just moving in."

"Want to risk it?" Eliza was sarcastic and angry, but her expression softened. "I'm sorry. Besides, if you think it's secure out here, try to imagine in there. No, that's no way out."

"But what are those?" Lainie indicated a line of neon-yellow blobs hanging on racks along one side of the airlock leading into the containment chamber.

"Containment suits," Eliza said. "You go in the airlock and as the seal is cycling you put those on – suits, hoods, booties, gloves, etc."

"Breathing apparatus?"

"Yes," Eliza said, looking up. "They would protect us from the gas. But it's moot. We'd still have to get past everyone upstairs. Not to mention any guards they may have posted."

"Get dressed," Lainie said. She'd begun clearing items from one of the lab benches.

Eliza made no move to comply. "Why did you come after me? It was a stupid thing to do."

"You didn't know what he'd injected you with," Lainie said as she turned to a low file cabinet and tested its weight.

"I had no idea," Eliza said. "Days before the raid he told me that he planned to take everything to a new lab, a hidden lab somewhere up north. That worried me, because I knew it would make him a fugitive. I talked to my former roommate about it. It was she who recommended I tip off the feds."

Lainie had stacked two small filing cabinets side-by-side on top of the cleared workbench. She was lifting others onto it as Eliza spoke.

"When I found him deleting his notes from the computer," Eliza said. "I confronted him about it and we had a big fight. He grabbed me, tied me to an office chair, and injected me."

Lainie now had several cabinets on the workbench and had hopped up onto it herself. She now set to stacking them in a pyramid rising toward the ceiling. Massive exposed exhaust vents crisscrossed the ceiling. She was building her platform up to one of the wide, round registers pointing down into the lab.

"As it happened the FBI raided at that moment," Eliza concluded. She looked at the contraption Lainie was building. "You don't expect to get out through the vents, do you? You have no idea where they lead, if they will even support our weight, what kinds of fans and filters and other things may be blocking your way. . ."

"Do you have a better idea? Now get dressed."

"No."

Lainie stopped. "Get. . .dressed. . .now."

"I'm not going anywhere," Eliza said.

"The hell you aren't," Lainie snapped. "I came all this way to rescue you, now I'm not leaving without you."

"There's nowhere for me to go," Eliza said. "You heard him. With the mutagen in my system I'm a grenade with the pin pulled. I'm dangerous. No, I'm deadly. I can't go out there, god knows who I might run into."

Not for the first time since Harkness's revelation that the virus in Eliza had been programmed for Middle Eastern DNA markers, Lainie thought of Simi. "Yeah, well you're sure as hell not going to stay here for whatever beta test Harkness has planned for you."

Eliza's eyes darkened. Moving slow, like a child being forced to dressed for church, she turned to her clothes stacked haphazard nearby and dressed herself. Meanwhile, Lainie ran to the airlock outside the containment room. She grabbed three full containment suits, complete with oxygen tanks and masks.

"We only need two," Eliza said, turning to put one on.

"I have a friend out there," Lainie said. "If she wasn't killed on the way here, or asphyxiated by the sulfuric gas at the bottom of the crater, she'll need one of these."

Before Lainie cloaked herself, she yanked power cords from some nearby equipment to tie the third suit into a bundle. While she was climbing into her own suit, she saw Eliza go to Harkness's laptop, the one he'd been tapping on since they'd gotten here. Finding a screwdriver in a nearby tray, she pulled the hard drive and stuffed it into her suit. She then smashed the laptop, screen-first, against the corner of the table on which it sat.

Lainie got back on the workbench and motioned for Eliza to climb up next to her. They wore their suits largely unzipped for now, their hoods hanging down their backs, their breathing apparatus hanging about their necks.

"I'll take the lead," Lainie said. "Stay close behind me. Lay flat on your belly to distribute your weight. Slide, don't crawl, to minimize the noise."

The makeshift stairway to escape was relatively stable, though it wouldn't do to go waving one's arms around. Crouching near the top, Lainie examined the big round vent. She found a hinge, and on the opposite side a latch. The latch was a slide pin and push as she did with all her strength it wouldn't budge.

Stopping to catch her breath, she examined the latch again. On her next try, she pushed up on the rim of the vent itself to relieve any pressure gravity was placing on the slide-pin. This time, with some difficulty, the pin slid and the register swung down. Lainie held it to keep it from swaying wildly as it fell. She then rose to her feet, stepped up the last level of the pedestal she'd built and inserted the top half of her body into the cavity above.

Immediately she came against resistance. Where the round casing for the vent met the main horizontal duct the junction was blocked. It gave slightly, but only slightly to the touch. It seemed mesh-like behind a sheet of foil honeycombed with many holes.

"What is it," Eliza called up. "Why have you stopped?"

"You were right," Lainie said. "There's a filter here. I can't seem to find a way to remove it."

"Try turning it."

Lainie put both of her bright-yellow-gloved palms on the filter and twisted. At first the filter dragged, but then it turned quite freely. But it did not come loose. She turned it for some time, feeling foolish, before she stopped to rest her arms. When she reached up again she tried hooking her fingers into the holes of the foil sheet and pulled, but they only broke the foil and made no other headway.

She wondered how long it had been? How long was the luncheon banquet planned to last? When would Harkness and Dreck return to find them still struggling with this vent?

In frustration Lainie punched up into the filter. It gave much more than she'd expected it to, stretching up into whatever emptiness was above it. Lainie placed her fists in the center and pushed. The filter tented up, higher and higher, but didn't otherwise budge. She kept pushing and soon, stretched to its limits the fibers of the filter simply held.

Finally, with one last push Lainie felt something give above her. She stopped to rest her arms again, then resumed pushing. There was more give and she felt something tearing. The filter began to rip and shred and soon she'd pushed her fists up completely through it. By pulling and ripping at the edges of the hole she'd made she cleared a hole big enough for them to climb through.

"Here we go," she called down. Pulling herself up, Lainie twisted and squirmed up through the hole and horizontally into the large square duct above. She pulled up the spare suit after her, then grabbed Eliza's arms and helped the girl climb in behind her.

"I wish there was some way we could close the vent behind us," Lainie said, "but the latch is on the outside."

"The stack of cabinets would be a dead giveaway anyway," Eliza said. "Okay, Rescue, which way now?"

They were presented at the moment with two options. But Lainie had already studied the layout of the ducts, at least as much as she could see along the ceiling of the laboratory. She'd already decided on a strategy, a starting direction, at least that far. Her plan was to move away from the sound of machinery, at least at first, surmising that the blowers would be at one end and the vents to the outside at the other.

She led Eliza, the two women sliding on their bellies, Lainie pulling the bundle of the spare suit behind her. She took the turns she guessed led to the way out at each juncture, and in very short order they came up against another filter, this time blocking their path. There was enough room in the enormous duct for Lainie to turn around, and she used her heels to kick out the filter. She then led on.

Very quickly she was outside the path that she'd been able to plan from the lab and guessed that last filter had been the final barrier, that they'd now left the lab behind. They'd passed beyond the hermetically sealed room and were now somewhere within the superstructure of the mansion itself.

She briefly toyed with the idea of climbing out the next vent into the house itself and finding some way out in more familiar, less claustrophobic environs, but she quickly ruled it out. Here they were hidden from view, on the path to what she hoped was an exterior vent. In the house proper there was no telling who they'd run into, how many, or how they might be equipped to overpower she and Eliza and return them to captivity.

Besides, as they continued their sliding, slithering way through the ducts, no more vents presented themselves. Instead, the ducts became more solid, less flimsy. It was getting close and hard to breath within them, but there did seem to be a general inclined to them, toward what she hoped was the surface.

"I was afraid of this," Eliza said.

"What?" Lainie stopped to look back. The other woman's face was red from exertion and filmed in sweat, much as Lainie imagined hers was.

"Do you feel the change in the walls here? How they've gone from a thin steal to a heavier, thicker alloy?"

"So?"

"This is an incineration duct."

"That doesn't sound good."

"If anything should be released into the lab, should the lab need sudden venting, this section becomes superheated, as a final bid to destroy whatever antigens might've gotten past the filters."

"How. . .superheated," Lainie asked, not sure she wanted to know.

"White hot," Eliza said, breathless. "Hundreds of degrees. Even a thousand."

"So if Harkness and Dreck return and discover how we escaped before we can find a way out, all they have to do is turn on these superheated ducts."

Eliza swallowed. "You and I would be white ash in a matter of minutes. Very long, very painful minutes."

Okay," Lainie sighed. In what she hoped was a jaunty tone, she added, "Well, let's not dwell on that, then." There was nothing for it but to forge on, and Lainie did so.

There was a very definite tilt of the ducts upward now. There were no more vents and there were no more branches. They were on the express route to. . .well to wherever these ducts led, if not out then hopefully somewhere near the way out.

The problem was the way was also narrowing rapidly. The ceiling angled down and the walls closed in. And it was not her imagination. She began to worry that the ducts would become too narrow for them to fit through, that they'd become stuck or have to turn back. Somehow she knew they wouldn't make it back to the lab before Harkness and Dreck or someone else discovered they'd gone.

Would they really superheat the ducts then? With their beta-test monkey in here with Lainie? She hoped not. But what was to keep them from finding another. Dreck had said the group here at the mansion were all eager to do their part to spread the virus. Would it be any difficulty at all in finding a replacement for Eliza? How far back would it set them? Would it be worth it to them? There was no way of knowing.

Now the duct was so narrow her shoulders were brushing the sides, the hood on her back scraping against the top. She could no longer see Eliza past her own body when she tried to look back. "How are you doing back there?"

At first no answer came. Then, "Not so good. Getting claustrophobic. Not sure how much further we can go before it's just too small anymore."

Lainie said nothing, but crawled on.

"Is it just me or is it getting hotter in here," Eliza asked.

"Don't say that," Lainie snapped, noting that there was considerably more sweat on her forehead than when they'd started.

"I'm not kidding," Eliza said. "It's getting hot in here."

"Shit," Lainie cursed. Eliza was right. The temperature was rising, and fast.

Now she was having to squeeze past the tight walls and low ceiling, arms ahead of her to help narrow her shoulders, squirming now more like a worm than a salamander. Panic rose in her throat. They were not going to make it. She was going to get stuck like a cork in a bottle, Eliza trapped behind her, unable to escape the fire that was closing in around them. A scream began to form in her throat.

She felt a breeze, actually had been for some time but since it was warm she hadn't given it any importance. But it was coming from ahead. Fresh air. Bucking her hips and knees she drove herself forward through the tight squeeze and saw a light ahead. She smelled sulfur, but not so strong as to make it impossible to breathe.

She wiggled and twisted and squirmed and thrust herself forward and came to a sudden downward turn to the duct. Forcing herself over the edge she took the chute and slid, picking up speed. Soon she was going too fast to stop herself. God only knew what was at the bottom.

An opening appeared ahead and she let herself careen toward it. At the last moment she saw the opening was hooded and ducked her head, yelling at Eliza to do the same, but cut off as the metal hood struck the crown of her head anyway, drove her chin into her chest and made her bite her tongue.

She felt herself pop out of the opening. She fell a short distance before landing hard on a dirt floor. The ground under her was tilted and she slid a distance before stopping. Seeing stars, she only just remembered to roll away to get out of Eliza's path. But as she did she found herself sliding again, not on dirt but what appeared to be a deep layer of fine sand or, from the acrid smell, ash.

She was in a cavern of some sort, with walls of black, porous rock. The floor descended precipitously like a bowl below her toward a sudden pit in the center, blacker than any starless night. It was upon this she descended as she slid. Panic stricken, she spread her arms and legs, desperate to find some way to stop her downward slide. This worked and she jerked to a sudden stop about ten feet from the edge.

Gasping to slow her pounding heart, Lainie looked back up at the vent hole above her, carefully so as not to start sliding again, and was amazed that she'd fit through it. She only just wondered why Eliza hadn't appeared yet, when with a screech the girl appeared and thumped to the ground. She slid face down, heels pointed right at Lainie's head. Lainie tucked her chin into her chest and clinched her eyes, ready for the impact.

Somehow the bright yellow boots didn't strike her head but grazed her shoulder.

Lainie was sliding again toward the pit, this time Eliza slightly above and beside her, both plummeting toward oblivion. Both screamed. Lainie grabbed Eliza's flailing arm and gripped it with all her strength. She dug in her heels but they found nothing but soft ash against which to grind. The blackness seemed to rise up to gulp them like the maw of some nether beast. Just as she reached the edge her heels struck something and her knees nearly buckled.

There appeared to be a ridged stone lip around the verge of the pit, and it was on this that her heels had caught, stopping her progress. She gripped Eliza's arm even tighter and the girl stopped sliding as well. They'd both stopped screaming somewhere between their slide toward certain doom and this stop. They met each other's eyes, Lainie supine and Eliza prone, their eyes wide with shock.

"Let's do that again," Lainie said.

"No thanks," Eliza groaned.

The temperature was still rising as hot air came blowing out of the hole they'd just dropped from. "We need to get out of here," Lainie said.

Eliza craned her head to look up, and so did Lainie. The jagged, porous walls rose and bent into a dome above them, and glistened with crystals. What light there was came from an irregular arch high on the far wall, where fresh air wafted in. Well, relatively fresh, as it was tainted with the smell of sulfur. There, clearly, was their way out. And the hot breeze coming out of the square metal vent in the wall from which they'd just fallen was getting hotter and more insistent.

"How do we get from here," Eliza said, a surprising amount of sarcasm underlying the fear in her voice, "to there."

"Very, as they say, carefully."

"How did I know you were going to say that?"

Lainie cast about her for any rock outcroppings or stalagmites to which they could cling in their climb away from the edge of the pit, but this was not that sort of cave. This cavity had not been formed over millions of years of water flowing and mineral-dense condensation forming spires and columns and stalactites hanging from the ceiling. This one had been formed relatively suddenly and quite violently during the eruption of the volcano outside. While the walls were decidedly rough and craggy, the center of the cavern was pretty much featureless.

Lainie tried shifting her feet. At first they found nothing of purchase but the rim of the pit. But as her heels dug a trough in the dust and ash they finally reached the rock beneath and there was enough there on which her boots could catch. Sliding her heels, she pushed back and was rewarded with a slide of her whole body up the slope away from the edge. She did it again, and yet again.

Eliza, watching Lainie, got the idea. On her belly, she used her toes and her fingers to shove through the silt on the cave floor to the rock beneath and crawl up. Together, side by side, they both worked their way up the side of the funnel toward the relatively level ground around the foot of the walls. It was pretty slow going, but steady progress.

By the time they were half way, they were both sweating and breathing hard in the steadily increasing heat, and by silent mutual decision paused for a rest. They said nothing, but huffed in exhaustion. After only a few moments they resumed their inchworm slide toward erstwhile safety.

Eliza made faster progress than Lainie, who lagged in case she needed to grab the younger women upon a backslide toward the pit. But neither slipped and Eliza made the level ground a full three minutes before Lainie. She stood, moaned and hugged her left shoulder, then reached down with her right to help pull Lainie the last few inches.

Struggling to stand, bracing herself against an earthen wall, Lainie took stock of where they were. She studied the walls rising above them and identified what she thought might be the easiest route to that exit high on the far wall. But easiest was not easy – she could tell they were going to have to climb, cling to the wall, and watch their step.

"Follow me," Lainie said. Eliza sighed much like a teenager being asked to take out the trash, but she nodded.

Picking her footing carefully, Lainie bent to the task of spider-climbing her way up and along the wall to the right, making her way toward the exit arch above. She looked back once to make sure Eliza was following, then never looked back again. She would have to concentrate on finding the safest path. Eliza would have to worry about herself.

"As much as possible," Lainie said, "put your feet where I put mine, your hands where I put mine." Eliza grunted in response, clearly already concentrating on the climb too much to answer verbally.

As they climbed, so did the temperature in the cave. The ducts were being superheated. How much of that heat would make its way out of that vent and into this chamber? Did it matter? At a thousand degrees, even if only half of the heat made it out here it would still cook Eliza and her like Christmas turkeys.

Lainie looked up to see what progress they'd made toward the exit and found it still depressingly far away and high. She also nearly lost her footing and pressed herself to the wall, gasping for air and for courage. For some reason an old climber's term an ex-boyfriend used to use came to her: "She's all tits and toenails." It referred to a first-time climber who was hugging the wall in fear, unable to move

Well Lainie was determined not to go tits and toenails now. By sheer force of will she made herself take the next handhold, make the next step. And the next. And the next. The heat was rising, she was drenched in sweat, especially in this yellow plastic suit, or whatever it was made of, but on she climbed, knowing it was that or die.

The igneous rock they clung to was sharp-edged, but luckily it was porous enough, the holes large enough to present plenty of finger-holds. It was finding a ledge on which to perch one's feet that was the challenge. The rock was craggy enough, but she had to look down to place a foothold, and that meant pulling out away from the cave wall far enough to see her feet, which made her heart pound like a wrecking ball.

Lainie forced herself not to look up again until she was absolutely sure she'd made at least some noticeable progress toward the exit. By now the heat was making it difficult to breathe and she took many short gasps instead of filling her lungs. When she did finally look up she found she was nearly beneath the arch. She had only to climb a few more feet and she could reach across and pull herself through.

She heard rubble give way, a sliding sound accompanied by Eliza's cry of terror. Lainie had to turn on the rock face to look back and down and feared she might see nothing but a bare cave wall behind her, no Eliza, by the time she managed it. But as slow as she was turning, by the time she'd turned, Eliza was there.

But only just barely. The girl hung a few feet below Lainie and to the right, fingers clinging to the rock wall, but feet dangling out over the drop. Even as Lainie looked, Eliza turned her eyes down, screamed again and clenched them tight.

"Hold on," Lainie screamed. "I'm coming."

"No!"

Lainie froze. "What?"

"Don't come down here. Don't come get me. You get yourself out of here."

"I'm not leaving you," Lainie shouted.

"Yes you are," Eliza bellowed. "I'm going to let myself drop."

"Don't you dare, Eliza Andrews."

"Listen," Eliza said, "you heard Harkness. I'm a walking bomb. I'm poison. You said yourself, who knows how many people have the DNA markers I'm programmed to kill? You can't always tell by looking. How many people don't even know themselves?"

"That's not. . ."

"Shut up," Eliza snapped. One of her hands slipped free and she screamed, casting up for another hold. Once she gained it she panted for a moment, catching her breath before going on. "I won't be responsible for those deaths, Lainie. I won't. Better for me to kill myself now."

"That won't stop them," Lainie called, "Harkness and Dreck. They'll just infect their volunteers, send them out, kill thousands or millions, just like they said."

"We can't stop them," Eliza said. "We can barely save ourselves. But I can stop me. I can make sure I never take a life. Not like that."

Suddenly, Eliza screamed as Lainie grabbed her right wrist in an iron grasp. Clinging as she was to the ledge, eyes either pinched closed or cast downward toward the pit, Eliza didn't see Lainie as she crept down, lower and lower toward her. Ever closer, until close enough to grab her.

"Let go," Eliza shouted.

"No," Lainiei defied her, meeting her now wide-open eyes with steely determination. "You want to let go, you take me with you."

Eliza tried to twist free and one of Lainie's feet came loose as she fought the girl to hold on. Both women screeched as gravel and dust fell beneath Lainie's loose foot. Lainie gazed down past Eliza's body and the black, fathomless maw of the pit yawned huge below them, hungry to swallow their lives up without a trace. Holding on by one foot and one hand, Lainie saw herself breaking loose, falling, twisting, screaming down into darkness and nothingness.

She managed to gain another foothold and she felt Eliza's wrist trembling in her grasp. The girl was losing strength. "Come on now," Lainie screamed. "While you still can!"

Eliza hesitated another second, then she hauled, her arms trembling, Her feet scrabbled at the cave wall, found purchase, and she forced herself up into a steady position. The two women clung there for yet another moment, panting, desperate to catch their breaths.

But the heat was rising and they had to move. Lainie once again returned to the ascent. If Eliza was determined to sacrifice herself, Lainie was helpless to stop her. But Eliza continued the climb behind her and together they made their way back toward the exit again.

Lainie finally found herself in reach of the ledge of the arch. With the last of her strength she hauled herself up and over the edge and onto a smooth shelf of rock. The sulfur smell was considerably stronger up here. She turned as she heard Eliza grasping for a hold on the ledge and grabbed the other woman's wrists. Between them they managed to get her up onto the plateau with Lainie.

They lay there for a few seconds more, feeling the knots in their muscles loosen one by one, like popping corn kernels. But even here the heat was becoming unbearable and they had to move out of the mouth of the cave. The sulfur smell was so bad that Eliza indicated their suits and they both zipped them up, flipped their hoods up and sealed them, and placed their breathers between their teeth. The quick turn of a knob on the hose at their right shoulder turned on the oxygen, but even without it the masks operated like simple gas masks, with biohazard filters and all.

Looking at Eliza, Lainie reflected how alien the suit looked. Then she turned to take stock of where they were. There was rock all around them, and a slope leading down below them and up. Eliza turned to start up the slope but Lainie stopped her and pointed down. "We have to find my friend," she shouted. "I at least have to try."

Eliza nodded and together they embarked on the rocky, precarious way down. Out away from the cliff-face they descended was the expanse of the crater in which the helicopter had landed, on the wall of which Dreck had built his impossible chalet hideaway. The horizon was dominated by rocky walls like the one they climbed now, the rim of the dormant volcano high above their heads. That, the dull yellow haze hanging over everything, and the two women in their containment suits, Lainie was struck by how alien was the entire tableau.

Having turned on the ventilation system, Lainie knew that Harkness and Dreck were now aware of their escape, and that destroying Eliza, no matter how valuable she was to them, was preferable to the exposure they risked with her at large.

The superheated ventilation system was meant to turn any errant bio organisms to fine ash. But how diligently would they seek to verify that Lainie and Eliza had, indeed, met their ends inside the vent? If they were indeed dust there would be little or nothing to verify.

Lainie had to assume they'd at least make a cursory search for any sign that she and Eliza had escaped. And to that end it was in their best interests to put as much time and space between them and that cave as possible. It was also possible that any search would concentrate on the cliff above the vent cave, logically assuming the two women would seek a way up and out of the crater. So by going down there was a chance they'd leave any search party behind them.

There was dust and grit between the crags of this lava-like surface. Was it enough to show footprints? Lainie had to assume so, and that I might eventually lead searchers down after them even if they first searched high. Which meant any advantage their current downward climb might afford them would not last long.

The wise thing would have been to climb to the top, as Eliza had started to do, and find a phone somewhere nearby to call for help. But leaving Simi behind, after all she'd risked to answer Lainie's call for help, was repugnant to Lainie, no matter how slim the chances that her friend was still alive.

The climb down was not hard compared the cling to the shear face of the vent cave, it was more technical, which was a rock climbing term for the number and complexity of obstacles they needed to navigate. Having been formed by eruptions when this volcano was active, the crater walls were uneven, presenting spires, ridges, and treacherous crevices into which one might turn an ankle.

During one of their rest stops Lainie reminded Eliza to take her time. "Slow is safe and safe is fast," she said. "It won't matter whether they capture us or not if we break our necks out here."

At some point Eliza froze below Lainie, looking off to the right. Lainie wondered why until she came up beside her friend, then she pressed down on her shoulder so that they both crouched low. Over the edge of a ridge between two spires about thirty feet below was the courtyard filled with vehicles and the chateau rising above it all.

While the activity below seemed intense, it was unhurried. Clearly their escape had been noticed, but the lack of urgency seemed to indicate the general consensus was that the superheated exhaust system had eliminated the two escapees. It didn't mean others weren't even now searching for them, only that the search was probably being treated as a formality.

Lainie tapped Eliza's shoulder and they continued their descent. Very quickly they were obscured from view of those at the chateau by the rough terrain. After several more feet Eliza paused again, this time in sight of the crater floor and the helicopter almost directly below them.

Before they'd resumed climbing down, Lainie heard a yell and looked upslope. There was someone dressed in jeans and a Hawaiian shirt, wearing a gasmask and a floppy fisherman's hat. He was pointing at her and shouting up. Lainie could not tell if he was armed.

She gave Eliza a shove, not enough to knock her off balance, but to let her know they'd been spotted. The two women climbed down as fast as they could. The next chance Lainie had to look up she saw at least four men making their way down to them, among them Conrad, her prior bully. He was carrying some sort of blunt cudgel. Lainie did not look forward to a closer look at it.

Now they heard more shouting from above, and it was drawing closer. The crater floor was still ten feet down. The helicopter stood on a circular, iron-mesh grate at the foot of the stone stairway leading back up to the mansion. Lainie and Eliza bore left, away from it. It would've made an ideal escape, had either of them any clue how to fly it. Lainie's only idea of this was the vague sense that piloting one was a vast deal more complicated than flying a fixed wing aircraft, which she had only the usual movie-watcher's idea how to operate.

They were near level ground when Eliza suddenly pitched forward and tumbled over sharp rocks and crags the rest of the way. Her hood came loose, as did her rebreather, and she cried out in pain. Lainie tried to rush to her, but before she could get to her another figure appeared.

Simi helped Eliza to her feet. As the girl reapplied her hood Simi turned to Lainie, fists raised, crouched for attack.

"Simi it's me," Lainie yelled.

Immediately Simi grabbed her arm and Eliza's and led them to the left, further away from the helipad. Lainie looked at her and realized she was holding her breath, only breathing in shallow gasps when she had to. They only ran about fifty feet when Simi led them into a vertical crease in the rock. She led them down a corridor open to the sky, then turned again into an A-shaped arch so narrow it almost looked like nothing at all.

They were in another cave, this one narrow but widening out into a round room about eighty-by-eighty feet. Simi had let them go and while she slumped against one of the walls and breathed hard, she did seem to be breathing quite naturally.

Lainie removed her hood and tried the air. It stank like week-old rotten eggs, but it was breathable. A noticeable almost constant draft blew through the cave from above and back out the way they'd come in. When Lainie looked up she saw a shaft so steep she couldn't see how far up it went, but the fresh air came from there. Another of Eliza's inversion shafts.

So this is where Simi had been hiding all this time. "How did you find this place?"

Simi smiled, "By luck alone, sister. I dropped from the helicopter mere feet before it landed. Already it was near impossible to breathe. I was forced to run toward the rear of the thing so not to be seen, and it turned out to be fortunate, for I was led almost as if by Allah himself to the path I led you on. I fell into this place more than found it. Here the air is foul, but I could breathe it. Hamdallah."

Lainie turned to Eliza and saw that the girl had moved to the far side of the cave. She had not removed her hood. "Eliza, this is my friend, the one I told you about. Simi, this is Eliza. Eliza, take off your hood."

Eliza shook her head rapidly, and immediately it occurred to Lainie why and she sobered. Of course, the virus. "Please, Eliza. You need to conserve the oxygen in your tank. Harkness said it spreads much the way a common cold is spread. That means it's not airborne, unless you sneeze directly into Simi's face."

"He could've lied," came Eliza's muffled shout.

Lainie supposed he could've, but why? When he thought he had them cold and was bloviating on his own genius? "I don't think so," she said. "It's up to you. I just don't know how long these tanks last."

A long moment passed where Eliza didn't move. Finally she lifted her arms, broke the seal, and took her hood by both sides, raising it until it flopped back to hang between her shoulder blades. She turned the valve of the tank off and removed her breathing unit. Her eyes were dark and bruised, haunted and retreating into their sockets.

"Pleased to meet you," Simi said, taking a couple of steps and offering her hand. Lainie stopped her. Eliza said nothing and stayed where she was.

"We need to talk," Lainie said. "You recall I told you that Professor Harkness injected Eliza against her will? Well, there's more to it. . ."

* * *

The three women huddled in the cave, Simi and Eliza as far from each other as they could get in the small area. Simi, already a serious person prone to quick anger, was clearly fuming with rage, and couldn't help but glare at Eliza, even though she had already conceded repeatedly that the girl had not injected herself. It was often hard to tell whether she was seething at Eliza, or at the virus that coursed through her.

For her own thoughts, Lainie was torn. They needed a way out, both to save themselves from Dreck's collective and to warn the authorities of the virus and what he planned to do with it. But it was also clear to her that with she and Eliza gone and confirmed by the searchers to be alive, not only would efforts to find them redouble, but so would the efforts to spread the virus. How much time did they have before the carriers were shipped all over the globe to spread their sickness far and wide? Whatever it was, Lainie was nearly certain it would be done long before they could get back here with the FBI, or the cops, or even the military to stop them.

"You need to get Eliza out of here," Lainie told Simi. When Simi looked at her alarmed, Lainie said, "Find some way to alert the authorities and bring them back."

"How?"

Lainie craned her neck. "Climb this shaft. When we climbed out of the vent cave, it wasn't easy but it was doable."

"And you? What will you do?"

"Stay here, try to decoy Dreck's people."

"Liar," Simi said. "I know you, Lainie Parker. You wish to go back to that lab and stop the Canadians from releasing this virus." Lainie said nothing. "And what if one of us should slip, or fall. How is one to help the other if we are not to touch each other?" Lainie hated to admit that Simi was right. "It makes more sense for you to take Eliza up. I am a trained operative. I will infiltrate the lab and prevent the propagation of this abomination."

"No," Eliza snapped. Until now the girl had sat quiet, sniffling occasionally. "I can't climb again. I almost didn't make it last time. I can't do it again. I won't. I'm going with you back to the lab."

"Oh no you won't," Lainie said. "We just got you out of there. I'm not letting you go back in again."

"You won't know what to look for. I do. Or at least I have a better chance than either of you."

Simi and Lainie looked at her, and Lainie wondered if the girl was up to it. She looked utterly broken. The thought of what'd been done to her had taken its toll on her, and the initial horror had given way to despair.

"We aren't all three going back," Lainie said.

"No," Simi said. "Eliza and I will go. You will stay."

Lainie wanted to protest, but on what grounds? On the grounds that Eliza was her friend, that she was hers to protect, not Simi's? That was pure ego, not pragmatism, and Lainie was ashamed to think that way. There was one legitimate protest, though: "But how? You can't touch each other, or even touch anything Eliza touches, in case you pass the virus."

Simi reached for the bundled spare containment suit Lainie had dragged along with she and Eliza in their escape. "This will protect me, will it not?"

"Yes," Eliza said.

"Unless your captured," Lainie put in. Why was she still feeling resentment of Simi for stepping in like this?

"If I am captured," Simi answered, "then whether a bullet kills me or this vile thing, I do not imagine it matters."

Lainie sighed. "Then don't get captured." Their eyes met for a moment, then they exchanged a brief hug. "So, I'm just supposed to sit tight and wait," Lainie grumbled.

"No," Simi said. "We will all wait until the cover of darkness. Eliza and I will find our way back to the lab, and you will get to the helicopter. You will find a way to operate the radio and call for assistance."

Of course. Lainie wondered why she hadn't thought of the radio on the helicopter. It seemed so obvious, now. "And what are you two going to do? How are you going to stop Harkness from injecting everyone here with the virus?"

"Simple," Eliza smiled. It was the humorless smile of a predator. "I will change their minds"

.

CHAPTER 9

They had initially landed in the crater in the small hours of the morning. When Lainie and Eliza had emerged from the vent cave the sky was bright with the dawn. By the time they'd reached Simi's hideaway it was pretty much mid-morning, Lainie figured. Which meant they had hours yet to wait for night again.

As they crouched, waiting, inchoate attempts at conversation fell flat and died quickly – each was lost in her own thoughts and not in the mood for commiseration. For her part, Lainie felt frustrated with herself, and with Eliza. In her hubris Lainie had imagined she and she alone could rescue Eliza and save the girl from her own bad choices, in spite of the improbable mounting dangers they found themselves facing. It'd been arrogance and her usual over-confidence. Eliza's earlier threats of suicide and now her stubborn refusal to let herself be saved felt like ingratitude to Lainie, and she was fast on her way to resenting the younger woman for it.

The darkness was near complete when night fell, but the containment suits featured headlamps above the forehead, like miner's helmets, only these were dotted LED nubs. Lainie followed her friends out of the cleft, along the trail back to the crater floor. Out here there was more light, not just from the stars above, but the helipad was well lit with amber floodlights. That light, diffused as it was by the rising steam and clouds of sulfur gas, actually lit up quite a circle. Still, when they turned off their head-lamps they felt relatively secure about not being seen. There was no sign of searchers and it appeared Simi was right in her conjecture that the collective would call off the search after dark.

When they'd suited up Lainie had noticed that Eliza's suit was torn in more than one place, either from the climb out of the vent cave or from her fall to the crater floor. Probably both. Either way, the sulfuric gas would penetrate. It didn't matter to her breathing as long as oxygen remained in her tank to dilute the gas, but prolonged exposure would irritate and eventually burn her lungs and skin.

Still, there was no helping that, because a cursory scan of Lainie's suit showed similar abrasions, though no actual tears. Even Simi's suit had suffered some from being dragged up lava-sharp walls and over igneous rocks and crags. They would simply have to move fast and hope to finish their tasks and escape long before the gas blistered their skin and made them ill.

Simi started the climb up the crater wall, made all the more precarious in the dark, and with a final wave Eliza followed her. The irony was not lost on Lainie that she'd gone to so much trouble to rescue Eliza from the clutches of Harkness and Dreck, just to have her go back in again. But there was a big difference between being held captive in the lab, and going back in under the cover of dark, accompanied by Simi, someone Lainie was coming to rely on implicitly.

Of course, it had occurred to Lainie to sabotage the lab, with Eliza's help, before they left it through the vent ducts, but they hadn't the time nor any element of cover. No, it was wiser to get out immediately and return later, when they were least expected. At the time Lainie had planned to go back alone, after having gotten Eliza in the clear.

But Simi was right, this was the better plan. Simi was stronger than her diminutive size suggested and a fierce fighter, she would keep Eliza safe. With them infiltrating that lab and Lainie going to the radio in the helicopter to call for help, they were covering each other – if either team failed the other might succeed. If they both failed, well at least they'd tried.

Lainie turned to the chopper. It sat in the ghostly-lit haze on the helipad like a squatting dragonfly ready to fly away, but of course there was no one inside and the engines were as inert as this volcano.

Lainie had to walk carefully along rocky ridges that mazed between pools of boiling sulfuric acid of differing sizes and shapes. She had to concentrate to keep her balance, but there were plenty of stepping places as long as she kept her head about her and looked ahead. Some pools had what appeared to be small islands broaching their milky, multihued surfaces that were perfectly foot-sized, but she somehow knew trying to use those as stepping stones would be a gigantic mistake.

She reached the helipad, which came to her chest, and though she'd been keeping a wary eye she saw no sign of a guard. That didn't mean there wasn't one, only that if there was he'd done a good job of staying out of sight. Lainie was able to climb onto the grated platform by stepping on lower struts that braced the pilons supporting it.

She was between floodlights now, but she was sure the light diffused by the haze put her fully in view, should anyone be looking. She went quickly to the chopper and tried the handle of the passenger (or copilot, she supposed) side of the cockpit. She expected it to be locked, but it wasn't and opened freely. With one last glance around to see if there was anyone on watch, seeing no one she climbed into the cockpit and closed the door behind her. She looked for an inner lock for it. The handle to open the door was recessed and had to be rotated nearly 180 degrees to open so presumably that kept it from being opened accidentally. Otherwise no inner lock.

She scanned the control panel for the radio. Frankly she just assumed she'd be able to tell it from sight, if for nothing than from the microphone hanging from it, but from the sheer dizzying array of dials, knobs, digital screens, analog indicators, and levers in front of her, down the center console between the seats, and lining the ceiling, the radio was not immediately recognizable. The was no palm-sized microphone connected to frequency and volume dials by a coiled cord like she imagined from television.

The recollection came to her that in helicopters, everyone, from the pilot to the passenger wore headsets and spoke in tin-plated voices to one another. Of course, the radio was connected to the communications systems integrated into those headsets. They certainly spoke to each other that way. But did passenger-headsets have access to radio frequencies like the pilot's, or only to intercom channels?

She looked for headsets in the cockpit and found none. There was, however, a helmet dangling from a hook under the console on the copilot side, where she sat. She looked inside among the padding and could see the patterns of holes on each side where speakers would align with the wearer's ears, but there was little more than a very small, square slot in the chin-guard – could that be the microphone? She imagined so – the mikes for cell phone weren't much bigger.

But holding the helmet did her no more good than holding a fork with no slice of pie in sight. It was useless unless she could figure out which controls operated the radio. The sea of controls surrounding her was intimidating.

Often, autistic children became overwhelmed by the cacophony of sights or sounds around them. It caused them to turn inward, to shut out the outer world and retreat into their shell. Lainie often encountered this during sub-rotations in graduate school, where she would substitute for teachers for class credit. Putting her face near theirs to get their focus on her, she told the child to focus only on small subsets of details in front of them, instead of trying to take in everything around them at once. When they have comprehended one small set of details, move on to the next. Don't let anyone rush them. Simply take it in small bites.

Small bites. Lainie noticed the miasma of machinery around her could be viewed in small, logical sections at a time, the natural division demarcated by seams between the equipment where it was inserted into the console. By focusing on only one apparatus at a time she found comprehending what was in front of her much less overwhelming.

The first thing she tried to find was a way to turn the power on. The panels and small LED screens were dark, it would be much easier to identify them if they were powered up and showing the information they had to impart. She looked in the logical place for an ignition, to the right of the control stick. There was no key slot, but there were a series of toggles, and right amidst them a rather important-looking, thumb-sized button. She pressed this, and with much *clicking* and *ticking* and *bleeps* and *bloops* the entire console came to life. It emitted a soft hum, as if a series of fans spun behind it all, keeping the electronics and power components from overheating.

The second thing she noticed was a curious, overall redundancy to the various screens and controls before her. With some exceptions, what stood before the copilot's stick appeared largely to be a mirror image of what was in front of the pilot. This simplified her search considerably. She knew, for example, that while piloting the craft, both pilot and co-pilot would need access to the same controls and information. But there was really only need for one radio. So she could spend much less time on the duplicated controls and more time on those that appeared to be single machines within reach of both operators. In other words, mostly the center console.

While studying the various components here she suspected more than once that she'd identified the radio, only to doubt herself. She knew there would be some sort of frequency indicator, and radio wave frequencies would be expressed as decimal numerals. There was more than one display here showing floating point numbers.

She noticed one with an LED display, a decimal followed by the subscript "MHz": megahertz. Lainie knew little enough physics but recognized a sine wave frequency. The number went up or down by .25 each time she tapped either the less-than symbol (<) or greater-than symbol (>) on either side of the screen, as well as by turning a manual knob below it. There was a progressive stack of five bars, smallest to tallest that anyone with a modern smart phone recognized as a signal-strength indicator, and other icons on the screen she didn't recognize. There was what was clearly a volume knob, and preset buttons that set the frequency to predetermined destinations. She felt safe in assuming she'd found the radio.

She decided not to use any of the preset buttons. God knew which recipients they were programmed to, and sending a mayday distress call to the mansion itself would be, of course, disastrous. Her initial plan hailed back to some of the old 70's movies her father had made her watch as a kid with truckers and car chases. Channel 19 was the setting for all public communications for CB (citizen band) radios. But did that even translate to aircraft radios? Were they even on the same frequency band? Probably not. This dial went no lower than 118 MHz, much less 19.

She knew that on CB radios there was a predetermined frequency for emergencies, but she couldn't recall what it was, if she ever knew, and she suspected it would be different here as well. She decided to pick a frequency at random. She spun the turn-knob once, shrugged, then turned to put the helmet on and make the call.

She broke the seal on her hood to push it back and was surprised that the air was only mildly tinted by the smell of sour eggs. Apparently, part of the soft hum she heard when turning on the console were air circulators throughout the cabin. She took a moment to breathe in the fresh air.

She was about to lift the helmet and place it on her head, but suddenly it wasn't possible. A burly, muscular arm appeared like a flash from behind her and encircled her throat, another pressing across the back of her neck, forcing her head forward. Dropping the helmet to her lap, Lainie gasped and let out what little squeals her windpipe would allow as it was being crushed. She pulled at the arm but it was a concrete collar as immovable by her as the abutment of an overpass.

"What are you doing, bitch?"

Conrad.

How he'd managed to get on the helicopter without her hearing him eluded her. She had been pretty focused on the console for a good while. Could she really have missed the sounds of someone opening the back door and coming in behind her? Certainly she had been wearing the containment suit hood, which did muffle sound somewhat, but enough? She would have been embarrassed if she weren't so desperate for air.

Lainie heard herself making duck noises deep in her throat as her lungs demanded service from her windpipe. Her vision was dimming, with little flits of sparks winking in and out across her vision. She knew she only had seconds before the sleeper hold put her out once and for all.

Flailing, she found her hands on the helmet in her lap. Grasping it like a lifeline she swung it over her head with as much force as she could manage. The impact, accompanied by a loud crack, wrenched the thing from her hands and sent it flying back into the passenger cabin. But the arm around her throat lessened, then slipped away entirely.

She turned and her uncertain vision showed her Conrad, gas mask pulled down around his neck presumably so he could whisper in her ear as he attacked her. He fell back in slow motion and slumped spread-eagle on the rubber floor mats behind her seat. Blood was drizzling from a gash in the center of a rapidly growing goose-egg above his left eyebrow. She stood between her seat and the center console, then fell back to her seat as her head swam and numbness threatened.

She let the blood rushing back to her brain reassert itself before she tried to rise again. She climbed all around the cabin, peering out of the windows, looking for a second guard or Conrad's backup. The light diffusing off the haze actually made it harder to see instead of easier, and if anyone else were out there they were making good use of it. She didn't see anyone.

She knelt beside Conrad and touched his neck. She detected a pulse, though strong or weak she had no experience to tell her. But at least he was alive. She tried to think of some witty rejoinder, like James Bond, John McClane, or any Arnold Schwarzenegger character, but nothing came to her.

In fact she didn't feel very pithy, she felt horrible. Certainly Conrad was among her adversaries in this ordeal, but aside from holding her prisoner he hadn't really done much to hurt her. Even though she'd delivered a well-placed blow to his man-parts back at the SDS building. He could have twisted her arm or kicked her, or slapped her around, but he hadn't. He'd seemed self-assured of his greater strength over hers and simply led her where he'd wanted her to go. On the other hand, he was a member of a group planning a massive global genocide.

Lainie had killed during the affair a year ago in self-defense, but had never struck anyone so personally, so hands-on before. She looked for and found a first aid kit stashed behind the co-pilot's seat. In it she found peroxide, gauze, and wrap-bandages. When she was done Conrad looked like a Civil war survivor with his blood-stained headband. She checked his pulse one more time, then went looking for her helmet.

When she found it, there was some damage. The chin-guard had been torn away, along with what she had assumed was the microphone. She looked around the cabin for an undamaged one but found none. Instead what she found was a much more compact headset hanging on the pilot's side of the center console, where she wouldn't have seen it from where she'd been sitting on the copilot's side. What, then, had the helmet been for? Perhaps she'd never know.

She sat again, this time in the pilot's seat, and resumed her chore of finding a way to alert the authorities and call for help.

There were several controls on the radio she didn't recognize – Vox/Squelch, Transceiver Xmit/Rcv, Pilot Iso/Norm – so she just decided to leave everything alone other than the frequency she'd chosen. Currently there was nothing but soft white noise coming through the headset when she put it on, adjusting the microphone on its extendible arm.

She didn't know if she needed to push a button to talk, so she just spoke: "Mayday-mayday-mayday. Please help. We need assistance at. . ." Where the hell was she? She suddenly realized she had no address, not even GPS coordinates to give anyone to find her. If she had her cell phone, its built in GPS might have a clue, but Conrad had taken. . .

She jumped up and ran to his supine form. As she searched him she repeated a mantra: "Please be here, please be here, please be here. . ." She didn't scream hooray or shout for joy when she found her cell phone in the lower-thigh pocket of his cargo pants, she just stared at the phone in her hand and whispered, "Well for God's sake."

She turned on the phone and looked at the signal bars. Of course, there were none. The phone had, indeed wiped itself when Conrad made too many attempts to break past her security, code. The service provider would have also suspended her service as a result, so she could make no calls. But the satellite-based GPS system on the phone worked independent of the cellular system. It should still be working, if it, too, wasn't blocked. GPS sometimes stalled on a cloudy day, never mind the cavernous walls of an inert volcano and the rising mists of gas spewed from boiling sulfuric acid pools.

She returned to the pilot's seat and tried her maps app. She watched as it showed her position the last time she'd accessed the phone, back at the airport in Jackson. She waited and tapped her foot, and just as she was about to despair the screen blinked, scanned over maps and centered on a remote, featureless splotch of landscape only just North over the Wyoming/Montana border, then zoomed in where a single road appeared to terminate. . .well, nowhere.

There was no address on the screen, no identifying landmarks near enough for her to give even that much direction nothing. She played with the app on her phone for what seemed like an hour but was more, she knew, on the order of minutes, and still found nothing to identify her current location. While thinking he had rested her finger on the little red teardrop indicating where she was on the map when the screen moved.

She looked to see what had changed. She knew that often touch-screen displays didn't just respond to taps and swipes, but less commonly to long-touches. Sure enough, this one had: map coordinates appeared at the top of her screen where an address would normally go: 45.01, -110.30. But these didn't look like any map coordinates she'd ever seen. Where were the degrees? Minutes? Seconds?

She tapped the search icon, and as if the thing read her mind, the latitude and longitude she'd learned in elementary school geography appeared below: 45°00'36"N 110°18'00"W. With this information she spoke into the headset again.

"Mayday-mayday-mayday. We need immediate assistance at forty-five degrees, thirty-six seconds North, one-ten and eighteen minutes West. Please send substantial police or military assistance. Over."

She repeated this twice, waiting a minute or so between. When there was no answer, she moved one-tick up the frequency dial and tried again. After several tries she got an answer: "Is this a lady or some kid messing around?" It was a male voice with either a gravelly tone or bad reception.

"My name is Lainie Parker. This is a dead-serious emergency. Can you please contact the police or military for me? Over."

"Well, lady, if you're really serious, the emergency channels are monitored for mayday calls."

"I'm not a trained operator. Which frequency is that? Over."

"Okay, ma'am, IAD is 121.5. MAD is 243.0."

"What's the difference?"

"IAD is for civilian distress, MAD is military."

"Thank you," she said. "Over."

"Yeah, well, you better be serious, kid, because they don't take too kindly to prank calls on this band. That's a felony, son. Over."

Lainie had no doubt. She didn't much care whether they came to help her or came to arrest her, so long as somebody came. She switched to the military emergency band, 243, and sent out her call again. This time the response is immediate.

"This is National Guard Armory, Idaho. Please call out and state the nature of your emergency."

And another: "Malmstrom AFB, Montana. Please give call letters and nature of emergency."

"Malmstrom, this is Idaho National Guard, you go."

Then silence. Lainie assumed "call out" was the same thing as giving her call letters, and it appeared that while two answered, the Idaho Nation Guard base was yielding the call to Malmstrom.

"Malmstrom, my name is Lainie Parker. I'm sorry, but I don't know the call letters for this. . .this helicopter. I am a civilian in extreme distress of a national security nature. Please call the CIA. Give them my name, they have a file on me." Oh, what a file they have. "Tell them Agent Cord Steele has been killed. Give them these coordinates –" she restated the map coordinates "– and tell them those responsible for the bombing of the SDS building in Idaho are here and planning a terrorist action. Tell them there are three civilians in distress. Tell them to hurry."

There was silence. Lainie almost repeated herself when the white noise spat and the man from Malmstrom responded. "Ms. Parker, please stand by. Over." He sounded calm but for the almost imperceptible crack in his voice. Probably the last sort of distress call they expected.

She waited. She chewed her nails. She looked out the front and side windows again for any sign of another guard: none. She checked her phone for any improvement in service: none. She looked at the piece of paper taped to the console in front of the pilot: indecipherable numbers and figures.

C'mon, she thought, come and arrest me for making a false report over national airways, if you want. Just get your asses here.

"Ms. Parker," the man from Malmstrom said. "We have the CIA field office in Utah patched through. Go ahead, Utah."

"Ms. Parker, this is Special Agent Derek Young from the CIA field office in Utah." He sounded like his name implied, young and green. And tired, as if he'd been awakened from sleep. "Would you care to repeat to me what you told the gentlemen from Malmstrom?"

Lainie repeated what she'd said, almost verbatim.

"Please hold the line," Young said, and the line went dead again.

Lainie had to believe that the wheels of rescue were moving faster in the background than it seemed to her speaking to these men. She hoped so. Because if not, their seeming lack of urgency could mean no help was coming at all.

"Ma'am," Young came back on the line.. "It may be of interest to you that Agent Cord Steele is not. . ."

The headset was yanked from her head. She turned to see Conrad on his feet again, standing crouched in the cabin behind her and glaring at her with rage-darkened eyes. She balked at first, but then his eyes seemed to roll back and he teetered that way. He caught himself at the last second with one backward shamble, then his eyes refocused.

"You don't look so well," Lainie said. "You should lie down. You probably have a concussion."

"Can't leshu call th'thorities," he said.

"You definitely have a concussion. Why don't you give me back the headset and you have a seat back there. I'll make sure they bring medical help when they come."

He looked from her to the headset in his hand, then with both mitts he folded the headset until Lainie heard a snap. Then he whacked the headset against the bulkhead next to him until pieces started flying around the cabin. In one final swing he missed, overbalanced, and went down again with a crash that shook the entire helicopter.

She went to his side again and it seemed he was once more unconscious. She picked up the shattered headset. With ear-cups hanging from wires and the microphone boom completely gone, it was quite irreparable. She examined every inch of the cabin, inside stowage and under seats, and could not find another.

"Damn it." What had Agent Young been about to say? Agent Cord Steele is not what? Is not employed by the CIA? Steele had told her he was on administrative leave, had he just downplayed it? Had he in actuality been fired instead? Steele is not reachable? She told Young that herself, though she hadn't gone into detail.

The sight of flames and smoke enveloping the building on which Steel stood, collapsing in a rain of debris, surely crushing him under mounds of rubble. She hadn't let herself think about him, and now she felt nausea and tears rising. She forced them down and looked around her.

She could no longer use the radio. She hoped Young would send help, but she had to assume, for the sake of her and her friends, that he was not. Better to save their own hides just in case. What good she could do was done here on the copter. She needed to climb the crater wall and keep an eye out for Simi and Eliza, in case it appeared they needed her help.

But she couldn't leave Conrad here. He might regain consciousness again, at least coherent enough to raise an alarm. She slipped his gas mask over his face and replaced her own hood and oxygen supply over hers. Opening the back cabin door, she grabbed Conrad's armpits and hauled him to the edge of the threshold. He was heavy, but she wasn't exactly weak, either.

Stepping down, she grabbed him again, his head lolling back on her shoulder, and hauled. At first he dragged horribly and she wondered if he might be caught on the rim of the door, but then his body overbalanced on the edge and came sliding down precipitously. Lainie stumbled back and fell to the helipad grating, Conrad on top of her. God, he was heavy.

Lainie pushed the big man's body off of her with a grunt, then stood and closed the helicopter door. Taking Conrad once more by the armpits, she dragged him along the length of the helicopter's landing skid toward the edge of the landing pad nearest the crater wall. Around the bottom of the wall there was room to walk without having to navigate the sulfur pools. It was the long way around to her destination, but easier, she thought, when dragging a body.

Lowering him off the edge of the platform was easier, then she dragged him, sweating and taking breaks, around the crater wall to the cleft that led out of the crater, toward Simi's airshaft hiding place. She managed to pull him along the cleft, feeling the wall in the dark for the opening to the cave Simi had taken them too, but she couldn't find it even with her head-lamp on. She began to think she'd passed it when her hand slid into open air. Reaching in further she was certain she'd found the air shaft.

In the utterly lightless chamber, the light on Lainie's head made shadows leap as she turned and leant the chamber a haunted, devious aspect. She dragged Conrad to the far wall and left him there. She removed his gas mask, certain he could breathe now with fresh air rushing in from the open chimney above. "Sorry, Connie," she said, "but this will at least slow you down, even if you do find your way out of here."

The floor shook violently under her as a thunderous crash sounded from what seemed like directly above her. It rumbled and the walls around her resonated in sympathy to the subsonic thud she felt in her chest. She cast about her, her light flailing wildly around the room as rocks and debris from above came careening down.

Lainie threw herself against the wall for what little protection that would provide and even that was trembling under her hand. Suddenly something heavy and hard struck her square on the crown of her head, sending radiant pain through her skull and down her spine to her knees, which collapsed under her. The light on her head went out with a static snap and all was plunged into utter blackness.

.

CHAPTER 10

Lainie curled like a pill bug into as tight a ball as she could, covering her head with her hands, as rocks pelted her from above, leaving bruises everywhere they hit along her left side. As she imagined the whole volcano coming down on her she felt her head. The lamp, shattered as it was, actually saved her life, protected her head, though she would develop a pronounced bump in a few minutes.

Luckily nothing so heavy fell on her again, and what did drop on her left only minor bruises as the rain of lava stone subsided. Soon there were only occasional sounds of settling stones far off in the darkness. She crawled over the now rocky floor to Conrad to check him. Using her cell-phone flashlight app she examined him and found no substantial new wounds, though he, too, would be spotted with contusions.

That explosion could only mean that Simi and Eliza had achieved their objective and destroyed the lab. She only hoped they'd gotten away before the explosion, which sounded huge enough from down here to have enveloped the entire mansion. Lainie needed to get moving on the chance they might still need help escaping retaliation.

Using her flashlight app, Lainie made her way over the floor, now treacherous with gravel that ranged from pea- to fist-sized, toward the exit. It was much easier to find one's way out of the cleft than in, and once she saw moonlight ahead she turned off and stashed her cell phone again. She turned off her own air supply to preserve it and donned Conrad's mask. The air wasn't quite as fresh as from an air tank, but it was breathable.

She worked her way to where Simi and Eliza began their ascent up the sloped crater wall and set herself to climbing it. The moon had risen above the rim of the volcano high above so that there was much more light than there had been. These walls weren't sheer, like in the vent cave, but sloped at a mere 45° angle, so she found the climb easy, even exhilarating, and she made good time. Long before she reached the point at which she and Eliza had been able to look over the chalet and its courtyard she heard the commotion.

There was an undulating orange glow on the rocks above and people shouting, even some gunfire. Lainie hurried up to her vantage and saw the chaos below. The entire right-hand wing of the chalet was fully engaged by spurting and sputtering flame reaching joyfully into the sky, washing everything in a sinister red hue. As windows shattered, blown out by spouts of fire, it was clearly spreading.

The courtyard itself was crowded with people, indeed it looked as if everyone who'd been in the house when the lab exploded was now here. Oddly there was a definitive line of demarcation where their group ended in a line mere feet away from three figures who were moving away from them. Lainie recognized Eliza, Simi, and Professor Harkness. Harkness walked between Simi, who held him by the scruff of his collar and held what appeared to be a gun to his back, and the rest of the people. Behind Simi huddled Eliza as the trio slowly moved step by step away from Donelly's group.

Donelly's group, the man himself and his son in front, advanced slow on the retreating three. Once in a while a gun would fire, and Lainie distinctly heard Harkness shout, "Don't fire! For God's sake, stop firing!"

The hostage standoff wouldn't last, Lainie knew, not with so many trigger-happy people climbing atop the trucks and RV's on the far side to get a better vantage. But worst of all she could see what neither Simi nor Eliza could, that they were not backing toward a way down from the clearing, but toward a promontory, an overhang that stood out from the crater wall, from which there was no way to climb. It was just a fifty-foot drop to the helipad below.

Desperately Lainie made her way that direction across the ridge above the courtyard on what she hoped was an intercept-trajectory to Simi and Eliza, to warn them that they were backing into a trap. For some reason Eliza was not wearing her containment suit. Simi was but had the hood pushed back. They were moving slowly, only glancing back the way they were headed occasionally, while Lainie moved as fast as she could manage.

Lainie came to an inverted wall she could not cross. She watched her friends move back until she could see them around it no longer. She desperately wanted to cry out a warning but dared not. It didn't matter to her that Donelly's people might spot her and come after her. She was worried about distracting Simi and giving one of the snipers on the far side the opening they needed.

Suddenly the air was filled with the roar of engines as a flight of perhaps eight or twelve helicopters flew past overhead, out over the volcano, already banking back, searchlights illuminating everything below like daylight. Thank god for the man from Malmstrom and Special Agent Young, Lainie thought.

Below, the mob was fraying at the edges, and then the entire crowd was in full-on retreat, sprinting to their vehicles and seeking escape. With only one road in or out she doubted they'd make it far. Already the choppers were hovering overhead and descending rapidly. Repelling lines unraveled themselves downward like strings of licorice.

But when she looked at Eliza and Simi they weren't celebrating, they were arguing. They held the professor between them and tugged him first one way, then the other as they shouted at each other. Eliza wanted to take him toward the promontory, and Simi, it seemed, wanted to take him back to the courtyard.

Surprisingly, Simi's grip gave way first. Eliza had something pointed at the professor, too small to be a gun or a knife, it had to be a scalpel from the lab. He did as she directed, walking toward the apex of the funnel, while Simi followed, seemingly trying to reason with Eliza.

Lainie couldn't watch any more, she had to intercept them. She was forced to climb down the slope to get past the barrier. On the other side, though she was lower, she could see the courtyard again. Air Force helicopters landed one by one as the collective group of Canadian terrorists scattered. Some tried to maneuver their vehicles toward the gate that led out, but got in each other's way and the tangle quickly became unmanageable.

Meanwhile Eliza, with her prisoner in tow, had backed into a V-shaped channel funneling them directly toward the cliff. Simi followed, arms spread as if trying to reason with Eliza. Lainie tried to shout again over the rumble of choppers overhead and could not even hear herself. She needed to get closer.

Thinking of Spider-Man, she worked her way horizontally along the slope toward where Eliza and Simi would be. Several times she lost sight of the courtyard below and twice she had to backtrack to get around some unsurpassable obstacle or other. After the second she could no longer see the courtyard. She moved as fast as she could and nearly tumbled more than once.

Then she heard voices above. She looked up and saw she'd been forced to climb below the level of the overhang onto which Eliza and Simi, from the proximity of their voices, must now be standing. They were arguing.

"No," Eliza screamed, her voice carrying with it the tears she must be spilling. "I will not let him go. What he did to me. . .I can't let him live to do it again."

"He will get justice," Simi shouted back, in command but cajoling. "I promise you."

"They'll use him. They'll use what he's made. I know they will."

"Maybe, but if you kill him now, you will be put on trial. You'll go to jail for the rest of your life."

"I don't care," Eliza screamed again.

Another sound below drew Lainie's attention. She looked down to see the helicopter on the landing pad below. There was a certain recognizable whine of revving turbines and the blades slowly turned, picking up speed. John Dreck looked up directly into her face, his smile tight but determined, as he climbed into the back of the chopper.

Lainie looked up again. She could see her two friends, and now Harkness had gone to his knees in front of Eliza as she struggled to get him to stand again, the scalpel at his throat. He was frozen, his face a sweat-shiny mask of dread. Lainie saw his hands were tied behind him, which they must've done when taking him hostage.

"Eliza," Lainie called, and the girl looked down at her. "If you kill him, there'll never be a cure. You'll have to live your life in isolation. With him, they can find a cure."

"There is no cure," Eliza shouted down. "The genetic mutation is permanent. Any attempt to undo it will only make matters worse. Tell them!" She shook Harkness but he said nothing, petrified.

The sound of the helicopter below had become deafening. Lainie couldn't spare a thought for Dreck's escape, as distracting as it was. She focused on her friend. Simi shouted and so did Eliza, but Lainie couldn't hear either of them above the scream of the helicopter. She saw Eliza back closer to the edge.

"No," Lainie screamed. She scrambled to climb the slope, to reach her friends before Eliza did something she couldn't take back. She entered a vertical draw that led her to the back of the promontory behind Simi. Eliza looked at her, face awash in tears, her expression less angry now. She evinced nothing but sadness and Lainie feared the worst even as it happened.

Just as Simi leapt at Eliza and her professor, Eliza flung herself and her burden backwards over the edge. Harkness disappeared from sight over the edge. But somehow Simi had gotten hold of Eliza's arm. Instead of allowing her to fling herself over the edge Simi's grip brought her back and she slammed against the rocks over the edge. Simi screamed as she herself slid toward the edge, and Lainie lunged onto her stomach, grabbing Simi's legs and holding them.

"My glove," Simi shouted, "it is slipping."

If the glove of Simi's containment suit slipped off, she would have to grab Eliza bare handed, surely exposing her to the deadly genetically engineered virus programmed specifically to kill her and her kind.

"Hold on," Lainie called. She struggled to climb up over Simi's back while still holding her from slipping over the edge herself. Just as she reached Simi's shoulders where she might've been able to take hold of Eliza and help pull her up, the seal on the glove ripped and the glove slipped off.

Eliza slid a short distance but clung to the porous lava-rock wall and stopped herself from falling.

"Take my hand," Simi shouted.

Eliza was still within reach, but she didn't reach out. She turned her sad, dim eyes on them. She didn't say anything. She didn't need to. The inversion air shaft that provided the chalet courtyard with breathable air was less effective here hanging over the fuming sulfur pools. Lainie saw signs that the others were breathing shallower like her. Within such shallow supply of oxygen none of them would retain their strength for long.

"Take my hand," Simi screamed again.

Eliza just looked back at them. Without voice, she mouthed the words, "I'm sorry." Then she pushed away from the edge and flung herself backwards, arms and legs spread as if in surrender, out over the void.

Lainie watched her fall as if in slow motion, never losing sight of Eliza's eyes as she fell. The young woman struck the rotor of the helicopter, which rocked forward on its skids and nearly slid off the platform. A fine red mist filled the air in a corona over the bright yellow floodlights. A mangled body pinwheeled out over the volcano floor, landed half-in, half-out of one of the acid pools, which spouted in protest. Then she slowly, unceremoniously slid the rest of the way in and disappeared.

*   *   *

Lainie sat on a metal crate of some sort amid a collection of helicopters in the courtyard of Dreck's mansion, which was still burning, emitting sparks into the sky when some newly weakened timber fell into the pyre with a crash. She could still hear some of the skirmishes that persisted in the distance between the airmen and what remnants of Donelly's terrorists hadn't been rounded up. Those prisoners sat in a group not far off, hunkered down, wrists strapped behind them with zip-ties.

Lainie felt nauseous. She could still see the sight of Eliza as she fell. One would've thought the rotor mechanism of the helicopter would be destroyed by her body falling into the blades, but the chopper lifted from the helipad well enough and swung up and away over the far wall of the crater. Lainie saw two air force gunships fly after it, but not immediately. It seemed already too late.

She looked down at her gloved hands. There were only a few red dots on the bright yellow, but suddenly they seemed intolerable. Lainie rubbed the gloves together, then on the legs of her containment suit. With greater and greater urgency she rubbed them, trying to obliterate the red dots. She didn't realize she was grunting and sobbing in rage until she saw men and women in uniform looking at her as if she had two heads. Simi appeared and folded Lainie into her arms and Lainie let her. She didn't cry, but her cheeks were wet.

"I could've. . .I should have. . .if I'd only just. . ."

"*Alsamt*," Simi said, smoothing Lainie's hair. "There was nothing either of us could have done. I saw it in her eyes when I first met her. She planned to do it all along. Maybe not just that way, but she knew what she planned to do long before I met her."

Lainie thought back to the vent cave, when Eliza had hung from the ledge over the seemingly bottomless pit. She'd wanted to do it then, but Lainie wouldn't let her. Lainie supposed, though, that if she was determined enough, there was really nothing anyone could've done to stop her. Short of tying her down, which wasn't feasible under the circumstances. She straightened and wiped her face.

"Thank you."

"Let's get you home," Simi said.

As they walked together to the chopper they'd been told would take them back to the base, some passing airman pushed a piece of paper into Lainie's hand. She would have stopped to look at it, but just then an airman was leaning from the deck of the chopper, offering her hand to help Lainie up. She absently stuffed it in her pocket and took the airman's hand.

The chopper ride was uneventful, during which Lainie remembered to call the rental company to tell them to pick up their car on the side of the road in the mountains outside Yellowstone, just a mile from a now demolished building. Everyone has their own mechanisms for staving off the worst of grief, and for Lainie it was focusing on mundane details.

At Malmstrom Air Force Base, Lainie went through the motions expected of her. She realized she was receding into shock – she spoke when spoken to, ate when food was put in front of her, showered, wore the olive flight suit that was left for her while her own clothes were laundered, slept when it was dark outside – but didn't much care. Her only goal in this whole ordeal was to protect Eliza, and she had failed. Simi's assurances aside – perhaps it *had* been out of her hands from the moment Eliza realized she'd been weaponized, genetically hotwired as the initial wave of a massive genocide – still, it felt like failure nonetheless.

One day later, rested, once again clean and in her own clothes, Lainie sat opposite Simi in the base canteen eating a premade, tasteless egg salad sandwich. She still felt numb. Simi coughed into her napkin, and Lainie reflected that she, too had found it hard to breath, dangling as they did over the sulfur pools. But her throat and lungs had recovered. So why hadn't Simi's.

Lainie moved like lightning, snatching the fist into which Simi had crumpled her napkin before she could stash it under the table. They struggled. "It is nothing, Lainie. It is only a cough."

Lainie tried to force Simi's fist open but the girl was quite strong and did not relent. When their hands broke contact Lainie only retained a small portion of the napkin that'd been protruding from between Simi's fingers. But even that small piece showed signs of a crimson stain.

Blood.

"I said it is nothing," Simi protested.

"Lieutenant," Lainie called to the security officer who'd been assigned to guard them – guard them or watch them? – who sat at the next table by herself. Lieutenant Shore looked up. "We need to get my friend to the hospital. Now." Lainie was now standing, dragging Simi to her feet, ignoring her protests. "She needs level five containment now, and she needs to be tested and treated for the virus we were to be debriefed about."

At the word *virus* the Lieutenant looked alarmed. When Lainie showed her the napkin fragment she looked terrified. She took the radio clipped to her belt and chattered urgently into it, meanwhile she led Lainie, dragging Simi behind her, out of the canteen and toward the cruiser she'd been chauffeuring them in. Under full siren and flashing lights, she sped through the streets toward the base hospital.

*   *   *

Lieutenant Shore stood at parade rest against the wall, one foot in the carpeted waiting area and one foot in the tiled hall. As Lainie paced the waiting room, her heart alternating between dead in her chest and beating wildly, she couldn't stop looking at the security officer's sidearm. She wondered again whether Shore was truly the liaison they'd been told she was, or a guard.

Lainie's thoughts were wheeling. It'd been hours since she and Shore brought Simi in. Lainie had accosted almost every nurse, doctor, and uniform who had the misfortune to pass down the hall outside, begging for any news about her friend, but it appeared there was none to be had.

When Lainie thought she'd certainly run mad, Lieutenant Shore's two-way spat static. She stepped into the hall and spoke into it, listening with it close to her ear. Was she concerned about disturbing the peace and tranquility of the hospital or was there something she didn't want Lainie to hear? Lainie knew she was teetering toward paranoia and tried to force herself to relax.

When she closed her eyes, for some reason she flashed on the image of John Dreck as he looked up at her from the helipad, smug, before climbing into the helicopter and flying away.

"Ms. Parker." Shore stood just inside the waiting area. "They'd like to see you now."

Lainie's blood ran suddenly ice cold through her veins and her feet were rooted to the carpet. She'd already lost Eliza. Could she stand to lose Simi, too? Gravity suddenly seemed to fight her and it was a Herculean effort to lift her right foot from the floor and place it in front of her left. But then she was so tight on Shore's heels she actually kicked her foot once.

"I'm sorry, but please hurry."

Shore led her through a series of swinging doors, the last of which was flanked by Air Force Security Force officers, not just armed with M-16 rifles, but holding them at an angle across their abdomens, at the ready. They let Shore and Lainie pass, so Lainie wandered who they were there to keep out. Or perhaps they were there to keep someone in.

When they entered the isolation ward Lainie only had eyes for Simi, who laid under a frightening array of machinery in another room surrounded by windows. Lainie rushed to the door but Shore and two doctors stopped her and held her back.

"You can't go in there without a containment suit," one doctor said to her.

"I had one but they took it," Lainie said. She sidled over to one of the windows and pressed her hands against the glass. Simi had tubes in her nose and mouth and more than one IV in her arms. They appeared to be feeding her clear fluid from one and blood from another. She didn't seem alive at first until her eyes flickered and craned toward Lainie. Lainie couldn't read her expression, but the whites of her eyes were bright red, and it brought tears to Lainie's eyes. "Oh God, Simi."

For some reason, Lainie flashed again on the memory of John Dreck climbing into the helicopter before flying away and escaping. Why did she keep seeing that image in her mind?

"Ms. Parker, I assume," someone said behind her.

She didn't turn. "Yes."

"My name is Doctor Forthinger. Your friend told us her name is Shima Ateem, but you call her Simi?"

"It's a term of endearment," Lainie lied. Simi was holding her gaze, and was she trying to say something around the tube in her throat?

"Yes, well your friend is suffering the rapidly debilitating effects of what appears to be some sort of ebola-like virus, but we've never seen anything develop this fast."

"It's a new strain."

"Yes, I gather. Now what can you tell me about it, it's origins, it's topology, you see. . ."

"Nothing."

"P-pardon me?"

"I can't tell you anything about it," Lainie growled. "The only two people in the world who could have told you about it are dead. Senselessly, stupidly dead." She said this flatly, without energy.

Simi seemed to be struggling to lift her head. She was definitely trying to say something.

"I see. Well then can you tell us what kind of contact you've had with your friend in the last twenty-four hours? Is your relationship, forgive me, romantic? Have you kissed? Made love?"

"God, no," Lainie snapped. "Look, Simi, I mean Shima, she wants to say something."

A couple of men in white containment suits had entered the room. As Simi struggled to sit up they pushed her down. She fought them but was clearly too weak.

"What are they doing to her," Lainie demanded. "Tell them to leave her alone. She wants to tell me something."

Suddenly Simi grabbed hold of the tube in her mouth and yanked. It came out, long and snaking. It was covered in blood, and a fountain of blood came spewing out of her mouth after it, splattering the floor. Simi took a deep breath and though she screamed it was muffled through the glass.

"RUN!"

Horrified by what she saw, it took Lainie a second to galvanize. In a split second the memory returned: Dreck peering up at her, smug in his escape, yes. But also, smug in victory. Now she saw it, what she didn't register before but what her mind was trying to remind her of. Dreck had something in his hands. Some sort of a white plastic case with a clear plastic lid. Inside were an even assortment of test tubes and syringes.

She spun around, but it was too late. Lieutenant Shore and another guard were behind her. They were wearing white containment suits. She fought them but they were stronger than she. One held her from in front while the other cuffed her from behind.

"No! Wait! You don't understand! He has it! He's got the virus! He's got the virus and the mutagens!"

They tried to lead her away but she dropped to her knees. "Please listen to me. He's going to do it. He's going to spread it around the world."

They picked her up pits and ankles, and though she kicked, they dragged her across the ward to another isolation room. They dragged her in and, with some effort, placed her on an exam table. "What are you doing? I don't have it. I'm immune. Don't you understand? It wasn't meant for me. It wasn't meant for us. It was meant for them."

They pinned her and fastened restraints to her wrists, ankles and forehead. She realized that she sounded like a lunatic and tried to calm down. "Okay, listen. Call the CIA. Call Agent Young in the Salt Lake field office. No, call Langley. Tell them I'm here. They'll tell you. They'll tell you."

Someone had stuck her arm with a needle. Light was fading. As consciousness melted away all she could do was protest in a steadily weakening voice, "No. Please. I have to find him. I have to stop him. Please." And then blackness enfolded.

·

CHAPTER 11

Unconsciousness was not complete senselessness. She thought she'd awakened at some point, until Judson Harkness walked into view and peered down at her. His face was impassive, his voice flat and emotionless as he said, "I'd have gotten away with it if it wasn't for you meddling kids and your dumb dog." Then she was out again.

The next time she thought she was awake, Eliza soon bent over her bed. "If you didn't agree it was the best way, you would have found a way to stop me." Lainie wanted to argue but the world faded away again.

And again, she imagined she opened her eyes. This time she heard the voice before she saw who spoke. "Hey, Sleepyhead. You up?" Cord Steele leaned over the bed and looked at her. There was something different about him, he didn't look like himself, but she'd recognize him anywhere.

Unlike the other two times, Lainie tried to move. She felt vague frustration the she couldn't. "Here," he said, "let me." And then her left arm was free to move again.

She reached up and touched the side of his face. "Aw Cord. Sorry got you killed. You wouldn't've done that to me." Her mouth felt filled with cotton.

"S'okay, Kiddo," he said, putting his hand over hers. "It happens. Listen, I need you to tell me what you want."

"Hmm?"

"Lainie, I got you. I got your back. You just tell me what you want."

"Oh, Cord, what do I want? I want to teach, I don't wanna be a pimp. *Un chulo de internet.* I want to have sex with you again. I want a car that doesn't blow up every time I try to start it."

Steele leaned closer. "Lainie." She felt him pinch her cheek, it made her wince and turn away. He took her chin and turned her face back to him. "I need you to tell me what you want. Right now. And I'll do it. Whatever it is. I got you. Do you understand?"

She tried to push his hand away and realized her right arm wouldn't move now. She realized she was still bound to the exam table they'd put her on earlier. Why? What had she been doing before. "I want. . .I need to get out of here. Need to find Dreck. Gotta find cure for Simi."

The effort to remember made her head swim and she felt herself go out again. The next time she dreamed she was awake both of her arms were free, And her feet. Something covered her face and she was in motion. She was still lying down and moving at the same time, a bizarre sensation. She reached up and pulled the cloth from her eyes and saw Cord Steele above her. Fluorescent bars flashed by overhead like the dotted line on a highway and Steele ran alongside.

He looked down at her and didn't smile. "Lie still," he said, covering her face again. "We'll be clear soon." Consciousness faded yet again.

She seemed to be clawing her way out of a tangle of hot, sweaty yarn. Her eyes didn't seem to want to open, but she forced them. She was in motion again, supine but not flat. There was wind-noise around her. She looked up. Dashboard. Door handle. Steering wheel. Hands, not hers, driving. Occasional lights flashing by.

Her head hurt and she closed her eyes.

Awake again, she was being stood up out of the passenger side of a car. She was being half-carried, struggling to make her legs work. With a beep, little green light somewhere, a door opened and she was inside. Bedroom. Beds, nightstands, desk, dresser, TV, bathroom.

Bathroom.

Suddenly she rushed to the bathroom and slammed the door behind her. Only a little vomit hit the bowl, the rest were dry heaves, but it seemed to go on forever and after, her stomach hurt all the way up to her ribs. Then something else struck her. Suddenly she was standing again. She tried to push the door open, then remembered bathroom doors opened in.

She swung the door open with a bang. "Cord Steele!"

He turned and looked at her, his crooked smile firmly in place. "In the flesh."

She ran to him and threw her arms around his neck, squeezing. "Easy," he laughed, "easy." She tried to jump up and wrap her legs around him, but they overbalanced and fell to the bed. She resorted to covering his face and lips in kisses. Steele pushed at her insistently. "You need to brush your teeth, kiddo."

She relented. She sat up, still straddling him, and he propped himself on his arms.

"But how," she demanded. "I saw you. You were on the roof when the whole place went *poof!*"

"I jumped."

"You jumped?"

"I dove off. You remember how the building fronted right up against the lake. I dove and I swam, like I never swam before."

She looked at him, really looked for the first time. His hair was no longer full and wavy, the cocky curl so characteristic of him no longer resting on his forehead. Instead it was buzzed close to his head, and there was a bandage around his neck. She touched his hair, ran her fingers over the fuzz of it and he ducked away, embarrassed. "Yeah, I was sort of on fire when I jumped. This was the better alternative to walking around with singed hair."

She touched the bandage. "Yeah," he said, pushing her hand away, this time looking serious. "It'll heal. Don't worry."

"Good God, Cord," Lainie whispered. "I thought you were dead."

"I sent word to you when Agent Young called me and told me what was going on. Didn't you get it?"

She started to say no, then reached into her pocket and pulled out the piece of paper the random airman had put in her hand back at the chalet. She opened it. It was a printout of an email.

"Ms. Parker," she read aloud. "As I started to tell you before we were disconnected, you'll want to know Agent Cord Steele is not dead. He sends regards and wants me to tell you he'll meet you at Malmstrom. Yours, Special Agent Young, Central Intelligence Agency, Salt Lake."

"You didn't read it?" Cord laughed. Lainie crumpled the paper, put her arms around his neck and kissed him again. "Um, I wasn't kidding. Your breath."

She covered her mouth. "Sorry." She jumped off of him and went to the restroom to rinse. She didn't have a toothbrush with her. Steele came to lean on the door jamb, watching her scrub her teeth with a finger.

"How did you get me out of there," she garbled around the digit.

That roguish smile took over his face. "Do I really have to say it again?"

This time they said it together: "Sneaky son of a bitch."

"Not a smart career move," Lainie said.

"I'm still on admin leave. Officially, I'm not here."

Lainie turned to him. "What is this place? Are we still on the base?"

He shook his head. "Motel in Great Falls, just off Route 87."

"Good. We have no time. Simi's life depends on us finding John Dreck."

"The billionaire philanthropist?"

"No time to explain," she said. "But he has. . .he might have what we need to save her life. If all he has is the virus, and a cure has to be extrapolated from that, then we are probably already too late. If he has an antidote or cure already, if Professor Harkness got that far, so much the better."

"Okay well shouldn't be a problem. . ."

Lainie shook her head. "Dreck has gone into hiding."

"Problem," Steele said. "With his resources. . ." He shook his head and shrugged.

"The government may have frozen his assets by now," Lainie said.

"Doesn't matter. Man like him, he's got money stashed all over the globe, friends. . .man like him could stay off the grid for a very long time. If we want to as well, and trust me after breaking you out of a government facility and level 5 containment, we do, then I can't use agency resources to find him. There aren't even really any favors I can call in without getting someone else in trouble. I'd rather not do that."

"No," Lainie said, her thoughts whirling faster and faster as the remainder of whatever drug they'd sedated her with left her system "I may know someone. Wait." Lainie looked down at herself for the first time since her head cleared. "I'm wearing a hospital gown."

Steele wagged his eyebrows at her. "I brought your clothes in from the car. They were in a bag in the containment lab marked for incineration."

"We need to find a place to buy an anonymous phone."

"Unless I miss my guess," Steele said, "we're going to need a few burners. I know a place. C'mon."

*   *   *

"Orin?"

"Lainie," Orin said, sounding happy to hear from her. The creator of the escort app Lainie proctored rarely had cause to hear from her. He worked his end – maintenance and enhancements to the app itself – and she did hers – interviewing and hiring new girls, referee when disputes arose, etc. There was rarely crossover, except the one time when a change he made brought the whole app down for four hours. Which is most likely why he asked, "Is there a problem?"

"No," Lainie said into the burner Steele had bought with cash from a small drug store. He bought four which, he said, was few enough not to send any red flags anywhere, but enough that they wouldn't need to buy more until they were far from Great Falls. The prepaid cell phones were a little more expensive in a place like that, he explained, but it was easier to keep one's face averted from security cameras in a small store, allowing him to leave no trace that even facial recognition could link him to the phones he bought, should it ever come up.

Both Lainie and he had, of course, taken the batteries out of theirs. Turning the phones off wasn't enough. If called upon to do so the service providers could still track them. Indeed, they could send a signal that would turn the phone back on and use it as a listening device. Such things took a warrant, of course. . .unless the affiant could claim it was a matter of national security.

"Listen Orin, I need some help," Lainie said. She had him on speaker and she and Steele huddled together in his rental car.

"S'up?"

"I need you to find someone for me."

"What do you mean? I'm not exactly a bloodhound."

"I need you to find him on the grid."

She was met with silence. Then, "You want me to hack. What makes you think I do that sort of thing?" Orin sounded cagey, paranoid.

"A hunch," Lainie said. "But if I'm wrong, I'm hoping you can hook us up with someone who can."

More silence. Then, "Are you working for the cops, or any law enforcement agency? You have to tell me if you are."

Steele rolled his eyes and shook his head – that was a canard passed around among prostitutes and drug dealers, but in truth the police and Feds were completely free to lie to others in the performance of their duties, including about their own identities. They only had to identify themselves in the case of entry, pursuit, or upon making an arrest.

"Orin, I can honestly say I am not." Lainie shrugged at Steele. It was true enough, as far as it went – he was on administrative leave, so technically not working as a Fed. At any rate, the CIA had no jurisdiction inside US borders.

"Ok, Lainie. If you jam me up. . ."

"Orin, it's me." In fact, she owed him and would, indeed, never betray him like that.

"Who is it you want me to find?"

"John Dreck."

He scoffed. "Famous guy like that? Why don't you ask me something hard?" They could hear his keyboard clacking through the phone.

"Well he's gone underground, if that makes it sexier" Lainie said.

"Really. Intriguing." He also sounded distracted as he hacked away. Lainie pictured skinny Orin, with his greasy hair falling into his eyes, his glasses slid to the tip of his nose, huddled over one of several computers clustered together, illuminated only by a bank of LED screens.

"I'll call you back," Orin said.

"My phone's. . .not working. I'll call you."

"Okay, give me thirty minutes."

Lainie hung up. To Steele: "How often do we need to toss these?"

"Every three or five calls or so," Steele said. "Or every time we move. Do you want to tell me what's going on, now? I thought I'd read your debrief when I got here, but I found out you were going to be debriefed tomorrow." He glanced at his watch. "Today, rather."

She looked up at him, "So how did you know where to find me?"

"Wasn't hard," he said. "Military bases are like small towns, gossip is oxygen. There were whispers all over the base about the cell of Canadian terrorist, of all things, brought in and locked up, and the two civilians who exposed them.

Conversation with a nurse in the hospital cafeteria and I found out about the two women in isolation."

"You got me out of that place."

"Yes."

"Why?"

"You asked me to."

Lainie cocked her head at him. "You know what I'm asking. You don't know what has happened since I last saw you. But you took me out just because I asked you to. You risked your career, even your freedom just because I asked you to."

Steele rolled his head, as if embarrassed, or as if he was trying to think of the right words, or both. "LP, you have the uncanny knack of inspiring loyalty in almost anyone you meet. Beats anything I've ever seen: Simi, her family, Eliza, this hacker of yours. . .me. If you ever led an army I would bet against every enemy you ever met." He sighed, shrugged. "You tell me you need me to get you out of there, I know you have a good reason, so I get you out. You want to hear something more complicated, I'm sorry. It really is that simple."

Lainie didn't know what to do with that, so she didn't respond. It was true that often people looked at her in ways she never imagined herself, put faith in her when she felt every bit on the razor's edge that they did. She felt as lost as anyone, but some friends did seem to turn to her for leadership, when what she really wanted was someone to show *her* the way.

Sure, she often took the lead while others were still standing still with indecision, but that wasn't because she felt in any way qualified to lead them. If she thought about it at all, she supposed she had an inner conviction that any action, even the wrong one, was better than none at all. Her father used to say, "If you stand in the middle of the road long enough you'll get run over." She felt that as long as one was moving, one could correct for mistakes. Standing still, all you could do was duck. And she was never one to stay on the defensive.

After long moments of silence, Lainie reached into the shopping bag where the remaining burner phones were, and drew out a pack of gum. Looking at him with a sly smile, she removed one piece, unhurried, deliberate, and chomped it between her teeth. Then she put her arms around his neck and kissed him.

When they came up for air, she filled him in on everything that had happened to them – Eliza, Simi, and herself – since leaving him on the roof of the building about to be demolished. He sat quietly and listened, didn't interrupt her, his face blank, absorbing details. When she was done he shook his head, said, "I'm sorry. About Eliza."

"I would have stayed at the hospital with Simi willingly if I thought there was anything I could do there to help her," Lainie said. "But the only two people I know who know enough about the virus to find a cure soon enough to help her are dead. The only thing I know to do is get a sample of the unmutated virus for them to study. And they weren't listening to me."

"How much time does Simi have?"

"I don't know." Lainie chewed her lip. "For all I know it's already too late. But I refuse to assume that. I'll keep running until I know the race is over."

Steele glanced at his watch again. "It's time."

Lainie called Orin.

"I didn't find Dreck, but I found one of his body guards," Orin said. "Guy named Von Donelly has accounts all over the social media landscape. Not racist, per se, but he has some pretty definite opinions about Islam. Anyway, his family runs the private security firm contracted to protect Dreck and all his properties and businesses. From Donelly's recent posts he's been moving around a lot in the last couple of days, especially just in the last twelve hours. He doesn't say it but you get the impression that they're trying to stay ahead of the process servers or cops or collections agents, something like that." Probably all three, Lainie thought.

Orin continued: "He mentions that as soon as his boss, whom he seems to worship like a rock star, picks up enough cash from various stashes around the country that they will be heading overseas to, and I quote, 'finally once and for all strike a blow, not just score a political point.' If Dreck is on the run, it's a good bet this Donelly's with him."

Steele nodded.

"Okay," Lainie said, "how does that help us find out where they are?"

"Most social media sites accept as part of the meta data for any posting, location stamps indicating where the post was sent from. Ostensibly this allows friends to meet and hook up. You can shut this off on a phone or tablet, but most people don't bother."

"Von?"

"His location data is active."

"So, where are they?"

"Well I can tell you where they are now: Denver, Colorado. But they're moving around a lot, and quickly. No more than four to eight hours in any one spot. They must be flying. I don't know why you want to know where he is, but I'm guessing he's going to be hard to pin down."

"Unless. . ."

"Well, I can tell you where they're headed. Maybe not next, but soon. I looked at the places they've been and compared it to an impromptu map I made of known Dreck properties, places he's most likely to have stashed cash. Based on the pattern of their movements I've a pretty good idea where one of his last stops will be before they leave the country, if the Donelly guy is telling the truth. It's just a guess, mind you, but I think a pretty educated one."

Steele entered the location into his phone as Orin recited it. "I have no idea how long it'll be before he shows up there," Orin went on. "But given their current pattern, I'd say no more than 24 hours."

"Thanks, Orin," Lainie said. "I owe you."

"No you don't," Orin said. "Friends don't keep track."

"You're the best."

"Now you're stating the obvious. Say goodbye, Lainie."

"Goodbye, Orin."

"Interesting guy," Steele said when they'd hung up. "Not only gave you what you asked for but anticipated what you needed before you knew yourself. Could use a man like him at Langly."

"They couldn't afford him," Lainie said as she thought of the stacks of cash piling up in her own account, knowing as junior partner she got only thirty cents out of every dollar their so-called dating app made. If she was raking it in Orin had to be using a snow shovel.

Steele held up his phone, showing the location Orin had given them. "We're going to need a plane."

*   *   *

Lainie felt less hypocritical this time when dipping into her pimp stash to charter them a plane and pilot and then, once they landed, a helicopter and pilot. As they tilted headlong over pine and juniper covered hills toward their destination as fast as their pilot said he could safely go within flight regulations, she felt justified in such extravagance in the interests of saving her friend's life.

As they zoomed in over the Donelly group compound north of Houston, British Columbia where Lainie had first met Von Donelly, though not formally, the pilot maneuvered skillfully, kicking the chopper back on its heels as it were and stopping at a dead hover directly over the mess hall. He then landed light as a feather in the quad out front.

The place looked deserted, right up to the moment that Lainie heard a familiar *snap* followed by the tinkle of broken glass. A thumb-sized hole had appeared in the helicopter's windshield. A matching hole had appeared the same instant in the pilot's left temple, which Lainie, sitting in back with Steele, only saw because he slumped over the center console.

"Sniper," Lainie shouted and dove for the door on her side. As she hit the dirt outside and rolled she caught sight of Steele from the corner of her eye. He, too, had bailed. Lainie wanted to sprint for cover but since she didn't know where the shot came from she didn't know which way to run. Steel sped past her, grabbing her arm as he went and leading her to the side of the building. One more silent bullet kicked up the dirt where her running left foot had just been before they found cover.

"Guess they're already here," Steele shouted – the rotors of the nearby chopper were turning at idle, which was still loud enough.

"Leonid!" Lainie all but hissed.

"Your ex-neighbor nee hit man?"

"Son of a bitch." Lainie looked around the parts of the ring of cabins and sheds that they could see from their vantage. "He must be traveling with Dreck, covering his ass. We need to find where the money is they came for. That's where Dreck will be."

"We're not doing anything until we take out that sniper," Steele said. "We're lucky the helo kicked up dust, obscured his L.O.S., otherwise if he's got any eye at all we wouldn't have made it across the clear like we did." Steele was speaking in that abbreviated slang soldiers use in the heat of battle, but Lainie thought she understood what he was saying: helo – helicopter, L.O.S. – line of sight, etc. "I need to know his position. He'll be on higher ground somewhere, but unless he fires again I can't get a bead on him. Maybe not even then."

"You need him to shoot again." Lainie heard Steele shout, "NO!" as she dove out into the dust-clouded clear again and made a beeline for another nearby building. She heard another shot ring out, but didn't feel any impact. As she pitched herself at her new cover she turned back.

Steele shook his fist at her, then mimed spanking a child and pointed at her. She stuck her tongue out at him. "Did you spot him?" She mouthed the words.

Steele put his fist beside his head and then raised his index finger: "I think so." He then showed her the flat of his palm: "Stay put." Shook his fist at her: "Or else." He rolled his eyes and she knew he didn't expect her to comply anyway. He then turned and, at a crouch, disappeared around the next corner of the building he hid by. Lainie tried to sooth her nerves by reminding herself that he was a sneaky son of a bitch, his words, but her heart still pounded.

She spotted movement out of the corner of her eye. Someone had emerged from a fenced in building across the quad. It was the senior Donelly, limping on his injured leg. He peered around as if trying to spot who it was that their sniper had shot at. He couldn't have heard the silenced shot, so they must be in radio contact with each other. Of course.

Lainie stayed perfectly still. The building he'd come out of was the only structure in the compound apparently cast from concrete, marked with water stains from the elements. It was surrounded by a chain-link fence, the gate of which stood open, and various ducts and conduits ran in and out in a tangle around it. From the top stood the tall tower she'd spotted last time she was here, arranged with solar panels disguised as pine branches to blend with the surroundings.

Some sort of power station, she guessed, If Dreck were to have a vault at this compound, as it seemed, of course he'd put it in the sturdiest building, possibly in an underground vault. Lainie needed to find a way to separate Dreck from his security detail, send them on a wild goose chase while she confronted him.

She sidled along the back of the cabin to the far end, looking toward the mouth of the dirt cul-de-sac around which the compound was built. There, parked side by side, were a helicopter with the Dreck Foundation logo painted across both doors on this side, and Leonid's van. So he wasn't traveling with them, but had met them here.

Lainie gauged the distance between her hiding place and the vehicles. Not knowing where Leonid was, she didn't know if that sprint was in his line of sight or not. Steele would kill her for risking it again, but they were running out of time. Any moment Dreck could finish emptying the vault here and leave with his entourage. She had to act.

She slid back along the wall again to her original spot to check if Donelly was still outside the power station and saw that he'd been joined by his son, Von, and another man. Sidling once again she returned to the vantage of the vehicles. If she could cause a ruckus there, she could not only eliminate their means of escape, but hopefully draw the men away from the power station, away from Dreck.

She bounced on the balls of her feet. This run would not be obstructed with dust kicked up by the helicopter like back inside the quad. But with any luck, even if it were in his line of sight, Leonid might be looking elsewhere when she ran. Or hopefully occupied by someone else. . .

She kicked off and beat her heels as hard as she could toward the parked vehicles. She was just halfway across when two silent shots hit the ground at her feet in rapid succession. One bullet struck the ground in front of one planted toe, and the other just where the other, raised foot was about to come down. These weren't just gunshots, this was a message. Two shots meant, "I want your attention." The placement of the shots said he could hit anything he wanted. And what he wanted was for her to turn back.

Her gut freezing, she spun and ran back toward her hiding place. Another two shots kicked up geysers of grit, striking in front of her again. Once more she turned and ran toward the vehicles. Again, halfway, the bullets kicked up dirt in front of her. Like a cat, Leonid was toying with his prey. But Lainie knew she dared not simply stop and stand, making an even easier target for him.

She gasped for air, her heart beating both from exertion and panic. He was forcing her into wind-sprints, and while she was by no means weak she wasn't in the shape of a football player. So she was stumbling every time she was forced to switch back, using her hands to keep her from falling completely.

She was slowing down, her lungs burning as she sprinted toward the vehicles for what seemed the hundredth time when only one shot came. But instead of hitting the dirt at her feet it flew past her with a *twang* like a passing insect, striking a tree another forty feet beyond her. In the far distance she heard an echo, a man's voice, "Ack!" She'd only heard an *ack* like that once before, from one of the victims of Cord Steele's signature monofilament garrote.

No more sniper shots came, and she finished her run toward the helicopter and the van. She didn't have time to rest as the Donelly's could come to investigate soon, but she couldn't stop herself from going to her knees up against the van, wheezing loudly in spite of her need to be quiet, dying for enough breath to stop her vision from threatening to blackout.

Thank God for Cord Steele. She acknowledged now it'd been foolish to try to run past a professional killer like that. She knew before she tried, but her desperation to find the virus in time to save Simi was making her reckless and she knew it. Was it enough to make her slow down, think things through better before she acted?

Probably not, she had to admit.

She was still out of breath but recovering when she pushed away and went to the fuel spout of Leonid's van. It was covered by a little trap door, which when she tried to open it didn't budge. She rounded to the driver's side and tried the door. It was locked. She cast about for and found a good-sized rock from those lining the drive. It took her three good, hard smacks to break the door window.

Reaching inside she opened the door, and a short search showed her the lever deep under the dash that popped open the fuel spout cover. She then went back to the rear where she removed the gas cap. The acrid smell of gas struck her nostrils. She looked around to see if anyone was watching before reaching under her sweater and unfastening her bra. Slipping the straps down her right sleeve and over her hand, she was then able to pull the bra free from her left sleeve.

Rolling one of the cups she pushed it and the accompanying strap down into the spout as far as it would go. When she drew it out it was moist with gasoline. She rolled the other cup and forced it into the spout, leaving the already soaked end dangling. She patted the pocket of her jeans and found the book of matches she'd taken away from Eliza at the diner what seemed ages ago. For some reason she'd transferred them from pocket to pocket every time she'd changed since then without any real superstition that she might need them later.

She lit one, cupping a hand to protect it from the mountain breeze. When she touched it to the dangling end of the bra the cloth lit readily enough, then traveled up the length much faster than she'd planned.

Lainie turned and ran. She heard a low roar and when she reached the corner of the building on the far side of the drive from where she'd come, she turned back to see a jet of blue flame spewing from the fuel spout. She was afraid it wasn't going to blow after all, giving her the distraction she needed, but just burn in a jet like this until it ran out of gas to burn.

Then the explosion hit. It wasn't the giant blast she expected, but it was enough to lift the back-end of the van off it rear wheels and drop it back again. And it made a noise she though sufficient to draw the attention of those guarding Dreck. But in jumping as it did, the van had also pivoted slightly toward the chopper. Flames from the explosion fell into the grass beneath the helicopter, catching fire there, too.

If the helicopter went up in flames, she suspected the resulting explosion would be considerably larger. Not wishing to stay within range to find out, Lainie turned and slid along the building she hid against, staying close because she couldn't know for sure that Leonid was permanently out of action. She crossed a short gap to the next cabin, then the next until she came within sight of the power station enclosure again.

Now, seeing it from the other side, she had a better view of the entrance. The Donelly's and the third man were talking in murmurs to each other, looking tense, as if arguing over which of them could leave Dreck and go investigate the van explosion.

The blast that came then could only be the helicopter blowing up. It was deafening, a sharp bang that hurt the ears and sent a brief spout of blue flame up above the rooves of the cabins and yurts. Without discussing things further the three men sprinted together out of the enclosure and toward the vehicles, out of sight of Lainie.

She crossed to the gate of the fence enclosing the concrete building, then to the open door. She didn't hear any voices inside, only the hum of machinery. She walked into a concrete entryway with no furnishings, not even carpeting, and another metal door on the opposite wall. There was a lock on the door, but it hung open. She peered in and found a small control room with a single office chair and a bank of electronics clearly meant for observing the performance of the machinery that regulated and distributed power to the small community of cabins. There was a large bay window on the far wall looking into another room crammed with two rows of racks, one along each wall to right and left. Each rack was burdened with blocky apparatuses whose purpose wasn't immediately apparent.

Prepper is a term for someone who, to varying degrees, plans and prepares for any sort of disaster from natural to nuclear. Communities of that sort are known for establishing an independent grid of power relay stations meant to pull and store power from the primary, municipal grid. If Lainie had to guess, these black boxes on the racks in the next room were nothing more than batteries meant to store and preserve power against the contingency of a prolonged power outage elsewhere.

That made this building less of a simple power station and more of a bunker, probably lined with lead to shield it from external electromagnetic forces. She only knew what little she did about such things because her uncle, her father's brother, was quite far down the road to being a prepper himself. After her father died, she and her sister – and her brother when he was still alive – often stayed with Uncle Danny when her mother decided she needed some *her* time, which was often. Danny loved the kids and let them eat some of the MRE's and other foods he'd stored for fun. Most of the food was middling to awful, but it was fun eating in the bunker, pretending to be hiding there from zombies. Especially when Uncle Danny would bang on the door and make growling noises, as if zombies were coming it to eat them. They would hide and scream and giggle all at once.

There was no light except that coming off the control console screens and readouts. In the electrical room beyond the glass were dim amber lights on each battery that gave the place a murky, unsettling illumination. Given the meager dimensions of the exterior, that chamber had to be the only room unless there was a cellar or crawlspace below, which she doubted.

Lainie looked at the metal door leading into the battery chamber. There was a placard on the door with an oppressive high voltage emblem on it. Her father's voice rang in her head, "It's not the volts that get ya, it's the amps." He'd been changing a lightbulb at the time. Lainie knew little about electronics, all she knew was high voltage signs were intimidating enough, she didn't want to know about the amps.

She touched the doorknob and snatched her hand away as if expecting to be electrocuted, but nothing of the sort happened. She opened the door, stepped in, then shut it behind her. The room smelled of electronics, that acrid, ozone-like odor that made one's nose twitch. And it was cold in here, not freezing but enough to raise goosebumps.

Seeing no one from this vantage, she peered carefully around the left bank of batteries. She heard shuffling noises from the far end. "Who's there?" a man called out from the dimness.

"John Dreck?" Lainie didn't think it sounded like Dreck.

"Parker? Jesus Christ, where'd you come from? Who the fuck are you? How'd you find us?"

"Conrad?"

"Seriously, I gotta know. Who do you work for?"

"Is Dreck with you?"

"Hah! Miscalculated there. You expected to find him here. He's smarter than that. He's back at the airport, on the jet."

Dreck not here? Lainie's heart sank. She wasted her time. . .Simi's time. . .coming here. She and Steele were at the airport just hours ago when they'd hired the chopper that flew them here. Dreck had been within their grasp then, had they known. The disappointment was palatable.

"He gave us a deadline to return with the loot," Conrad went on, "or he'll leave without us." Then: "Parker? You still there?"

Lainie nearly turned to leave, then thought she should do something to delay or, if possible, stop Conrad and the others from leaving the compound, rejoining their boss, protecting him. She thought of somehow locking or blocking the door to this room, but realized all Conrad had to do was break the observation window to get out. The next door? She recalled no lock on it, the door back out to the anteroom opened inward, so no way to jam it closed.

"Sorry about your head," she said. "How are you feeling?"

"Had a headache. Gone now."

"So what's in the vault," she asked.

"Vault? Just a safe. What you might figure – diamonds, highest value for the weight."

"How much?"

"Oh, I don't know. Enough to fill a small valise."

"Don't supposed you'd give it to me?"

"Um, most likely not. Unless you can give me a good reason. Immunity, maybe? Witness protection?"

"We might be able to arrange something." Never mind that she had no authority to make such promises.

Suddenly two massive hands grabbed great fists full of her sweater from behind, spun her around and slammed her up against the wall. Her head swam, but from here she could see that the banks of battery racks did not back up against the wall entirely, there was a space there wide enough for a man to sidle past. The shadows had kept her from seeing it before. It was along this darkened slot he'd snuck up on her.

Conrad bodily turned her to face him, pinning her wrists above her head. Now that she thought of it, his voice had gotten louder as he spoke, she had just thought he was exerting himself, emptying the safe. New she knew he'd been sneaking up on her. He had nothing on Cord Steele for stealth, she'd just been stupid, un-alert.

Each time she tried to bring her knees up to kick him, his leg came up with hers and blocked it. "Awful white-hat of you," he said, his face inches from hers, "to bandage my head, carry me to that airshaft so I didn't suffocate slowly on fumes."

She struggled but he was much too strong for her. "I'm conflicted about that," he added.

"Then let me go and we're even."

"Not that conflicted. Tell you what I'll do. I'll strangle you instead of beat you to death. It's a softer death. Your lungs will ache a little, maybe your head, but then everything will go numb and you'll go to sleep. Really not a bad way to go."

Looking into those eyes, Lainie felt real terror. She didn't want to die, couldn't afford to die, not with Simi hooked up to machines, receiving blood transfusions and antibiotic taps and morphine drips, only to die anyway.

Lainie's knees buckled and she slumped in Conrad's arms. As he shifted his hands to get a better grip on her and keep her from falling, she suddenly lifted both knees, placing her full weight on his hands. She planted her heels on the wall behind her and kicked back as hard as she could. Between his shifting grip, her weight, and her strength against his balance, Conrad was thrown back. Lainie fell to the hard concrete floor, but he stumbled against the far bank of batteries, flailing backward to catch himself.

There was a sub-aural hum Lainie felt in her skull more than heard. Arcs of electricity spat and flashed around Conrad as his body first froze rigid, then began jittering and flailing amid spouts and little tinkling showers of sparks.

.

CHAPTER 12

Lainie smelled piss and burning flesh. She planted her nose and mouth into the crook of her elbow and fled from the room. The lights flickered before blinking out entirely, but Lainie found the exit by the sunlight. Her blood was rushing, not only from the stress and fear of action, but in a visceral reaction to seeing Conrad die. She had a connection to him, of a sort, after seeing to his health and safety briefly at the volcano. For him to remain determined to kill her in spite of that filled her with an odd mixture of hurt, sadness, and rage. He didn't have to die, but in deciding to kill her he immediately absolved her of any remorse over having to defend her own life.

Still, she remained shaken.

Now, with Conrad dead and Dreck out of reach Lainie was at a dead end. She felt despair, an unfamiliar feeling to her, threatening to close in around her now, wanting her to give up. She tried to stave off hopelessness. She and Steele might be stranded here, their pilot dead, but so were three more enemies. They were still in danger.

She just wondered how she was going to find Steele, when yet again he appeared as if bidden, this time from around the corner of the buildings by the road, sauntering toward her, grinning his crooked grin, the very image of the jaunty, self-confident rascal he was. In spite of his cropped hair, he looked his old self, no sign of the darkness that had been bowing his shoulders and shadowing his eyes of late.

"You seem pleased with yourself," she said.

"That depends," he said. "How many more of them are there?"

Lainie glanced over her shoulder, "Conrad's dead. Three went the way you just came from. I haven't seen anyone else."

Steele said, "Those three are neutralized: Your guy Von, nuther guy named Lars, and guy they called Dutch. And Dreck?"

She told him Dreck stayed back at the airport. She turned to look at the helicopter they came in, still sitting in the quad in front of the mess hall bungalow. "I don't suppose you know how to fly a helicopter."

"Nope."

"Wait," Lainie said.

"What?" Steele trotted after her as Lainie ran back to where the destroyed vehicles were. As she rounded the corner and the mouth of the cul-de-sac came into view she saw the blackened, burning husks of both the van and the Dreck Foundation helicopter.

Nearer the buildings, in the shade, three men sat trussed with bonds that seemed invisible until they glinted briefly in the light – Steele's monofilament. If they tried to break free with any force at all they would only succeed in severing a wrist or ankle and bleeding to death in the dirt.

Lainie pointed at Von and said his name, "Von," looking at Steele. Steele nodded. She pointed at the elder Donelly: "Lars?" Steele nodded. She pointed at the odd man: "Dutch." Steele nodded again. Lainie shook her finger at Dutch. "He's a helicopter pilot. He's the one flew us away from the SDS building before it went up."

Dutch looked at them wide-eyed, but didn't bother to deny it. Lainie remembered his name, if not his face because it'd remained hidden behind goggles and a gas mask last time she saw him. But it stood to reason he was the one that'd flown

Dreck and others away from the burning chalet back at the volcano and here again from the airport.

Steele took one of three pistols he'd taken off the men from his waistband and handed it to Lainie, who pointed it at Dutch while Steele unbound him. "You're going to fly us back to Dreck," Lainie said.

Dutch only had to look at the gun once, nodded.

"What about us," Von snapped.

"You fellas can wait here for the RCMP," Steele said, "who will be on their way very soon."

Back at the rented chopper, while Dutch was doing his pre-flight check and Lainie, in the co-pilot's seat, kept the gun on him, Steele lay the body of the dead pilot in back, on the floor. He covered the corpse with a silver heat blanket from the survival kit, less for his comfort and more for their own. By the time that was done Dutch was revving the engines and the rotors were turning.

All three wore headsets. As they lifted off and tilted East, Steele spoke into his mic, "You are under arrest, Dutch. Understand? You're going to jail. For how long, whether you get time off for cooperating with us, well that depends on whether you get us to Dreck's private plane safely or not. Follow?"

Dutch said nothing, but nodded once. Apparently a man of few words, Lainie reflect.

To Steele, she said, "You sure seem to be feeling your oats again."

He smirked at her. "I think taking time off was the wrong thing for me. Jumping off an exploding building, stalking a professional sniper, taking down the other three one by one while they each wondered where the other had gone. . .that's my jam. I feel like myself again for the first time in months. What happened in Afghanistan, I realize now it wasn't me. It was the enemy, they killed Whirls, not me. I no longer blame myself."

Lainie beamed at him. She happened to glance down at his groin, then did a double-take. When she looked back up to his face again, he colored a little, but shrugged. "As you say, feeling my oats."

Lainie laughed, then turned back forward again.

The helicopter was flying low enough to rustle the leaves of trees it passed with its downdraft. "Why are you flying so low," Lainie asked.

"Stay under the radar," Dutch answered.

"Why?"

"You'll see."

"Tell me now," she said, raising the gun to the level of his head.

Dutch glanced at her from the corner of his eye. "We're not exactly landing at an airport."

She saw as he banked down over what looked for all the world like a storybook farm, with green pasture, verdant orchard, white beam fence, two-story gabled house, red barn with white trim, horses, cows, even sheep and chickens. If Dreck did, indeed, hide here, it was truly the unlikeliest place for any authorities to look for him.

"Is Dreck in the house," Lainie asked.

"No he's in the jet, in the barn," Dutch said as he lowered the craft toward the wide gravel drive leading out of the structure to the road in front. Sure enough, when she took another look, Lainie saw the slender nose of a good-sized jet protruding out of the open double-doors of the barn. It was a sleek black with gold trim, and as they descended it was clear this barn was huge, well large enough to accommodate a full-sized jet.

"Land us over to the side of the barn." Steel instructed, kneeling between the pilot and co-pilot seats, "out of direct line of sight. They no doubt have a lookout who saw us coming, but we don't want them to see Lainie and I just yet."

Dutch did as he was told, landing the chopper on a patch of dirt on the opposite side of the barn from the house. "Leave it idling," Lainie said. Steele grabbed the scruff of Dutch's shirt and led him to the back of the craft, where he used a length of his garrote wire to tie the pilot to the frame of the bench seat.

Steele handed Lainie one of the guns he'd been collecting from Dreck's minions so now she had two, and led the way out of the copter. They headed for the rear of the barn where a matching set of double-doors were only open wide enough for a person to walk through. Before they went in Steele eyed the house, but if there was anyone watching from there they did not shoot or raise any audible alarm.

Just inside the doors, high above their heads, was the tail of the black jet, slanting down to the body. The enormous wings were within a yard of each wall. It had been a precision piece of ground taxiing on uneven ground to slip the plane into this barn for parking.

Steele motioned for Lainie to stay here and slunk up the left side of the plane. Lainie stepped out far enough to see the fold-down gangway was extended. There was a guard leaning against the rail at the foot of it swiping his finger along the screen of his cell phone, playing some game or other.

Steele slipped under the plane, his hand over his head tracing the smooth underside of the machine as he stalked, silent as death, up to the underside of the gangway. From there he tiptoed closer to the guard until he was directly behind him. He reached up with both fists, and while Lainie couldn't see the hair-thin monofilament between his gloves she knew it was there.

But Steele hesitated, seemed to think before throttling the man, and returned the garrote to his pocket. Instead, he reached around and pulled something from behind the low wall of the foldable staircase. It was an assault rifle, left unattended by the lax guard. By the time the man turned around Steele had it aimed at him.

Brief words were exchanged and the man's shoulders sagged. Without raising the alarm he turned and knelt with his back to Steele, put his hands on the back of his head. Steele raised the rifle and slammed the butt across the crown of the guard's head, who in turn slumped to the dusty wooden floor of the barn.

Steele turned and motioned Lainie forward. When she reached his side, running at a crouch, he said, "Apparently there are no more guards. Only Dreck and a woman inside."

"Do you believe that?"

"I don't take it on faith." He grinned his broken grin. "Wait here."

Steele trod soundlessly up the stairs – how did he move so silently? – and disappeared inside. Only moments later he called from the interior, "Lainie."

She went up and entered the plane. Its opulence was blinding to her, ivory carpets, cream-colored walls, black seats, and everywhere gold-colored metal trim and fittings. The plush seats were arranged in circular tea groupings with low tables between them. Steele stood about half-way back with the rifle raised. Beyond him, at the point of his gun, sat two people. In one seat sat a stunning brunette in a black mini-dress with gold trim, clearly a flight attendant of some sort. Across the aisle sat Dreck. On the table before him were files and papers, more than one cellular phone, and two laptop computers.

Dreck's face was red as he held his hands up at shoulder height, but he smiled. Granted that smile was clearly forced, but it was his attempt to appear, at least, that he was still on plan A, even though clearly he could not be. "Ms. Parker," he sneered. "Why the fuck am I not even surprised?

"Y'know I have some of the best hackers in the business on my payroll, rivalling even the NSA, but not a one of them could punch even so much as a pinhole in your cover as some unemployed graduate student. Your legend is even so detailed as to include some ludicrous cover within a cover as the administrator of some underground wireless app that hooks men up with hookers.

"It's the most comprehensive, detailed, and ironclad backstory I've ever come across."

"That's because it's all true."

"Please," Dreck said, "tell me who you really are, who you really work for."

"I told you," Lainie growled. "I am that unemployed graduate student doubling as the proctor of a dating application online."

"Bullshit."

Lainie sat in one of the seats facing his. "Please," she said, "don't do this."

He looked surprised He hadn't been expecting this simple, straightforward request. "What are you trying to do?"

Lainie tried to hold his eyes with hers. "I'm asking you not to release this virus. I'm asking you to give me what I need to help my friend. My sister. One to whom I owe my life"

"She has it?"

"Yes. And I love her no less than you loved your father."

"If she has it then she's one of *them*."

Lainie took a moment to keep herself from spitting in his face. "She's Iranian, raised in Kuwait and later France. But she's not a terrorist. No one in her family is." This wasn't strictly true, Sayed had been her cousin after all. Still: "She's innocent. Her only crime was trying to help me save Eliza from you and Harkness. There is no one I know with a bigger heart. Please, let her live."

Dreck folded his arms. "'A world of millions was lost because of mercy for a few.' In every war there is collateral damage. It's the blood of the innocent more than all the carnage of the guilty that makes men strive the harder for peace."

"Please," Lainie pleaded.

"If your friend has it, she's dead."

Lainie glowered at him. "Where's the virus?"

He smiled and leaned back in his seat, as if he had all the time in the world. "Do you ever read fiction, Ms. Parker? Ever read classic spy thrillers, James Bond, Matt Helm, like that? One of my favorites, Alistair MacLean's *The Satan Bug*. I've named it, you know, our virus. I call it the Lucifer Strain."

"Where is it you son of a bitch," Lainie said, standing and stepping forward past Steele. She wanted nothing more than to smash his smug face, but in case he'd hidden the virus somewhere she didn't risk rendering him unable to speak. She did, however, raise both of her guns and aim them, one at each of his knees.

Dreck's smile faltered. He pointed back toward the rear of the cabin. Lainie headed back while Steele kept his rifle on Dreck and, marginally, the attendant. Lainie found a restroom much roomier than that found on almost any public airline, a galley, and beyond that a door leading into a bedroom with a double bed and rich accoutrements.

One glance around showed her a safe in the wall to the left about waist high that stood open. She went to it. Inside were several small flat clamshell cases that when opened, proved to be full of diamonds. This, then, was Dreck's easily negotiable stash of wealth, that he planned to take with him to whatever non-extradition hidey-hole he was running to.

She searched the rest of the room. No sign of the little plastic case full of test tubes and syringes. Lainie marched back out to the main cabin and whacked Dreck on top of the head with the butt of her gun, not hard, but decisive. "Where are they?"

"Ow." He rubbed his head. "In the galley. In the fridge. Where else?"

Lainie went back to the galley. It was roomy compared to the cramped space on commercial planes, and the refrigerator was, while recessed into the wall, apparently full sized. Inside were perishable groceries. Pushed to the left side was the plastic case. Looking through its transparent cover all insertion slots seemed occupied by full test tubes and syringes. Nothing seemed missing, or partially empty. Hopefully that meant he hadn't had the chance to infect anyone else yet.

She carried the medicine caddy out and stood in front of Dreck. "Tell me," she said, "Which is which in here?"

He seemed to consider lying to her, then shrugged. "The syringes marked Lucifer double-oh one are the unmutated virus. The tubes marked AP-X47 through X52 are the mutagens."

Lainie turned to Steele. "Where's the pilot?"

Steele kept his vicious-looking rifle aimed at Dreck. "Not here. I'm guessing Dutch is both the helicopter pilot and the airplane pilot."

"Let's tie Dreck up, then get Dutch to fly us back."

Steele nodded and handed her the rifle while he tied up Dreck. When he turned to the attendant, who looked petrified, Lainie stopped him. "She's okay," Lainie said. To the woman, she added, "You cooperate and there won't be any reason for you to share his fate."

The woman nodded quickly and waved her hands.

Lainie nodded to Steele, who nodded back and left to go fetch Dutch.

"If my friend dies before we can get back to Malmstrom," Lainie said to Dreck, "I'm going to see to it the rest of your life is hell." She didn't know how she could, but she meant what she said, or at least she'd try.

Suddenly he leaned forward, showing real interest for the first time. "Tell me, how long after exposure did symptoms assign? What symptoms presented first, and in what order? In what timeframe did they intensify? And please, try to be detailed and exact."

His purely clinical queries infuriated her. She stepped up close to him and lifted the gun in her right hand, placing the muzzle less than an inch from his left eye. "I should kill you, right here and now."

"But you won't." His eyes were wide and his eyelashes quivered.

Lainie realized he was right. To shoot a man was horrifying enough to her. To do so at such close quarters, and him tied and helpless, was simply further than she was able to go. She stayed for a moment longer, as if to bluff him, then stood straight again.

"Why won't I? I don't need you. I have your unmutated virus. We'll take it back to Malmstrom, they'll synthesize an antidote, and Simi will recover."

Dreck seemed nonplused, then burst into peals of laughter. "Oh my god! You're a fucking idiot!"

Lainie's rage died stillborn as her head exploded in sudden pain. The hit came so suddenly she went out as if someone had simply flipped a switch.

*   *   *

She didn't know how long she blacked out, but when she came to, her vision was narrow, ringed by clouds. She was on the floor of the plane, but sitting, propped up against the bulkhead. Dreck sat across the aisle, the assault rifle laying over his lap. He was smiling at her as she blinked, trying to clear her vision.

"That one'll give you a concussion for sure," Dreck said, his voice jiggling, as if he could hardly contain his glee. "Never turn your back on an ex-Marine."

"Who?"

"Sheryl. The woman you told your henchman to leave untied."

"Oh," Lainie said. "Are we. . .are we in the air?" She could hear the whine of the turbines, the hiss of recirculated air, the rocking of the floor beneath her. "Who's flying the plane?"

"Sheryl."

Lainie felt ashamed. Not only had she let sympathy for another woman cloud her judgement, she'd assumed the pilot of the plane was simply a flight attendant. She'd never thought of herself as a chauvinist before.

"I'm amused," Dreck said.

"Clearly." Lainie's vision-cloud was receding, but not fast enough.

"You assumed all you had to do was bring the virus back to some lab somewhere and they'd whip up an antidote like that." He snapped his fingers. "Then you could save your friend and all the other poor souls infected with the base, unmutated virus and be the hero. Sorry, heroine."

"All the other. . .?"

"Why, didn't you know? Everyone your people arrested back at the crater? All my mules? They are all already injected with it. Of course they were! How stupid and unprepared do you think I am? All they lack is the right mutagen to weaponize what's already within them. They will eventually be released by your courts on bail – I will see to it each and every bond is paid. Then all they need do is contact me to let me know where to send them their dose of the mutagen.

"I know what you're thinking. You can't send such chemicals through the mail without sending up all sorts of red flags. That's why we, Harkness and I, made the mutagen soluble in juice, or soda pop. Hell, we can send the mutagen in a mason jar of grandma's preserves."

Lainie groaned. All of Simi's and Eliza's efforts to destroy the virus, failure. Eliza had given her life in vain. Though to be fair, she had to admit, Eliza didn't sacrifice her life to stop the spread of the virus so much as to not be the cause of its propagation.

Dreck leaned over as if to catch her gaze. He enjoyed watching Lainie's failure dawn on her. "But that's not so amusing as what brought you chasing me across the country like you did."

"All I wanted to do was find a cure for my friend. What's so funny about that?"

Dreck crossed his legs and sat back. "You see, Harkness estimated that the virus would kill the victims, that they'd bleed out and die within forty-eight hours. I don't know how long ago your friend has been exposed. But even could you bring the virus back so that your lab could synthesize an antidote, you dummy, that sort of thing takes, what? Months at the very least."

He inhaled with relish and sighed. "Poor Miss Parker, your mission failed even before it began."

.

CHAPTER 13

Lainie glared at him, fighting the almighty fight to keep the burning lump in her throat from bursting out in a scream of rage and helplessness. She felt her face wet and supposed she was losing that battle, but she still fought it and refused to let loose. Not, dear God, in front of him, of all people. Finally she raised her knees and dropped her head between them to keep him from seeing the pain in her face.

"Aw, chin up, Kiddo," he said. "You did have a chance. You just didn't know it." When she didn't respond he sounded disappointed, "You could have succeeded. You were just after the wrong thing."

"What do you mean," she managed to croak out.

"Me," he said. "To quote the immortal Val Kilmer, I'm your huckleberry."

Lainie glared up at him again. She'd had enough of his gloating, his toying with her emotions, and was getting angry again. "What the fuck are you talking about?"

He chuckled. "Ms. Parker, how can you so consistently underestimate me? How stupid would I be if I didn't have Harkness create both the right antidote and *vaccine* even before we moved to phase four? And to make sure I was the very first to be vaccinated?" As realization spread across Lainie's face a smile radiated across his. "That's right, Ms. Parker. An antidote to the virus, mutated or not, can be synthesized from my blood in mere hours."

"Damn you," Lainie grated. "Damn you, damn you."

Dreck finally seemed to achieve the satisfaction he was seeking and glowed at her in pure joy. He stood and started toward the cockpit-end of the plane. He turned back as an afterthought. "The seatbelt indicator is off. Please feel free to move about the cabin. I have no fear of you. If you manage to find a way to bring down the plane, you'd die with us. Even if you are willing to sacrifice yourself to stop me from propagating the mutagens, are you willing to kill me, your only chance to save your friend?

"I know heroes like you, Lainie Parker. You can't give up hope. So, you'll bide your time in hopes of catching us off guard later. Until then, help yourself to some champagne and caviar from the galley. There are even peanut butter and jelly sandwiches, if your tastes run more pedestrian." He went into the cockpit and closed the door behind him, taking all of the guns with him.

She hadn't asked him why he didn't kill her. She already knew the reason. He didn't consider her a threat. Maybe there was still a bit of his hypocritic oath left in him, but she suspected he'd kill her if forced to.

Of course, he was right. If he was indeed telling the truth and he was the only source of a cure for the virus in hours rather than months, then she needed him. Alive. Whatever she did to get herself out of this jam, it couldn't involve endangering his life.

She tried to haul herself up into a nearby seat and her vision swam, threatened to go dark again. The next time she tried she took her time. Once she was finally seated she lifted the screen over the window next to her and looked out over blue. Above a lighter blue, below a dark aquamarine.

They could be flying over a lake, she supposed, but her guess was the ocean. Houston had, indeed, been Dreck's last stop in his tour of hidden stashes around North America and he was now headed west. Or south, perhaps, after flying out to international waters. Either way, each moment took her mile upon mile further away from Cord Steele and whatever assistance he might've been able to render.

She was well and truly on her own.

Her head still hurt, but she knew she couldn't just sit and nurse her wound. Concussion or not. She had to find some way to regain the upper hand. The plane vibrated under her. She tried to get up, but the floor pitched under her and she fell back into the chair. She was sobering up a little. Was that her imagination or had the plane really lurched suddenly?

There was a loud rattle as the plane shuddered again, then tilted severely to the right. She looked out of her window. She was sitting behind the wing, and what little she could see of it told her nothing. She forced herself, holding onto the backs of the seats for crutches, to move to the right side of the plane and opened the shade.

She didn't have to strain to see the wing, pressing her forehead as hard as she could against the plexiglass. It was as obvious the plane was in distress as the black sooty cloud rushing past this window. The turbine on this side was smoking, probably on fire as well.

The plane shuddered and lurched again and Lainie nearly fell as she hauled on the backs of the seats like the rungs of a ladder, forcing herself forward, toward the cockpit. When she finally reached it, she banged on the door. After a moment Dreck opened it from inside, reaching back because he was still strapped into the copilot seat. "Go back to your seat," He yelled at her. "Strap yourself in."

The blue horizon through the windshield ahead tilted drunkenly up, then down, and side to side. Sheryl was pitched in an heroic struggle with the yoke, trying to keep the plane level and in the air.

"What's wrong with the plane," Lainie demanded.

"Your henchman wasn't any too happy to see us taxi out of the barn," Dreck spat. "He ran in front of us, threw something at the engine intake as we went by him."

"Looked like a ring of ordinary car keys," Sheryl grated as she pulled then wrenched the steering to one side. "Didn't affect us at first so I didn't think anything of it. But then the engine started grinding, then halting, and now it's on fire."

While Lainie was terrified of crashing, she felt a certain pride in Cord. He hadn't been trying to endanger her, just stop the plane. He couldn't know the engine would give no signal of distress until they were out over water.

"Johnny," Sheryl said, "You need to get out of here."

Dreck and his pilot exchanged looks, then he nodded. He stood, pitching back and forth with the increasing wild yaw of the airplane, then launched himself at Lainie. He bore her back and, pedal as she might backwards to keep from falling, she fell square on her back and smacked her head on the floor.

Already having a possible concussion from the prior blow, once again her vision blinked out, then swam back into focus, slow and with uncertain edges. There was wind now, and lots of it. The door was open. Dreck was fastening the last buckle of a parachute around his chest. He looked back at Lainie and grinned, then turned and crouched, bouncing on his toes, choosing the right moment in the pitching and tumbling aircraft to leap clear.

Once again Lainie found herself struggling to stand. The plane was rocking and rolling so much now that once or twice she felt her feet leave the deck before coming back down again. She pushed herself toward the door, Only to be thrown back again just fingertips away from grabbing him and preventing him from jumping.

The plane lurched again and Lainie was flung hard against Dreck's back. Just like that, the pair of them were out the door, falling face first into up-rushing wind and the moist air vapor of clouds. She hadn't been thinking of jumping, and it very well might have been he who left the plane deliberately even as she struck him, rather than having been flung unceremoniously free, she couldn't tell which.

She was acutely aware of the fact that she didn't have a parachute, nor anything to break her precipitous fall. Now, not only was Dreck her last hope to save Simi, but her own life as well. She clung to him, arms and legs wrapped around him like a chimpanzee to its own mother.

"Let go, y'damn barnacle," he screamed, fighting to dislodge her. "You're covering the chute. You'll foul it."

He punched back with his elbows, which sent them both into a tumble, ass over teakettle, flipping and spinning out of control. Now he was screaming, the pitch of his voice revealing both his rage and his terror. Meanwhile it was all Lainie could do to cling tighter to his back, even scrabbling for a better grip.

Dreck was flailing, in full on panic now, twisting and swinging, desperately doing anything he could to dislodge her. The world around them spun and twirled, and Lainie reflected in some insane clarity that between the plane spinning out of control and this, she should be well and truly immune to motion sickness ever again. If she lived through this fall.

Dreck finally landed a good solid elbow into her right side, causing her grip to slip, and she grabbed madly for another purchase. Her hand closed around something dangling from the pack on his back, but it didn't help her hold on, it instead came loose in her hand.

She heard a ripping noise and the pack between she and Dreck suddenly shifted. As she let go of whatever had come loose to put an arm around his neck, a small parachute about the breadth of a beach ball came out of a widening tear in the pack, As it flung itself into the sky above them, Lainie though that was just too small a chute to carry even one of them, much less both.

Then, behind it came a great sheet of cloth, sunset orange in color gradually fading to flame red, the main chute. She'd see enough parachute drops on film to know there would be a mighty jerk as the parachute canopy deployed – wind resistance drastically reducing their speed to a fraction of what it was now. She clung even tighter.

When the line snapped taught, their tandem flailing had them on their backs falling tail-end first, so that not only were they jerked to a near stop, but flipped violently one way, then the next. In spite of her determination to hold even tighter Lainie was very nearly dislodged.

Dreck, on the other hand, let out a yelp, then stopped flailing entirely. Indeed, he went so entirely limp that Lainie found herself calling out his name. She allowed herself to reach of his face and feel it. There was no defensive turn of the head or twitch of muscle, and to the best she could tell by touch his mouth hung slack. He was clearly unconscious, but whether he was still even breathing or not she simply couldn't tell under these chaotic circumstances.

The ocean below seemed to be rushing up at them at the speed of a windshield careening toward a bug, or pair of bugs. This was far from the serene drift through cotton clouds and azure skies she'd seen in movies and on TV, but then what did she expect, given how this dive had started?

Still, she craned her head following the taught lines to see above them. The first alarming thing was that not all of the lines were taught, some slacked and snapped and snaked in the wind. When her eyes reached the canopy above she saw the problem. Whether because of her interference with the clean deployment of a parachute or some other mishap, the thing had not completely deployed. It had not spread and embraced the air as it should have.

Part of the square expanse of sunset-hued nylon above had folded back in on itself, and as a consequence a good quarter of the chute was flabby and slack, fluttering as if itself in a panic of falling. It looked like Lainie's heart felt as it sank in her chest down into her stomach.

She wasn't looking down and so was not prepared when they crash-landed. When they hit the water together it felt like hitting wet concrete. Lainie blacked out yet again, only to open her eyes on a hazy sunlit sky. She was floating on her back on the chute, which she must've somehow managed to climb to before winking out, though she didn't remember doing it. The cloth, spread as it was across the surf, buoyed her up and kept her from sinking. But it was even now collapsing under her and sinking. Lainie righted herself and swam, looking for Dreck.

She didn't see the man anywhere on the surface, and as the canopy was steadily pulled under she realized what it was that was anchoring it down deeper into the water. It had to be Dreck's unconscious. . .or dead body. She grabbed at the last of the parachute before is disappeared under the surface and pulled on it.

She reeled in the cloth hand over hand, still kicking her legs to tread water, until she encountered the course lines. Then she pulled on those, again hand over hand. Eventually she felt weight and pulled harder. But she was exhausted, and he was heavy. If she didn't have a concussion before the fall she certain had one now.

She cast about her and saw beachline behind her. Either they had been flying south along the coastline toward South America as she had suspected, or Sheryl had tried to steer the plane back toward dry land as soon as she knew she was going to have to make a crash landing. Probably some combination of the two.

At any rate, Lainie swam as hard as she could toward shore, and each time she felt the tug of Dreck's weight on the line she pulled him along behind her. This seemed easier than hauling him up. She swam as hard as she ever thought she could, her lungs bursting with the exertion, and her injured brain fogging in and out on her.

The next time she looked up, the shore seemed even further away. How could that be, she was swimming straight toward it? Perforce, she chose to believe it was only a mirage or optical illusion, that she was indeed drawing closer to land. She had to believe that, because she wasn't going to give up in any case.

How long had it been, she wondered as she paddled and pinwheeled her arms against the weightt? How long could someone remain underwater and still be revived? She knew CPR, she had to as the medical part of her degree, but she didn't know that. How long was the record? The longest time someone lay drowned before being revived?

Suddenly her hand, as she reached out for more distance, struck sand on the downstroke. She forced her knees under her and was able to stand. She hauled the parachute behind her as hard as she could as she stalked her way up the sand. She imagined she looked like some insane fisherman dragging in with all his might the whale he'd caught on his fishing line.

When she glanced back she saw Dreck in the surf and she dropped the lines and ran to him. She hauled him by the shoulders of his jacket to get him out of the water, and she fell on her rump. She scrambled around him and rolled him over. His lips were blue.

Shoving a finger down his throat she threw aside any effluvium in his mouth, then bent her lips to his, pinching his nose, and blew. Lather. . .rinse. . .repeat. . ..

She didn't know if he needed to be alive for them to extract what they needed to replicate the antivirus in his system, and at the moment that didn't matter to her. Yes, she had been prepared to kill those who sought to release such a horrible plague on the Earth, doubly so those who stood in her way from saving Simi's life, Dreck included. But killing someone in self-defense was one thing, simply standing by and watching them die when you could do something to prevent it was quite another.

Between her exhaustion and her exploding headache, Lainie fought unconsciousness as she worked to save Dreck's life. Her vision swam in and out of focus, and more than once she came to, resting her head on his chest instead of performing CPR. During one such dim-vision moment she hallucinated helicopters flying nearby along the coast. One broke formation and came their way.

The next time she came to she was on her back. Her head and shoulders were in Cord Steele's lap. She looked up into his face, but he was looking to the right. She followed his gaze to a group of men dressed in back assault gear, guns slung over their backs. They huddled around Dreck, who was on his hands and knees vomiting seawater onto the sand.

"You okay," Steele asked. When she looked back to him his impossibly blue eyes were on her.

"I have a headache," she said.

"And one hell of a goose-egg on the back of your head to match it."

She looked to Dreck again, who was even now being handcuffed. "We need to get him back to Malmstrom."

"We will," Steele said. "Forthwith."

CHAPTER 14

When next Lainie saw Simi the normally diminutive woman looked positively miniscule. Gray skin, emaciated cheeks and eye sockets, clouded pupils, and lips like tree bark, Simi lay perfectly still. "Is she. . .is she. . ."

"She's alive," the doctor behind her said. Lainie felt as if he restrained himself from adding, *but barely*.

She sat in the chair proffered by a nurse and pulled it up close to the side of the bed. Simi was still in quarantine, but Lainie refused to put on a containment suit before coming in. If she was to be infected, herself, then she already had been. Either the antivirus even now being synthesized from Dreck's blood would save Simi or it would not. It was out of Lainie's hands now.

Dreck had stashed the full complement of virus syringes and mutagen vials in a fanny pack, and it had not been compromised by his dip in the ocean. Steele had scolded Lainie for leaping onto Dreck's back and pushing him out of the plane, as if that was what she'd done, when she'd already told him it was more accident than design.

She tried to lift Simi's hand into hers, but the bones rolled against each other like a bundle of twigs and she let go, fearful of hurting her friend further. The doctor explained to Lainie that she herself had contracted the mutated virus from

Eliza. It didn't affect her because the mutated virus was programmed for those of Middle-Eastern descent. So even if Eliza had been careful not to touch Simi, which Lainie was sure she had been, so guilty she felt for carrying it in the first place, Lainie herself could have passed it on to her friend.

"I'm so sorry," Lainie whispered, choking. "It was me. I'm so sorry."

There was a commotion behind her and she turned as someone rushed in carrying a syringe. The woman hesitated, her face strained behind the plastic of her containment hood. She addressed the room full of doctors and Nurses, "Please understand I've never been asked to synthesize something like this in such a short time."

It'd been four hours since the lab had received the vial of Dreck's blood and the unmutated virus to compare it against. They already had the Mutated virus from both Lainie and Simi.

She went on, the quaking in her voice revealing her nervousness, "Much less to use it on a human subject without any prior testing. This may not work, and it could make her worse."

"She can't get worse," Lainie snapped. "She's dying. If you kill her while trying to save her, you're still a hero in my book. Now please, give her the antivirus."

The virologist looked at the doctor and he nodded. She moved forward and found a place among the tubes and wires surrounding Simi's face to apply the needle to her neck. Lainie wished she'd hurry as the woman injected the yellowish fluid into the artery there slowly and steadily.

She stepped away and everyone in the room looked at Simi with signs of resignation, not hope. Lainie couldn't stand it. "Now please," she said, "leave us alone."

Everyone filed out, Leaving Lainie and Simi alone. Lainie put her chin on the edge of the bed inches from Simi's parchment-like cheek. "Cord wanted to be here, but he was ordered to the Utah field office for debrief. I don't think he's in any trouble, they just want to know what has been going on."

She reached up and brushed moisture away from her friend's eyes. "I'll have to go, too, sooner or later. But I wanted to see you." She sighed. "I love you, sister." It was the first time she'd used Simi's word for their bond, and she found it wasn't awkward at all. In fact, it felt so right, that soon she was tearing up. "Get better soon." She sniffed. "This bad world is better with you in it."

*   *   *

Agent Young debriefed Lainie in a conference room at the field office. He was an attractive middle-aged African American man with the soft voice she remembered. The conversation was exhaustive, in which he had her tell her story repeatedly, often out of sequence, and during which he asked many questions.

After he closed his laptop and turned off the video recording equipment, he said, "Off the record, Ms. Parker, I think you are a remarkable young woman. I don't know many men with the guts to do what you did. If you were my sister or my daughter I'd be reading you the riot act right now, for being irresponsible, reckless, and even a little suicidal. But since you're not, all I can say is good on ya. Good on ya, Ms. Parker."

As they stood Cord Steele sauntered into the room. He greeted Lainie with a chaste kiss on the cheek and shook Young's hand. To Lainie he said, "We have one more thing to talk to you about."

She looked from Steele to Young and back again. "What is it?"

As the ranking agent, Young took over. "We'd like you to consider becoming a private contractor for the CIA."

"A what?" Lainie kept looking back and forth between them, as if watching a tennis match.

"As such," Young went on as if she was following what he was saying, which she doubted she was, "you would work for us, taking on assignments, basically doing what you do."

"What I do? I'm a school teacher."

219

"You have a PhD in education, with a minor in special education."

"All right, a glorified school teacher."

Young gave her a patient look. "All of us here in this room know you're a lot more than that. I've read the file we have on you, Ms. Parker. The Al-Serehmni affair, the Dreck incident. And what I can't read on paper Agent Steele here vouches for. You're smart, and more than just book smart, you think critically, you have an innate knack for strategy, you're stubborn, determined, you're a goddamned Mack truck in high heels if even half of the stories I hear are true."

Lainie felt like she was blushing. "I don't wear pumps, they hurt my feet. I think you over estimate me. I don't want to be a secret agent. I want to help disabled children. I want to be a teacher."

Young nodded. "And you'll be free to do that. You can work at whatever day-to-day job you want. When we call, as a contractor, you can either accept the assignment or not, it's entirely up to you."

"Why me?"

Steele chuckled, said, "Lainie you have a knack. The CIA just wants to harness that. Plus, between you and me, they want in on the loop next time you go pissing on the campfire of a cell of terrorists, or whatever."

"Look," Young said, "think about it, okay? There're still background checks and other criteria to sort out. Until then, you can take your time. Let us know."

She shook Young's offered hand. When she turned her back on him she gave Steele a look meant to convey: *what the hell?* Steele just shrugged and grinned that mischievous grin. She hung back to press him for answers, but he stepped toward the door. "Well, I have some other meetings before I head back to Langley. Call me." And he was gone.

Lainie said farewell to Young and saw herself out. On the elevator down to the ground floor she felt rather confused. Steele had barely said goodbye and he was off again. They really hadn't had much chance to talk after they separated at

Malmstrom. She'd hoped to be able to decompress, preferably with him, maybe over a beer.

In the cab on the way back to the hotel that the CIA was paying for, her cell phone pinged for the first time since it had self-wiped in response to Conrad trying to break her security code. She looked at a message from her service provider informing her that her account was now reactivated. "About time," she murmured. No sooner had she gotten that message and a cascade of tones sounded, one tumbling after the other, for so long she began wondering if they'd ever stop. These were notifications telling her she had uncounted missed calls, unviewed texts and unread emails.

She sighed and was about to put the phone away when one voicemail caught her eye. It was from Eliza. The timestamp was the night she died. She must've left it some time between when she and Simi had left Lainie to go destroy the lab, and her death.

Lainie felt a chill as she pressed the play button and put the phone to her ear. At first there was just breathing, then:

"Okay, Lainie, you aren't going to like how this ends. How it has to end. But you already know why. We already talked about it back at the cave with the pit. I'm not going to repeat it here. I couldn't go through with it then because I saw in your eyes how much it would hurt you. But I still knew it had to be done.

"You'll get this message after everything is over, I suppose. So the only thing left is to tell you how much you've meant to me in my life. Everyone in my life I depend on dies. My parents, grandpa. . . when Judson, Professor Harkness, betrayed me he was as good as dead to me. Everyone except you. I know you are embarrassed by your work at Capri, and with the dating app. I'm here to tell you to be proud.

"What you've done for the girls, for me, you gave us control. You didn't force anyone into this line of work, they would have done it anyway, but if not for you probably for some fucker rapist who would beat them any time they got out of line. You gave us the dignity to be our own bosses. Not just the financial freedom to pay off student loans, but empowerment to take control of our own lives. Our own sexuality, yes, but so much more than that. You were always there when we called, always with a steady, supporting hand. You are more than just our boss, you are our den mother."

Eliza's musical laugh came over the phone. "I suppose that sounds kind of juvenile. Anyway, that's how I feel. Anyone else could oversee the app like you do, but no one else could ever make us feel safe and looked after like you did. That's what you gave me when I was alive. Please don't forget that."

Simi's voice came over the line, faint, as if she was whispering from a few feet away, "All right, it's time."

"Goodbye, Lainie," Came Eliza's voice. "And thanks."

The voicemail ended. Lainie wiped her eyes and put the phone back in her pocket.

At her hotel room she inhaled deeply as she closed the door behind her, then exhaled long and loud as she leaned back against the door. She kicked off her shoes and took two steps into the room before she noticed there was someone on her bed. Her smile was broad and unrestrained. "How'd you get in here," she asked, then held up a hand. "No, don't say it."

Cord Steele smiled back and raised a bottle of wine in her direction. "Drink?" He was reclined on an elbow wearing one of the fluffy white robes left by the hotel for customer use.

"God yes," she said and climbed onto the bed, pushing her back against his chest. "What do we have here."

"Snacks," he said, flourishing his arm over the goodies laid on the bed before them. There were grapes, cheese, sesame crackers, corn chips, salsa, chili-cheese dip, and an assortment of candy bars from the vending machines. "Sorry it's not fancier."

"It's perfect," she said, grabbing a chocolate bar with almonds and tearing it open.

"Also sorry for the abrupt goodbye earlier. If you're going to work for the CIA, best keep anything we have under wraps. It's not against regulations, precisely, but in the interests of not complicating things. . ."

"I agree, she said, reaching behind her and pulling his head down, kissing him.

"Mm," he said, smacking his lips. "Chocolate and grapes. Not as bad as you might think.

She laughed and turned herself around to face him, kissing him long and sensuously. He kissed her back, groping for the buttons on her dress, even as she fumbled with his belt.

*   *   *

Just as Lainie closed the car door after settling in, her cell phone rang. She answered it with all of the jubilance and buoyancy she felt at the moment: "Lainie Parker speaking."

"Ah, Dr. Parker. Zis iss Dr. Reisin, do you remember me?" The woman rolled her R's so profusely Lainie was thrown for a moment, Then it dawned on her, The Reisin Clinic for Developmental Impediments. The job she'd applied for what seemed like an eternity ago.

"Dr. Reisin," Laini said. What she wanted to ask was, *why the hell are you calling me*? But what she asked instead was, "What can I do for you?"

"Dr. Parker, it is my fery kreat pleasure to offer you de position of Associate Resident at The Reisin Clinic for Developmental Impediments."

"Me." Lainie was stunned. She would have been given the bum's rush from the place, she was sure, if she hadn't run out on the interview herself. "Why?"

"Well, it zeems zat ze parents of my patient, Jeremy Jacobson, vere quite taken viss you. It zeems zat zey vill not vork viss any osser doctor but you. You zee, your unsolicited diagnosis of zere zon's condition, as intrusive as it vas, vas, in fact, precisely correct. But zey vill only vork though our clinic if I am to hire you."

Lainie's phone chimed. "Hold, please," she said. She looked at the notification. It appeared yet another deposit had been made by Orin into her account, her share of profits from the escort app. The amount was even greater than the last one, adding to what she had once dismissively referred to as her primp stash.

Placing the phone back to her ear, Lainie said, "I'm sorry, Frau Doktor –" overenunciating the German inflection "– but I simply couldn't take the cut in pay." Laughing, Lainie hung up the phone and dropped it into a slot of the center console.

She pressed the ignition button of her brand new, mere minutes off the showroom floor, gleaming copper Aston Martin Vanquish convertible. The engine rumbled to life, vibrated and whined under her, and Lainie felt like purring with the vehicle.

She turned to the passenger beside her and the two women smiled at each other. Lainie and Simi both slipped their wrap-around sunglass on and Simi tugged at the ties of her head scarf to tighten it.

"Ready," Lainie shouted.

"Go for it," Simi screamed.

Lainie squashed the gas pedal to the floor and the sleek machine fishtailed, kicking up dust, before throwing itself forward with every bit as much joyful abandon as the women felt, launching like a horizontal rocket upon the long, winding open road before them.

ABOUT THE AUTHOR

Kevin Paul Tracy has been writing fiction and non-fiction since grade school. He has travelled extensively spanning half the globe and has held just about every odd job you can think of, from cave spelunking guide to pinsetter. He currently lives in Colorado with two very charismatic St. Bernards.

You can follow Kevin at:

http://www.KevinPaulTracy.com

http://KevinPaulTracy.Blogspot.com

http://www.Twitter.com/KevinPaulTracy

http://www.Facebook.com/KevinPaulTracyWriter